Call of
LOVE

By Lee Haven

2023

Butterworth Books is a different breed of publishing house. It's a home for Indies, for independent authors who take great pride in their work and produce top quality books for readers who deserve the best. Professional editing, professional cover design, professional proof reading, professional book production—you get the idea. As Individual as the Indie authors we're proud to work with, we're Butterworths and we're *different*.

Authors currently publishing with us:

E.V. Bancroft
Valden Bush
Addison M Conley
Michelle Grubb
Helena Harte
Lee Haven
Karen Klyne
AJ Mason
Ally McGuire
James Merrick
Robyn Nyx
Simon Smalley
Brey Willows

For more information visit www.butterworthbooks.co.uk

CATALOGING INFORMATION
ISBN: 978-1-915009-36-4
CREDITS
Editor: Nicci Robinson
Cover Design: Nicci Robinson
Production Design: Global Wordsmiths

Acknowledgements

My deepest thanks and gratitude go to Nicci and Victoria who believed I had a story to tell when I arrived at their writing retreat in Spain in 2019. They patiently listened to the ideas in my head and helped me turn them into a novel. I'm grateful for every moment they spent teaching me what they know about writing and sometimes even about the English language.

Thank you, Nicci, for all the hours you spent editing my manuscript and pointing out all those little, and sometimes big, things that were in my head but hadn't made it to the page, and for finding and eliminating all those not-so English sentence constructions that seemed to creep back in.

To my mom and dad for their love and encouragement through the entire process and for always supporting me in this crazy and amazing journey.

All the wonderful and critical friends I met through writing in the Hatchery and through Swallows. Your encouragement, constructive comments, and high spirits kept me writing.

Margaret Burris for proofreading my novel and finding all the errors I couldn't.

Nicci for creating a beautiful cover when I was quite overwhelmed with the process.

And last, but certainly not least, my better half, AJ, for her love and support throughout this process, and for listening to me and encouraging me to keep going even when I didn't believe I could do it.

Without all of you this book would never have been possible.

Dedication

To my mom, Maggu.
Thank you for all the countless hours you read books to me as a child. All those magical journeys into the pages nurtured my imagination and love of books.

Prologue

Four and a half years ago

A FRESH BREEZE BLEW in over the river and ruffled through Parker's hair. A strand loosened and fell onto her face. She resented not having any gel to glue her hair in place that morning. It wasn't normally that long, but she'd let her hair grow out a bit during her last assignment to put the people she'd dealt with at ease. Between that and being laid up in the hospital the past couple of weeks, her hair had grown long enough to need a bun, for the first time since she got out of bootcamp. She pushed the offending strand back where it belonged and hoped that she still looked presentable.

The spring air was cold, but the sun warmed her face when it managed to peek through the clouds. Each time she drew another breath into her lungs, she felt less claustrophobic and little by little, she felt free and alive. Today's follow-up appointment had taken her to the Navy Yard, and she'd decided to stretch her legs and enjoy the solitude before she headed home. Happy memories from a time long ago drew her in the direction of the Navy Museum, a place she used to visit with her best friend Kate when their lives were simple and their friendship innocent, before they became lovers, and before everything fell apart.

She stopped when she came close to her intended destination and saw two civilians reach the park bench first, their backs turned. With the women settling in right where she wanted to go, she had half a mind to change her path since she was in no mood for company. But even from behind, there was something oddly familiar about them that made her pause. She crouched behind some nearby shrubbery to observe them from a safe distance.

A young girl joined them with an art portfolio under one arm and a backpack slung over the other shoulder. "I can see why you love it here so much, Kate." The girl dropped the portfolio on the bench.

Could it be Kate? Parker's breath hitched and her heart beat up in her throat. She hadn't recognized her niece Zoe all bundled up in her coat and scarf. But her voice was unmistakable, even though she'd only spoken to Zoe on Skype two or three times a year for the past seven years. She just hadn't been able to abandon Zoe entirely when she left. After all, Zoe was the last tenuous link she had to her sister. Even though she'd stayed mostly away from Zoe since arriving home not wanting her niece to become too attached to her before she'd leave again. The third person there was her mother, Helen, who she was trying to avoid just for a little while longer. Her mother had hovered over Parker ever since she arrived home, even to the extent where she'd begun to work from home while Parker was back.

Kate's long red hair was picked up by the breeze and reflected the occasional glint of sunlight. Parker had imagined this moment a million times, where she'd finally see Kate again. Each time, Kate had been the one spotting her, seeking her out. There'd been a hundred different things she'd wanted to say to Kate, to explain to her why she hadn't been able to do what Kate had asked of her and had abandoned her dreams instead. But now her mind went blank. All she could focus on was seeing her face again.

"I loved to come here with Parker. I was a bit younger than you are today when my dad last brought us here." Kate sat down next to Zoe on the bench.

"Why did you never tell us you liked to come here? We could've brought you." Helen held out a travel mug to Kate.

It somehow felt wrong to eavesdrop on them, but her body didn't want to move.

"I think the thought of coming here after my parents died was too painful." Kate shrugged. "I've come here a few times in recent years. Mostly to feel close to Parker, you know?"

Helen nodded and flipped open her own travel mug.

"But Parker is in the Marines, not the Navy," Zoe said. She drew a long, thin pencil box out of her pack.

"You're right." Kate ruffled Zoe's hair.

"If you miss her so much, why haven't you been over since she came home?" Zoe asked.

Parker's throat went dry, and she moved a little closer. She didn't want to miss one word of that answer.

Kate looked at Helen. The movement was so small, Parker almost missed Helen shake her head. What the hell did that mean?

"How did it go?" Helen asked.

Kate shook her head and shrugged. Parker considered walking over and demanding to know what was going on.

Zoe sat up straight and put her hands on her hips. "Do you guys really think I don't know you have secrets from me? I'm not a baby anymore. I'm almost ten."

Helen opened her mouth and closed it again but said nothing.

"Is she really home?" Kate asked.

"Yup, she is. She has a funny limp. I think she doesn't want anyone to know because she's trying to hide it. But she didn't fool me." Zoe nodded and set pencil to paper, leaving the portfolio open on the bench.

The little color Kate had in her cheeks faded further. Parker resolved to go over. She wanted to pull Kate into her arms and whisper that everything would be okay.

"I don't think this is a voluntary visit," Helen said.

Parker halted after she'd only taken a few steps.

"I think she was finally thinking about it, coming for a visit, I mean. Well, she didn't shoot me down right away when I asked her during the last time she called to speak to Zoe."

"Why didn't you tell me?"

"I didn't want to get my hopes up." Helen sighed. "I didn't want to get your hopes up either. You wished for Parker to come home from the very day she left. I was there. I saw your heart break into even more pieces when Parker got on that bus."

"No one can see someone else's heart break," Kate whispered.

"A mother can see her child's heart break, and you're my daughter in all but blood. You know that, right?" Helen squeezed Kate's arm.

Parker was grateful that her departure hadn't destroyed the bond between Kate and her mother. If anything, it seemed to have grown stronger since she'd left. It was her father's words that had pushed her into leaving, but it was obvious that her mother felt the same way too.

"A couple of weeks ago we got a call from the State Department," Helen said.

Fucking bureaucracy. She'd been furious when she found out her parents had been officially notified about the incident that had landed her in the hospital. More so when she'd heard the doctor phone them after the surgery that repaired the bullet hole in her leg. Even after she'd given specific instructions not to contact her family again. She'd wanted to give the doctor a piece of her mind, but she was too fuzzy from the post op drugs to do anything about it.

"What does that mean?" Kate asked.

Helen looked away from Kate. "They're the people who call when something goes wrong."

"Wrong?"

"They informed us that there was an incident involving our daughter, but they couldn't give us any more information at that time."

And they shouldn't have given you that much information. She only wanted them to be notified if she died in the line of duty.

Kate hunched her shoulders. "I wish you'd told me."

Helen reached out toward Kate, but she moved away. Parker was struck by the expression on their faces. Helen looked full of rejection and pain, while Kate's expression spoke of betrayal and old hurt. How was it possible that Parker had cost the people she cared about so much agony without even being there? They should have been better off without her, without her hurt and guilt making them miserable every day.

Helen reached out a second time and this time, Kate stilled. Helen slowly stroked her cheek. "Sweetie, we didn't tell you because we didn't have anything to say that would have made it bearable. Eventually they informed us that Parker was in the hospital. But they wouldn't give us any more information without her consent. With all the things you have going on in your life, we didn't want to worry you any more than necessary. I love you. We love you. The last thing I wanted was to cost you more heartache."

Parker strained to hear when Helen let go of Kate and looked away, her next words lost to Parker. She edged closer to make out what her mother was saying.

"I often ask myself if there was anything we could've done differently that would have changed things. The last thing a mother wants is to see her children suffer. If I could change the past, believe me, I would."

Parker inhaled sharply. She couldn't quite believe what she was hearing. If her mother didn't want to see them suffer, why all the drama and rejection in the first place? An apology would be nice but just knowing she was welcome in her parents' house would go a long way. Parker thought about walking over and sitting down with them. Listening to their private conversation didn't feel right, but something stopped her. There were probably things her mother wouldn't say if Parker was beside her.

"We got one other call from a US Military hospital in Germany after that. It was in the middle of the night. They told us Parker had made it out of surgery on her leg, and they expected her to make a full recovery," Helen said. "Imagine how shocked we were when Parker just showed up at our front door a few weeks later. We had no idea she was coming."

"Parker has been home for what, three days now. Why hasn't she bothered to let me know?" Kate hung her head.

It was a fair question. The truth was that Parker simply didn't know what she could say that could undo the last seven years. And she certainly didn't want to try that over the phone, should Kate's old number even work.

"I think whatever she's been through has taken its toll. She's been sleeping a lot, and to be fair, you had your own things going on," Helen said. "I hope that she'll call when her appointment is finished, and we can take her home. You'll get to see her then."

Yes, the painkillers would make her sleep, but she hadn't been taking them, preferring the pain over the oblivion the pills offered. The questioning eyes of her parents' watchful gaze made her feel like an exotic animal in a cage, so she'd pretended to be asleep. Helen had offered to listen multiple times if she needed to talk but talking was the last thing Parker wanted to do, either about the incident or about why she'd left her life behind in the first place. Like a reminder, the scar on her left side started itching. She touched it lightly but didn't scratch. She needed to leave it alone if it was ever going to heal.

Parker stepped closer, and Kate squeezed the back of her neck before she began to turn around. Parker had seen Kate do the same thing hundreds of times growing up, and she'd never been able to explain it. Kate had simply claimed she could feel Parker approach. The recognition gave Parker just enough time to duck behind a nearby shrub.

What am I doing? Hiding like a coward wasn't optimal, but having Kate think she'd been listening in all that time wasn't what she wanted either. Her position behind the hedge made it harder to see Kate scanning her surroundings, but she still saw Kate draw her eyebrows together, the way she always did when she tried to make sense of something. Parker was comforted that some things never changed. She felt the internal pull Kate had on her, like Kate was the center of her gravity.

Get a grip, Parker. Get your butt off the ground and walk over like you had always planned to meet them here. You wanted to do better for her.

The breeze turned into a sudden gust that picked up a couple of pages from Zoe's portfolio that lay open on the bench between her and Kate.

"Oh, crap," Zoe said.

Zoe reached for the pages, but they were already out of her reach tumbling through the air in Parker's direction. She was ready to step out of hiding and catch them when a loud metallic bang forced her onto the floor. Pain seared up her left leg and was followed by the acrid smell of burning flesh. The almost empty, cool Navy Yard turned into a hot, rocky desert that provided no cover from flying bullets everywhere. Her heart beat so loudly she could hear little else, and her breath came in short irregular gasps. The apparition turned white around the edges before it receded, and she found herself huddled on the ground in the Navy Yard surrounded by pavement and greenery. Sweat beaded on her face and neck, but her hands trembled so badly, she couldn't manage to wipe it away before it trickled into her eyes.

Parker saw Kate jump up. She could make out the vibrant patches of color drifting toward her. Kate covered half the distance between Parker and the bench and managed to catch two of the three pages. The last one stubbornly stayed out of reach, flying over her head. With a determined leap, Kate managed to pluck it from the air.

Kate and Zoe were so close to the spot where Parker lay prone on the ground that she could smell Kate's scent on the air. The sweet mixture of jasmine, green tea and citrus chased off the pungent stench of freshly seared flesh and pulled her fully back into the present.

Zoe hugged Kate, but something seemed off. Kate's face was neutral, but Kate favored her right side, and her eyes betrayed the pain she was obviously in.

"Can you help me with the shading?" Zoe took the pages from Kate. "I can't seem to get it right."

Kate scanned her surroundings, and Parker held her breath. They were so close, Kate was sure to spot her cowering on the ground.

"What is it?" Zoe asked.

"I thought..." Kate shook her head. "Never mind."

"So, can you help me?"

Kate held her hand out. The tremor was slight but enough to devastate an artist, Parker knew. How much worse had Kate's condition become? And why had no one mentioned it to Parker?

Kate balled her hand into a fist and stuck it into her jacket pocket. "I'm sorry, pumpkin, today isn't a good day. Maybe another time."

"Don't you think I'm getting a little old for that nickname?"

"I don't think so." Kate slung her left arm around Zoe's shoulders, and they walked back to the bench.

Parker swallowed hard. Kate must be much worse than the last time she'd seen her. That shouldn't be the case. Kate's condition should have stabilized, actually improved, with medication. Kate had promised her she was fine before Parker left. Kate had loved drawing and painting for as long as Parker had known her. Her pain made Parker want to help her in all the ways she could. It was time for her to get off the ground and do what she came here to do.

Her whole body was still shaking and wouldn't comply with her desire to rise. Her legs were too weak to allow her to stand. Emptiness settled around her like a leaden blanket. She had nothing to offer. Just as when Parker had left, Kate had made that very clear, and Parker was even more useless now. If their circumstances had changed at all, they'd become more hopeless than before. Kate had enough to deal with, without having to consider Parker's problems. All she'd ever wanted for Kate and their family was to be happy, even if that meant she wasn't part of it. She managed to stand and looked over to them. Kate had her head thrown back in laughter while Zoe tried to escape Helen's attempt to straighten her jacket. If that was the last time she'd see her family, that was the image she wanted to remember, a snapshot of happiness in time.

She turned around and was relieved that no one was there to witness her little episode. There was only one thing she could do to not complicate their lives, and that was to go back to her own. She walked off in the direction she'd come from without looking back, just like she'd done seven and a half years before.

Chapter One

PARKER'S BREATH CAME IN short gasps when she clung to the punching bag. Worn from overuse and patched multiple times it had been her sparring partner for the last two hours. Her workout gear was drenched in sweat and her muscles protested when she wanted to let go. Pain was the only thing that seemed to give her relief from the constant emotional hurt these days, allowing her to escape for a few hours by numbing the ache in her soul.

Her mind was still on the assignment they'd returned from earlier. An uncooperative witness had delayed their return to base for two full days. Thanksgiving was fast approaching, and the base felt oddly quiet with some of the personnel on leave for the holiday. Her new commanding officer reminded her that she was overdue for a break and had even tried to tempt her with time off over the holiday, but she'd refused. She hoped that, like her previous CO, he would eventually stop asking.

She'd missed the passenger flight out due to the delay, and she'd secretly been relieved. There was nothing left for her Stateside. Her last trip back had driven that point home. There was just one thing she wanted, and she couldn't have it, so there was little reason for her to go anywhere. The military was her life, her family, and her home now. She was right where she needed to be. Her legal aid, however, had been crushed that he'd missed his chance to get home.

Sometimes she wondered if the confrontation with her own mortality and the events leading up to her one and only home visit had something to do with her overwhelming need to flee. After three days with her family, she'd begged her superiors for an assignment that would take her out of the city. Her desperation to get away had eventually landed her in this desert hellhole, deep in enemy territory. Outside, the air was so hot and dry that it felt like she was breathing with her head pressed into the rough desert sand that surrounded her.

Parker laid on her back and stared at the lazily swinging heavy bag above her head. This had always been her ritual to calm down. It was almost as good as a long run through the wilderness, but here she wasn't permitted to go outside the wire, and the barren surroundings weren't her kind of wilderness for a run anyway. A thick forest or a state park was much more to her liking. She loved running but going in circles around the base, like so many of her fellow soldiers did, only agitated her more.

The bag had almost stopped swinging above her, letting her know that it was time to get up for another round. Maybe then the exhaustion and pain in her muscles would quiet her mind long enough for her to drift off to sleep for a few fitful hours.

A metal-hinged creak signaled someone opening the heavy rec room door, followed by a gush of hot air rolling over her overheated, sweat-dampened body. It left her freezing when the AC kicked back in after the door fell shut. Heavy boots walked into view, and she lifted her gaze to see her legal aid, Lieutenant Caleb Callahan—Kid to everyone—staring down at her. "I'm really sorry you missed your flight, Kid. I know you were looking forward to Thanksgiving with your family." Parker pushed herself up into a sitting position.

"It was hardly your fault. Nobody could know that it would take that long to get his statement." Kid held out his hand to help her up.

"I'm still sorry that you'll be stuck here for the holiday."

"But I'm not. I can go out on the cargo plane bound for DC." A smile briefly crossed his face before settling into a frown.

"What's wrong? That's great news."

"It is. But my sister Jazmin had to change our plans because something came up at work, and my parents decided to stay in

Florida. I just got the message, so I'm not sure what I'm going to do. Stay with my sister and meet up with friends or go to Florida to see my parents."

"I'm sorry, Kid, that sucks. What are you doing here anyway? Don't you have to get ready?" She wanted him out so she could continue her workout.

"I need to pack and finish my paperwork." He grimaced. "The CO asked me to find you first and send you over to his office. He wants to see you ASAP." Kid picked up her towel and threw it at her.

"I thought you and your sister had planned the family meet-up over the holiday for ages. Didn't you say that you both applied for leave early?" She had no desire to see her CO, already having an inkling of why he wanted to see her. Maybe she could buy herself a few more minutes talking to Kid instead.

He sighed. "I thought she had. But now she's volunteered for some special project, and she had to cancel her time off."

"She didn't talk to you about it first?"

"She must've had a good reason for joining the project. She was obviously willing to sacrifice our holiday plans for it. Some patients can't wait. She's a doctor, after all. But when I asked her for specifics, she was very vague. I don't think she is telling me the whole truth." His gaze turned distant. "I can feel it. Something's off. She never behaves like that."

"I'm sorry, Kid. If you need ..." She trailed off. She wanted to offer him her ear, but she wasn't any good with her own personal stuff, much less that of others.

"Thanks, but I'm good and you have to get going. Move your butt!"

Parker flicked her towel at him. "Don't let anyone else hear you talking to me like that." Even though they held the same rank in different branches of the military, she was still his mentor while he retrained. But they'd been through hell together and made it out alive, which was why she let him get away with his informality when they were alone. He knew she'd give him hell if he slipped up in front of witnesses. It took Parker five minutes to make her way to her CO's office, barely enough time for the incessant heat to dry Parker's sweat-dampened hair.

"I should've told him to hose you down on the way." Her CO, Colonel Muñoz, wrinkled his nose while she was still standing at attention in front of his desk. "At ease, soldier."

She didn't relax. Being called to the CO's office was almost never good news. Muñoz eyed her quietly, and the moment seemed to stretch on forever.

He slapped his hand on a file folder laying on his desk. "Do you know what this is?"

She had no clue and decided to keep her mouth shut.

"That was a question, captain!"

She looked him square in the eyes. "Sir, no, sir."

"It's your personnel file," he said. "You're a very mysterious woman, Captain Snow."

His opening made her bristle, but she remained silent.

"You currently serve under the Naval Judge Advocate General Corps, yet you're a Marine. Your record says very little about how that came to be."

Sometimes she wondered about that herself. Command had told her to go, and she went. That was the military way. An order didn't need an explanation.

"Your service has been exemplary, and you have the promotions and commendations to prove it. You earned a Medal of Honor for heroic actions under fire," he said. "You never complain, even over particularly difficult assignments, and the word *leave* seems to be missing from your vocabulary. The only scuttlebutt I hear about you is that you're an incredibly dedicated Marine."

The tension between her shoulders built, though she was happy that the rumor mill had nothing more to say about her. She had no idea what he was getting at, but she had the sense that something was off. Why was he questioning her assignment? She wasn't breaking any rules. She'd technically only ever bent one rule when she joined the service under the Don't Ask, Don't Tell policy. Back then, she'd put her head down and kept her personal life to herself. Thankfully, that was a thing of the past and she could be herself now. Her conduct while in the Corps had never been questioned, not even when she'd been captured and held hostage by the enemy.

Muñoz picked up a loose sheet of paper. "I received orders that reassign you to Navy JAG headquarters in DC, effective immediately. I'll be blunt. This caught me by surprise. With both Lieutenant Callahan and you gone, I'm left without a legal advisor on base. Did you request this?"

Parker shook her head. She'd no idea where that had come from. She'd extended her tour, and her time was nowhere near up yet.

"Did you hear me? You're going home, captain."

"Yes, sir." She wanted to beg him to let her stay or at least be sent some other place than the capital. That would put her much too close to her old home for comfort.

"I want you on the cargo plane that goes out tonight, together with Lieutenant Callahan. You'll need to be packed and ready to ship out by 2100." He leaned back in his chair. "You must be happy to make it back home in time for Thanksgiving. You can have real turkey for a change. Maybe they'll even let you spend it with your family."

She needed almost all her training not to look away in shame. Spending the holiday with her family was the last thing she wanted. "I'll go where I'm needed, sir," she said, more forcefully and clipped than she'd intended. But lying wasn't her thing, and she wouldn't tell him that she was thrilled when she wasn't. Nor was she about to tell him she'd rather stay when so many would be happy to go home in her place.

Muñoz smiled. "You're a lot like me, Snow. Married to the Corps. If they wanted us to have a family, they'd have issued it with our dog tags."

She smiled back. Family was the reason she'd run to the Corps in the first place.

"Get out of here and get your things in order. And Captain Snow, get a shower before you get on that plane." He held out some papers to her. "Dismissed."

She took the transfer documents and left. The papers weighed heavily in Parker's hand as she headed toward her living quarters to get packed. The fifteen-minute walk would give her time to wrap her head around what just happened. Why did they have to send her to DC of all places? Parker groaned and hoped whatever the reason was that it kept her busy over the holidays, at least until she could figure out how to avoid her family altogether. The beauty of the life she'd chosen was that she had little of sentimental value, so she had little to pack. The few items she really cherished were safe in a storage unit in DC. She packed up her few belongings quickly into her pack and deployment bag.

Kid drove up in a Jeep to pick her up. "You need some help with that?" He took the other end of her deployment bag and helped her load it.

"Thanks."

"Don't mention it." He got back into the Jeep. "I take it you aren't coming back?"

"Probably not." She shrugged. "Who knows?"

"Wait, Captain Snow!" A Marine she didn't recognize jogged up to her and held something out. "This just came for you."

Parker took the envelope and looked at it. Her name was written in barely legible handwriting.

"Letter from home?" the Marine asked.

Parker turned the letter over, but it didn't have a sender other than a military post code, like always. "Sort of." She pocketed it and got into the car.

They made it just as the pilots started the preflight check. The rapid unfolding of events had given her little time to think or analyze what was happening.

"Are you coming, captain?" Kid yelled down from the loading hatch they were about to close.

It was tempting not to get on board. The fine hairs on the back of her neck stood on end, and she felt the same sense of foreboding she'd experienced right before she'd been shot and captured, like something was about to shift and change the fabric of her life forever.

When she walked past the loading hatch, she turned around and looked out over the place that had been her home, and beyond into the darkened desert where she'd learned to survive and trust her instinct. She didn't feel like she was leaving a war zone. Instead, it was as if she was heading away from safety and into a battlefield.

Chapter Two

THE TRANSPORT PLANE OFFERED little in the way of luxury flight accommodation for passengers. Parker's ride home was a folding seat with the metal hull of the airplane acting as a backrest. She'd checked her seat buckles three times already. Dread had taken up residence in the pit of her stomach, and she swallowed repeatedly to combat the nausea it brought on. She was stuck here for approximately the next sixteen hours with no fresh air. She needed to get her stomach under control quickly.

Part of her wanted to be in Washington already to find out why she'd been called back so much earlier than expected. The other part wished she could go back into the gym and lose herself in strenuous exercise until every cell in her body was ready to shut down from exhaustion. Then she'd never need to find out what waited for her on the other end of the flight.

"You look a little green around the gills. I didn't take you for someone with flight anxiety." Kid leaned forward in his seat.

"I don't have a problem with flying."

"Oh? You could've fooled me." He pointed at her hands gripping her seatbelt. "That doesn't look like the behavior of someone who likes flying."

Parker looked around but they were alone in the cargo area, and the crew didn't seem to pay them any mind. She forced her hands to relax and placed them on her thighs. "It's not the flying."

"Then what is it? And why didn't you tell us you were leaving the base permanently? We would've thrown a party with the guys."

"I can't tell you what I don't know," she said, wanting an end to the conversation.

"What do you mean?"

She knew he wouldn't stop asking until she'd given him a satisfactory response. She rolled her shoulders to loosen them up. "That was why I was called into Muñoz's office. That's all the notice I got."

Kid was silent for a moment, and she hoped that would be the end of the discussion, but Kid had all the makings to become a fine lawyer one day and part of that makeup was knowing what questions to ask and when. It amazed her how clearly she could see the pieces fall into place in his mind.

"So, if you didn't know, and you don't have a problem with flying, then you just don't want to go home, do you?"

She sighed. Why did they have to be alone? She wanted to shut him down but couldn't bring herself to reprimand him for using the skills she'd taught him.

"I'm right, aren't I?"

"More or less. I don't want to abandon you over here. You have to come back when your leave is over."

He scrutinized her and shook his head. "No, that's not it. You don't have to worry about me, I'll be fine." He leaned back. "Do you already know where you'll go next?"

She exhaled slowly. He hadn't pressed her for a more detailed answer, as if he could sense that she was about to end their conversation.

"Looks like DC for now, but I'm not sure what'll come after that." If she had any say in the matter, she wouldn't stay in DC for long.

"Oh, that's great, isn't it? Didn't you grow up there?"

She refrained from rolling her eyes, wishing that she hadn't shared any personal information with him. "Yes, I grew up there, but that doesn't mean I like going back there."

"Can I ask you something personal, Snow?"

She nodded.

"Is your family in DC? Are they alive?"

"Why would you ask that?"

"When we were injured, my family was all over me even before we were shipped back to the US. They came all the way to Germany and didn't leave my side until I left Walter Reed. You never had a single visitor, not even after we made it to the military hospital back home." He shrugged.

"How would you know? I don't recall us sharing a room."

"People talk, you know." He looked sheepish. "Apparently a wounded Marine with no visitors merits scuttlebutt, and even half deaf with my blown ear drum, I heard enough."

"I'm so sorry." Even though Kid had recovered most of his hearing after two surgeries for his right ear, it was the reason he no longer sat in the pilot seat of an aircraft.

"That really wasn't your fault."

"I can still feel bad for you. You lost what you loved most. Do you remember telling me that flying was all you ever wanted to do since you were a little boy?"

His familiarity should've bothered her, but it seemed so inconsequential after what they'd gone through in captivity.

He shook his head. "I really told you that, when?"

"When they put us on an airplane to Germany. You were running a wicked fever and had enough medication in your blood that you were out for most of the trip. I'm not surprised you don't remember." She tried to swallow the rapidly growing lump in her throat. This wasn't something she liked to remember, much less talk about.

"Yeah, you're right. I don't remember much of that day." He rubbed his ear.

They looked away from each other, and she happily took that to mean their conversation was over. When Kid had started retraining as a lawyer and first been assigned as her aid, she'd feared that he'd bring up their shared past. But he hadn't, and that suited her just fine, so she wasn't sure what to make of their personal heart-to-heart now.

"I've never properly thanked you, Snow."

"Yes, you have. And so did your parents." She remembered the visit his parents had made to her room, with the vibrant Mrs. Callahan insisting she'd come visit with her for a while so Parker wouldn't feel so lonely without her family there.

"That's not what I mean. If I hadn't met you, I'd probably have punched my ticket, taken medical retirement, and gone back to the civilian world. I would've given up and pitied myself over the loss of the dream life that was taken from me. Instead, you inspired me to stay and retrain to be a lawyer."

The sudden show of gratitude made her uncomfortable. "You'll start hating me soon enough for it. Wait until you start studying for the bar."

They shared a humorless laugh.

"Don't remind me." He rolled his eyes. "You haven't answered my earlier question by the way."

"Huh?"

"I asked if your parents lived around DC?"

"Last time I checked, they did." She slid her hands under her thighs to avoid succumbing to the urge to check on her seatbelt again.

Kid tilted his head. "If your parents are still there, why didn't they visit you when you were in the hospital?"

The faint copper taste in her mouth told her that she'd replaced fiddling with her seatbelt with biting her lower lip. She loosened her jaw. She had no desire to open that particular box. "We aren't really on speaking terms."

"Why?" Even the dim light couldn't hide the rapid reddening of his cheeks. "Sorry, not really any of my business, is it?" He scratched the back of his head.

No, it wasn't, but she decided to answer him anyway. She had the urge to see if he would have the same reaction as her family. "I fell in love with my adoptive sister."

"Oh." He swallowed a couple of times, but he didn't say anything else.

That was pretty much the reaction she'd expected, and it put an abrupt stop to their conversation. She pulled the folded envelope from her pocket. "Don't sweat it. My family and I are better off not talking."

"It doesn't bother me that you're gay." He rubbed his ear again. "I need you to know that. Jazmin is a lesbian too, but you knew that."

She nodded and focused her attention back to the letter. She slipped her knife into the small opening under the flap and split the envelope open. The low sound of paper slicing satisfied something inside her after the uncomfortable conversation. She hoped whatever was inside would take her mind off things and lift her mood.

She unfolded the paper and grinned at the almost illegible handwriting that had grown so familiar in the past four years.

Hello, my dear sister,
You have no idea how much joy I feel every time I get to write those words. I'm grateful fate put you on my operating table that day in Germany.

Parker suppressed a laugh and rolled her eyes instead. Her brother knew how she felt about his belief that the Universe had anything to do with bringing them together. She had no time for fate.

I just made you laugh at me, didn't I? All joking aside, I'm happy to hear you're doing well, but please be careful over there and watch your back at all times. It worries me when you tell me you leave the base with just your partner and no backup. I know you can take care of yourself. But I'm your big brother, and that means I'm entitled to worry. Live with it.
I'm sorry it's taken me so long to respond. They don't

call the military postal service snail mail for nothing. So maybe you're right, and just switching over to email makes more sense. But handwritten letters are nice. I find them so much more personal than a quick email that takes someone less than five minutes to compose. Still, you'll find my email address at the bottom of this letter, but it won't get you out of enduring my crappy handwriting from time to time. There's nothing like a letter from home when you're surrounded by temporary base facilities in a foreign land with an unfamiliar culture.

I almost missed your last letter. It arrived after I'd moved onto another location, so it needed some time to catch up with me. When it finally arrived, I was about to move into my own apartment, and I forgot to write between work and all the moving arrangements. I'm sorry. Please don't think this isn't important to me. It took me so long to find any of you, and it makes me so happy to connect with you.

My request was granted, and I'm now working in Bethesda, Maryland. Thanks to you, I now live closer to our parents than I ever have. But after your last letter, I'm not quite sure if I'm ready to meet them just yet. I can't believe how they treated you and Kate when they found out you were in love. It's just so unfair. You really shouldn't defend them for their actions. Kate is your adoptive sister—so what? It's not like the two of you are blood related.

Parker had to smile at Mark's anger. It was nice to have someone who finally had her back. There had been countless times where she'd tried to reason with her parents and Kate's aunt, Colleen, with the very same argument. But she may as well have argued with a wall. They didn't want to hear it. Society said it was wrong— they were effectively sisters and shouldn't have such feelings. And they all agreed with society. Anger and defeat still battled inside her when she remembered their words: *You can't be in love with Kate. She's you sister, and it's just not right.*

But she loved Kate, and she couldn't stop that. Why was it wrong that their feelings had evolved when they had grown older? She pushed her thoughts aside and continued reading. Staying on an endless looping road of what ifs wouldn't help her. Not even the question of what if her brother had been around back then, standing by her side having her back. She was just happy to have a tentative family connection back in her life through Mark.

So I'm wondering how much of it relates to their love for social norms and how much of it is homophobia. You say they aren't, but I can't be certain. I'm ranting, aren't I? I'm sorry. I just don't feel comfortable making contact with them right now.

The funny thing about being adopted is that you hope you have that perfect birth family out there that misses you and is looking for you. And from what you've said, they may have looked for me, but I think they aren't all that perfect, and I need a bit of time to mentally catch up with that.

Her heart sank a little. He'd wanted to meet their parents so badly when he'd first sought her out a couple of months after she'd been released from the hospital. He'd told her his incredible story of being adopted and that after seeing her face and reading her medical record, he believed she was his biological sister. Even though she knew she had a brother that had been given up for adoption, she thought his first letter to be a cruel joke and had ignored it. Only when he'd gotten in touch again six months later to ask if she'd agree to a DNA test to prove his theory had she answered him. He also confessed that he'd made the call to her parents knowing that it went against her wishes. He'd hoped to feel some kind of connection if he heard their voices. Knowing why he'd done it had diminished her anger, and she eventually forgave him. It had taken a while for her to get used to the idea that her brother was suddenly in her life. She could understand that he needed to wrap his head around the shifted image of his family, but she was worried that her story would keep him from making the connection he'd searched for his whole adult life.

Thank you so much for the family photo you sent me. I know you said it's very old and that Zoe is no longer a baby, but I'm also aware that it's probably the only one you have and that it was maybe even your only copy, judging by the analog quality of it. Jeez, I can't believe I have a niece who's fourteen already.
I know you said you don't want to come back home for a visit any time soon, but I'd love to meet you someday soon. Maybe we can plan coinciding leave and meet somewhere halfway. Germany is beautiful, and I know my way around a few places after spending some time there. I'm sorry, I have to go now, or I'll be late for work. Let me know what you think.
Cheers, and don't forget to cover your butt.
Mark

Parker folded the letter and slid it back into her pocket. She pulled out her phone and stared at the digital version of the photo she'd sent Mark. He was right; it was the only photograph she'd taken with her when she snuck back to get the papers that allowed her to start a new life. But she'd made copies throughout the years so the original could stay safely behind in storage. If only she could have done the same with her heart.

Chapter Three

THE AIRCRAFT CAME TO a standstill and the loading hatch opened. The early morning air chased away the lethargy of the long flight. Sleep hadn't been kind; her mind had been too busy to allow it. Kid looked like he'd slept like the dead through most of the flight and had just come around from his slumber.

She disembarked the plane with her pack on her back and her duffel in hand, and she and Kid made their way down to the tarmac. Between the long flight and lack of cool-down after the workout session, her muscles had seized up and left her stiff and aching. Her body was letting her know she wasn't eighteen anymore.

"Are you okay?" Kid looked sideways at her.

She rolled her shoulders. "Yeah, I'm fine. Just not used to all the idle time and inactivity."

"Don't you think occasionally slowing down and appreciating life is worth it?" He adjusted his grip on her duffel. "I do."

A chill ran down her back, and she didn't think it was entirely due to the weather. She hadn't allowed herself to slow down since she'd been released from the hospital. Parker stood on the tarmac, taking in her surroundings. It felt a bit surreal being on US soil again. The pale half-moon grew fainter by the minute, giving way to daylight. The sun battled its way over the horizon, tinging everything in a reddish golden light and throwing long eerie shadows.

It was familiar and yet so different from what she'd left behind in the Middle East. The desert was pitch black and quiet at night. The first orange glow of the morning sun turned the land into a dull gray surface that slowly filled with activity as the rising sun infused the landscape with color. The sheer breadth of the facility and the level of activity this early in the morning made her feel smaller and more insignificant than when she'd stood on the barren desert back east with nothing but parched land as far as the eye could see.

"Good morning, I'll be your ride today." An ensign stood next to a vehicle and saluted them.

She and Kid returned the salute and the greeting.

"I only expected one." The driver looked from one to the other and looked a bit helpless.

"You know whom you were expecting?" Kid asked.

"No." He took Parker's duffel from her and put it into the back. "I'll just take you both, and you can sort it out in the office."

When they got to base, they freshened up and changed into dress uniform before heading to the judge advocate general's office. The door opened, and Admiral Jacob Pike filled the space.

Both she and Kid saluted. "Good morning, sir."

He answered their greeting and settled his gaze on her. "Captain Snow, I need to speak with you." He half turned and looked at Kid. "And who are you?"

"Lieutenant Callahan, sir."

"I don't need to talk to you. Go, enjoy your leave." Pike stepped aside to free his doorway.

"Do you want me to wait, Snow?" Kid whispered.

She shook her head. They hadn't managed a proper goodbye yet, but she didn't want to make him wait to enjoy his vacation. They could talk later if what was happening called for it. "He's right; enjoy your time off." She walked past Kid and into Pike's office.

"Close the door," Pike said.

He settled behind his desk, and she stood at attention, waiting. Her skin crawled, and she was colder than she'd been outside. This was where she'd find out why she'd been called back early.

"At ease, captain. Sit down." He gestured toward a chair.

Her body didn't obey the order. She'd never been asked to sit by anyone ranking that high.

Pike looked at her for a moment before he got up, walked around his table, and sat in one of the visitor chairs. "Please, sit down."

She couldn't outright refuse his invitation, so she complied. The simple act made her even more wary of what was to come. Her stomach gave a tiny flip flop in response. She was glad she hadn't eaten for hours, or she might've been sick.

"Captain." He regarded her for a moment, seemingly equally uncomfortable. "How are you this morning?"

Something must be really wrong for him to ask such a personal question. There must be a way she could politely refuse to answer to keep the conversation professional. She had no desire to explain her urge to be anywhere but in DC, but she couldn't think of one. Instead, she said, "Fine," and hoped he'd move on.

"I wish there'd be an easier way of doing this, but there isn't. You have a family situation, an emergency of sorts."

Dread settled around her heart and squeezed it tight. What could be going on at home that called for this? Different possibilities ran through her head but none of them made much sense. She wanted to ask but the words wouldn't come.

"Captain Snow," he said, "there's no easy way to put it. Your sister, Kate, is in the hospital, and the doctors don't think she has much time left."

White noise filled her ears and made her dizzy. *No, it can't be Kate.* Heat rushed through her body. Her uniform felt too tight to properly breathe. She needed fresh air, and she needed it now. She made herself stand up, and she took a few unsteady steps toward the door.

"Did you hear me, Snow?" Pike got up and took her arm. "Captain?"

"Sorry, sir. Did you say something else?"

He guided her back down into the chair and offered her a glass of water. "I said you have a lot of leave saved. Go home and find out what's happening. Take two weeks for now. That's an order.

After that, we'll see if you're ready to resume your work or if you need more time."

She left the office and stumbled outside. The fresh air cleared her head, and she let it wash over her, relieved when it helped her regain some of her composure. The rest of her conversation with Admiral Pike had melted into a stream of meaningless words. All she needed was to find out what was going on with Kate. It was crazy early, but she pulled her cell from her pocket and pressed it against her ear. She prayed that Kate had the same old number, but the probability of that was small. The call connected and a tinny voice droned in her ear, "The person you are calling—" She hung up. The phone was switched off, whoever had that number.

When she'd gotten onto the plane, she had no intention of going to see any of her family, including Kate. But now all she could think about was getting there as fast as possible. She needed some answers.

She walked off the base and onto the street. Before she'd decided where to take the bus, she spotted Kid standing at the curb.

"You look like you got bad news," he said and walked toward her.

She clenched her jaw, unwilling to share what she'd just learned.

"It's okay, you don't have to talk about it, Snow. Just know that I'm here if you need someone."

"Thanks." She hoped that her face wouldn't betray the rollercoaster of emotions whizzing around her head.

"Do you have anyone coming for you?" he asked.

Her hand went to the phone in her pocket involuntarily. She itched to get it out and make another call. She owed her family better than to show up unannounced, though she was pretty sure they expected her this time. She dropped her hand back to her side. "No, I don't think so."

"Jazmin just finished her night shift, and she's picking me up. I'm sure she wouldn't mind dropping you off somewhere downtown."

"Thanks for the offer, but I don't want to cause you any extra hassle with your sister. I'll be fine on my own." She longed for the anonymity and time the bus ride would offer to settle her emotions.

A maroon station wagon rolled to a stop, and Kid clasped her shoulder. "My ride is here. Give me a call if you want and take care of yourself in the meantime."

He got into the car. She was about to turn away when Kid stuck his head through the window.

"You sure we can't drop you off somewhere?"

She leaned down and looked inside the car. Jazmin was dressed in rumpled scrubs and gave her a tired smile. "No, thanks though." She had no interest in becoming embroiled in a confrontation between the two of them about their cancelled Thanksgiving plans.

Her phone was back at her ear before Jazmin's car was out of sight. She'd redialed Kate's number and got the same result. Before she could make a call to her parents to inform them of her arrival, the battery died, and the screen went black.

Parker's knees went weak, and she wobbled under the weight of her gear. Her life was about to change. Was her dead phone a premonition of what was to come?

Chapter Four

BY THE TIME PARKER walked down the street of her childhood home, she'd been mistaken for a man more than once. The dress uniform in combination with her height did an excellent job of disguising her few feminine features, almost as well as her desert camo. Her androgyny had come in handy in the Middle East and provided her with a certain freedom without compromising her security. Here, she'd usually correct people, but she couldn't be bothered today. Her thoughts were filled with worry about Kate.

It took her longer than she'd expected to make her way home. Going on a bus in uniform had earned her stares from some passengers. Even now, she could feel eyes on her. Curtains shifted back in the windows she passed, curious occupants tracking her way down the street.

Her surroundings looked and felt different but also the same. The streets used to be alive with children from the neighboring family homes, but now they were quiet, with only the rumble of an occasional passing car engine disturbing the peace. The low hanging sun in the sky reminded Parker that it was still early. Most kids would be in school right now.

Maybe it wasn't the neighborhood that had changed so much but her. Leaving had changed her. She'd grown into herself, become comfortable in her own skin. This version of herself probably wouldn't fit in around here. When they'd disembarked, the sun had fought the night's sky with quiet persistence. Now, it fought to climb over the rooftops and provided a special show of light and shadow.

Her childhood home came into view. She wondered if Aunt

Colleen still lived in the house across the street. She hadn't spoken to her since the day she'd walked out on Kate. The driveway was vacant, and the house looked like it could use some repairs. Despite it already being fall, the front yard looked like no one had tended to it in years. The shrubs close to the neighboring property seemed out of control. The cherished red maple tree had shed its leaves, littering the ground and part of the walkway to the house. With the streets and other front yards reasonably devoid of leafy remains, it became clear that this state wasn't a recent thing.

Parker sighed. She might never know what happened here. She'd forfeited the right to know when she left and didn't look back. A part deep inside her wanted to know anyway. She turned to the big family home across the street. It had barely changed. The window frames had gotten a new coat of paint, and maybe the front door had a new shade of dark blue. The curtains in the front room were drawn, and the driveway was empty. Maybe no one was home.

She made her way to the front door, not sure if she hoped someone would answer or not. The front door opened before she could ring the doorbell and revealed her mother, dressed in an impeccable suit. She recognized her mother's figure despite her face being hidden in the shadow cast by the open door. She stepped outside and the sun revealed her mother's once raven black hair, so much like her own, was now streaked with grey. Deep circles under her eyes marred her beautiful face and made her look like she was recovering from a draining illness herself. The worry lines around her eyes and mouth were more pronounced than Parker remembered from their last Skype call five months ago. But who was she kidding, those calls had been few and far between. Her mother's face was silent testimony that she hadn't been sleeping well.

So many questions flooded her mind, and a simple hello seemed to be stuck in her throat. She couldn't do anything but stare. Her mother came closer and hesitantly raised her hand.

Her fingers brushed over the ribbons on Parker's uniform, briefly lingering over the first one that held her Medal of Honor. It hadn't been there the last time she'd been home. Her mother lifted her hand, and Parker thought she would stroke her cheek but instead she ran her fingers over Parker's head.

"Your hair." Helen met Parker's gaze. "Every time I see you, your hair is shorter than before. I keep expecting you to be completely bald."

"Really, Helen, my hair?" She wanted to claw her words back when the sad expression on her mother's face drove home how much she disliked their estrangement. But it was her choice. Parker hadn't been interested in conditional love. Her mother's deep voice was similar to her own, though the smoky quality was much fainter and hidden by the thickness of unshed tears.

"It's so short."

"I like it short." Her usual pixie cut, that she wore slightly longer on top, was at least three weeks overdue for a trim. Before she could say anything else, her mother enveloped Parker in a bone crushing hug, gear and all.

"I'm so glad you came home." Her mother buried her face into Parker's shoulder.

The tears her mother had suppressed when she first opened the door found their way out and onto Parker's neck. The urge to push her mother away and tell her that those tears were a decade too late almost overwhelmed her. She'd only done what her father had told her to, her mother had to know that.

Her mother's shoulders heaved. "I'm sorry we handled you and Kate so poorly. I wish we could go back and change the past. We've lost so much time."

The words registered on Parker's mind but didn't manage to penetrate the numbness that had settled over her since she'd left the base. They stood in an awkward embrace for some time, making Parker's back hurt and her left thigh spasm. It was the first time the old injury was giving her trouble since she went back on active duty.

Her mother slowly let go of her. "If you'd let us know you were coming, we would've picked you up."

"When was I supposed to let you know? Before or after I left the office of my superior who ordered me to come here? Somehow, I think you've known I was coming long before I did."

"I have no idea what you're talking about. I would've appreciated a call, that's all I'm saying. But not one in the middle of the night again."

"I barely missed the small hours," Parker said, gesturing to the rapidly rising sun. "I got orders to report to DC. There wasn't exactly enough time for a social call before my flight left and a visit wasn't on my agenda before I got here."

She didn't tell her mother she wanted to see Kate and only Kate. "Helen, I need to know what's going on." Parker was about ready to come out of her skin. Pike's words had dropped like a bombshell, leaving her in a state of pseudo-reality where her mind desperately sketched out the worst-case scenarios in vivid color.

Kate had been the center of her universe for so long that she couldn't imagine a world where she didn't exist. Not being able to see her or being near her was one thing, but the thought of living in a world without Kate in it threatened to suffocate her.

Parker's mother opened the door wide and motioned for her to come inside. "Why don't you take your bags to your old room and freshen up? There are clean towels in your bathroom."

"I need answers first." Parker said.

"You need a shower." Her mother wrinkled her nose.

Parker wanted to object when her mother insisted she freshen up before they talked. The need for answers stretched her nerves thin. But getting the shower over with would be much faster than starting an argument. Besides, the travel had left her sweaty and grimy, and cleaning up would make her feel at least a little better. Getting out of her uniform and under the cold shower was oddly freeing. Entering the house in uniform had made her feel like a fish out of water, the same as last time. She'd never meant for those two parts of her life to intersect. It made her glad that she remembered to bring the old pair of jeans she'd stuffed in the bottom of her deployment bag and hadn't touched since she went overseas. They still fit well enough and with one of her green USMC T-shirts, she looked more like a civilian. The soft fabric on her skin felt like an embrace of a long-lost friend.

Parker made one last attempt to finger-comb her damp hair into order, but the short strands didn't want to obey. She didn't know why she was bothering. No one here would care or notice a few hairs out of place. She jogged down the stairs. "Can we talk now, Helen?"

"I really wish you would call me Mom." Helen's eyes shimmered and she turned away.

Parker ground her teeth together and shook her head. She hadn't called her that since the day she'd left this house. Her parents lost that privilege when they gave Parker that final ultimatum. "I didn't mean about me. I want to know what's going on with Kate."

"Sit down." Helen pointed toward the breakfast bar. She poured a cup of coffee and added creamer. "How do you take your coffee?"

"Black." *Like my soul.* Parker settled on a stool.

A few moments later, her mother put a cup in front of Parker together with a cream cheese bagel. How could her mother think she could get anything down? A lead balloon had taken up residence in her stomach the moment Admiral Pike had broken the news, and that left little room for anything else. "Can you please tell me what's going on?" Parker closed her hands around the ceramic mug and let the heat slowly warm her icy fingers.

"In a moment. You need to eat first."

"I'm not hungry." The unexpected attention of her mother left her out of sorts. Parker had done a damn good job taking care of herself for the past decade.

"When was the last time you had food that requires more

preparation than opening a plastic wrapper?"

Parker exhaled and glared at her mother. She noticed her own rigid posture mirrored in her. Maybe having to talk about whatever was going on was as hard on her mother as it was for Parker, waiting for answers. Her mother took a seat at the breakfast bar and faced Parker. She took in her mother's appearance and suddenly wondered why she was at home if she wasn't expecting Parker. Her parents ran their own law firm. For as long as she remembered, they were out the door before seven each morning and seldom came home before ten.

The early mornings and late nights had changed after Zoe, their first granddaughter, was born, but as far as she knew her mother hadn't stopped working at the office altogether. "Why are you wearing shoes in the house? And why are you not at work?"

Her mother flexed her hands. "I've been working from home for the past couple of months. I only go into the office if I have to. Most of my work I can do here in the study."

It took Parker's finely honed self-control not to hurry her mother on when she stopped. Instead, she took a sip of the too-hot coffee and burned her tongue.

"I promised Colleen I'd check in on her this morning. That's why I was ready to leave the house when you showed up."

"Sorry, I didn't mean to keep you." Old hurt made Parker's words much sharper than she meant them to be.

"No." Her mother's shoulders drooped, and her brow furrowed. "You're not keeping me. I can't put into words how glad I am that you're here."

"Why, Helen?" she asked softly.

Moisture escaped from the corner of her mother's eye, and she wiped at it. "I was afraid you wouldn't make it in time. She's really bad this time, honey."

Kate was why she had been called home. How bad had she gotten?

"They told us to call the family together." Helen held onto

Parker's forearm with surprising strength.

"Who told you?" Cold tendrils crawled up Parker's spine.

"The doctors. Kate started to display the first signs of liver failure seven months ago. It became readily apparent that there was nothing they could do to stop it." Helen looked away and toyed with her cup. "She was evaluated, and her name went onto the transplant waiting list. But the list is long, and the average waiting period for a transplant is well over a year. Colleen, your father, and I got tested to see if we would be suitable to serve as a living donor. Sadly, none of us is a match." She shook her head. "Kate declined badly about a week ago. The doctors think she doesn't have much time before she's too weak for any kind of surgery. It's unlikely they'll find her a transplant in time. She's in the hospital to help her manage the side effects and pain."

"Kate needs a transplant? Why wasn't I told about that? I may only call twice a year to check in on Zoe, and sometimes I don't even manage that. But it doesn't mean I wouldn't have liked to know. You could have gotten in contact with me. You think I'm such a heartless monster that I don't care what happens to her? She was so much more than my best friend, even before her parents were killed in that car accident." Parker tried hard to control her rising voice. She couldn't keep her whole body from tensing, as if she was getting ready to do battle.

Her mother visibly recoiled and slid off the chair, putting distance between them. "That's something you should ask Kate."

"I asked you, Helen." Did her own mother really think her capable of violence? Or was it a reflex to shy away? Helen showed the same behavior that Parker had seen in people who'd been abused. It was hard to admit that there were things she didn't know about her own family, because she'd been forced to leave instead of staying and learning how her family functioned after she reached adulthood. "I'm sorry, Helen. I didn't mean to upset you."

"It's all right." Helen tugged a strand of hair behind her ear.

Parker couldn't sit still any longer. Her nerves were too raw. She pushed her untouched bagel away and got up. "I need to see her. Please, Helen. I need to see her now."

The coffee soured in Parker's stomach when she tried to picture what she was going to find when she saw Kate in the hospital. The details of what she'd just learned didn't want to compute with what she'd been told about Kate's condition as a teenager. She needed more information. She needed to know that there was a sliver of hope for Kate.

Chapter Five

PARKER STRODE DOWN THE long hospital hallway, her mother barely able to keep up with her in her heels. Parker didn't care. Kate was so close now. Before she reached the door located at the end of two intersecting hallways, it opened. An older woman stepped outside and closed the door behind her. It took her a moment to comprehend that she was looking at Aunt Colleen. It was her hair Parker noticed first. Only here and there were reddish streaks visible among the gray tresses that hinted at the once vibrant color. With clothes that looked half a size too big on her slender frame and worry lines carved deep into her face, Colleen looked far older than her fifty-seven years, a few years younger than Parker's mother. The dark circles under her eyes didn't help. It took everything for Parker to not stare open-mouthed at her.

Colleen stared at her like she saw a ghost. They stepped toward each other but stopped like neither of them knew how to greet the other. She wished the rules of engagement in civilian society were as clear to her as those of a military encounter. *Get a grip.* Colleen had been like a second mother to Parker throughout her teens. The disconnection from her former life bothered her more than she'd expected.

Colleen embraced her with surprising strength. Parker didn't move but then loosely circled her arms around Colleen. Bony shoulders poked her through tailored clothing.

"I won't break if you give me a real hug," Colleen said.

It shamed Parker that Colleen could see right through her. They separated when her mother caught up. She and Colleen exchanged a hug that looked a lot less awkward than the one they had.

"Hello, Colleen. You look like you haven't slept at all last night."

Colleen shrugged and shook her head. Parker had never seen that woman shrug. She and Kate had gotten hell for shrugging as teenagers. The gloom and unspoken grief hung in the air around the two women like it was a tangible thing Parker could touch.

"Rough night?" Helen squeezed Colleen's arm.

"Kate's asleep. The pain kept her up all night. We can go in, but you have to promise not to wake her, Parker," Colleen said.

Parker reached for the handle. Colleen grabbed her hand stopping her.

"Promise me, Parker," Colleen said. "Or we wait until Kate wakes up."

"I want to see her now."

"You can't say anything, Parker, I mean it. Her sleep isn't very deep right after she drifts off. And you don't know what waits on the other side of this door."

"And whose fault is that?"

Both women looked away and said nothing.

"I promise, okay? I'll stay quiet." Neither of them had the slightest idea on how well Parker could control her outward reactions. It had taken her a while to perfect the skill, but now it was second nature. She didn't switch off her emotions, like so many others did. She just put them away in a safe place to examine them later when she was alone.

Helen frowned. "Are you sure you don't want to wait? We can come back later."

"I need to see her."

"I hope you can find it within yourself not to run out when you do."

Parker clenched her jaw. "I didn't come all this way to run."

Colleen opened the door, and what she saw was nothing she could've prepared for. Monitors and machines surrounded the head of the bed on either side, softly humming. Kate's skin had a yellow tint, an odd contrast to her Irish red hair that lay braided over her left shoulder. The shiny tresses Parker remembered were gone, and what was left seemed lifeless and dull. Kate looked almost like a ghost. Her body formed a fragile outline beneath the blanket, and her hands were way too thin. Only the shallow chest movement and the steady heartbeat displayed on one monitor indicated life.

Parker stepped closer to the bed and held her hand over Kate's skin, checking that she was still warm, but she stopped just short of touching her. The promise she'd given to Colleen rang in her ears like an echo. Rooted in place, she watched Kate's chest rise and fall. The movement hypnotizing her, and her breathing fell into a slow rhythm with Kate's.

"You can sit down. It'll be a while before she wakes again," Colleen whispered.

Time seemed to stretch and contract in odd patterns while Parker sat and watched Kate sleep. Passing through several time zones with no sleep left her disjointed. Her body yearned for rest while her mind refused to settle.

The cloak and dagger way of getting her home had told her that things were bad, but she couldn't believe what she was seeing. Fear would overwhelm her as soon as she allowed her emotions out of *that* little box in her mind. But she couldn't risk setting them free just yet. She needed a clear head and to stay functional if she wanted to help Kate.

She wished she'd insisted on knowing how Kate was on one of her calls with Zoe. But she knew they wouldn't have told her. For the first time she asked herself if there had been a different path to the one chosen, one with a different outcome. Parker hung her head. She would never know the answer to that question.

They sat in silence until her mother left to get some food. The smell of disinfectant grated on her nerves and brought back old memories. Without any distraction, she had to do her best to keep them at bay with sheer willpower. Every muscle in her body tensed and made her back spasm, but she didn't dare to move in case she woke Kate.

Colleen lowered her knitting. Parker could see something was on her mind from the look in her eyes.

"You've grown up, Parker."

Parker looked at Colleen and inclined her head toward Kate to remind her of the warning Colleen had given earlier.

Colleen smiled. "The doctors will be in any time now with another round of medication."

Parker nodded.

Colleen placed her knitting on her knee and sighed. "Talk to me. Please."

"We haven't seen each other since I was nineteen. Of course I've changed."

"That's not what I mean. There are people in their fifties that are still children. They may look all grown up, but they're not mature." Colleen patted her knee. "Yes, your physical appearance has changed, but you've matured beyond your years. I see an old soul shine in your eyes every time you look at me, one that has seen far more than anyone probably should have."

"Likewise."

"What do you mean?" Colleen asked and placed her hand over Parker's.

Parker had been subconsciously rubbing at the scar tissue on her thigh. "I recognize a kindred spirit when I look at you now."

"I don't know much about what you've been up to these past ten years, but I don't think I can come close to what you've experienced."

She covered Colleen's hand with her own. "It's not a competition. Being stationed in a war zone isn't the magic key to maturity. I chose that path. You probably had to do the same when you were kicked out by your parents for falling in love with a girl." It must've been hell for Colleen that her parents wanted their sixteen-year-old daughter dead or locked in one of those gay conversion camps, cut off from everything, including her brother.

The reflection of memories seemed to swim in Colleen's eyes. "That makes my reaction to realizing you and Kate were in love even worse." Colleen choked. "We didn't kick you out, but our behavior drove you away just the same. I don't know what happened to you since you left, nor do I have the right to ask, but you look like you've paid your dues."

Parker looked away. "You don't know that." The harsh slam of the front door in her face echoing through her memories was still all too vivid.

"You've sat ramrod straight for the past four hours, and the only movement is your hand rubbing over your thigh every time Kate moans. Tension is rolling off you in waves."

Parker looked back at Kate and felt powerless. Every time Kate moaned, cold tendrils of dread squeezed a little tighter around Parker's heart. For so long, Kate had been the love of her life, her reason to breathe. She still cared deeply for her.

"There's something you should know."

Parker tilted her head but didn't look back.

"Kate has a severe case of Wilson's disease and end stage liver failure as a result." Colleen shifted in her chair and pulled her hand away. "I'm trying to tell you that she's suffering, Parker. Things aren't looking good."

The tiny hairs on Parker's neck stood on edge, and a chill ran down her spine. Banging filtered in through the closed door and reverberated in the room. She flinched and lifted her shoulders a fraction of an inch to regain control. *What was that?* Colleen seemed to be unaffected by the sound while it almost made her ears hurt and the light made her want to squint her eyes shut. She wasn't a delicate person however the lack of sleep was catching up with her and turning her senses into a hypersensitive mess.

Movement in the corner of her eye made her look back to Kate. Parker's eyes started burning, and her vision blurred. She clenched her fists on her thighs, and the icy coldness of her hands seeped through the fabric of her jeans.

Parker thought she'd imagined the movement when Kate's eyelids sluggishly blinked open and revealed unfocused blue eyes. The copper-tinted edges clouding her irises were a silent testament to the dreadful disease that was stealing Kate's life.

And yet, everything faded away when Parker looked into Kate's eyes. Her sparkling baby blues were dull and lacked any sign of recognition. Looking into Kate's eyes had always made her soul feel at peace, but today it left her untethered like someone cut loose her reason to *be*. The heaviness in her heart amplified when Parker saw the growing confusion in Kate's eyes.

Parker knew her despair didn't show on her face, she was too controlled for that. Inside, she was reeling from the emotional assault that had her adrift and overwhelmed. She managed to tap into the place in her heart where she held all the shared affection and love she'd once had for Kate. The memories calmed her mind, and she smiled.

Kate's trembling hand lifted a few inches from the bed. "Parker?"

Parker's heartbeat rushed in her ears, and her throat tightened. *You recognize me.* Kate blinked and struggled to sit up. Colleen got up, raised the bed, and helped Kate to sit, blocking Parker's view.

Kate looked at Colleen. "I thought I could feel Parker's presence," she said softly. "That's new."

"I'm here." Parker reached around Colleen and wrapped her fingers around Kate's hand.

Kate's cool fingers slipped between hers and squeezed lightly, but Kate kept her eyes fixed on Colleen. "Is she real?"

Parker's heart skipped a beat before it gave another painful squeeze. She wanted to scream, "Yes, I'm real, god dammit," but she clamped down on that need. She tried hard to remember all the things she'd read or heard about Wilson's disease to get a better idea of what Kate might need from her. She'd tried to find out some new information after seeing her mother and Zoe with

Kate nearly five years ago. She'd dismissed her findings, thinking that if things had gotten that bad, someone would have told her. It was clear now that she was wrong but why had they'd kept it from her? It irritated her that Kate's case seemed to be one of the few that didn't respond to medication and no one had bothered to tell her.

She mentally shook herself. There was no point obsessing over questions she had no answers to. She was here for Kate. She would count it as a small blessing that it wasn't too late for that. Parker had to believe that there was hope for her as long as she was alive. And even if that hope was faint, Parker vowed to find it and hold onto it for dear life. Maybe it was time to repair things with her family too. And if she really was too late, at least she'd get to say goodbye. A lump formed in her throat, and she furiously blinked away a tear that stubbornly clung to her lashes.

Colleen squeezed Kate's shoulder and stepped out of her line of sight. "Yes, Parker is here."

The deep crease between Kate's eyes smoothed out. "Parker, you came?"

"Of course I came." And she would've come a whole lot sooner.

"Stay?"

It was ironic that such a simple question could be so loaded. Parker wanted to say yes, she'd stay. But she didn't know how permanent her assignment in DC would be, especially since the situation with Kate seemed to be the reason for getting her here. Who knew what came after her two weeks were up? She didn't want to make a promise she couldn't keep. Before she could settle on an answer, she was interrupted by a sharp knock and the opening door.

Parker didn't bother to look up. The heavy footsteps told her it wasn't her mother who'd returned.

"Could you wait outside Miss Cane's room, Mr..." The doctor's voice trailed off when Parker turned to face her. "My apologies, ma'am."

Parker stood at attention at the word "ma'am." "No problem, ma'am."

"There's no need to stand at attention." Pink tinged the doctor's cheeks as she looked Parker up and down.

"Force of habit."

The doctor nodded. "I'm familiar."

Parker guessed the doctor was in her early forties and had once served in the military.

She held out her hand. "My name is Doctor Miller. I'm one of Kate's physicians."

"Parker Snow. It's good to meet you." Parker held out her left hand since Kate didn't relinquish the hold on her right one.

"I have to ask you to wait outside until we're finished."

"We understand." Colleen tugged on Parker's arm.

Kate's grip tightened, surprising Parker with the sudden show of strength. Colleen pulled on her other arm to make Parker move. It left Parker in the middle of a tug of war. She couldn't bring herself to release Kate even though she felt the impatient stares from the nurses and Doctor Miller.

"No." Kate gripped Parker's hand tighter. "She's not going anywhere."

Parker bit her lower lip not to laugh. She didn't want to go, but she also didn't want to openly defy the doctor's order. "How about I wait outside and come back in when the doctor's done?"

"No!"

Kate's stubbornness brightened Parker's gloom. She still had plenty of fight in her. Parker looked at the doctor on the other side of the bed and shrugged.

"There's nothing you can say to me that Parker can't hear."

The doctor looked first at Kate and then back at Parker. "Fine, if it's what you wish, Kate. Ms. Snow can stay." The doctor waved over the two nurses. "But you must stay out of our way."

"No problem." Parker pointed to the far side of the room. "I'll wait over there until you're done." She loosened her grip on Kate and took half a step away before Kate tugged her back. "It's okay, I'll be right over there. You'll still be able to see me."

"Please don't let go."

Kate sounded like a helpless child, and it stopped Parker from disentangling her hand. She looked from the doctor to Kate and back again. The fear she had seen in Kate's face made the blood run cold in her veins. The doctor on the other hand nodded slowly and gave Kate a reassuring smile.

The doctor exhaled. "Okay, we'll make it work."

The death grip on her hand loosened enough that blood flowed back into her fingers and made them tingle. "Hey, Kate, relax." She reached out to stroke her cheek like the old days but changed her mind at the last moment and gave Kate's shoulder a gentle squeeze instead. "I won't leave, and I won't let go of your hand either until you're ready." Parker moved her thumb in small circles over Kate's wrist. "But I'd like to give you as much privacy as I can."

Parker looked out the window and softly hummed to herself to drown out what was happening behind her. The unpleasant smell of the antiseptic stung in her nose and made her eyes water, blurring the skyline outside. The sun in the sky transformed into harsh fluorescent lights from another time and place. The memory pressed against her consciousness, wanting to come out. Parker gritted her teeth and pushed the memory behind a thicker mental wall.

Being here distorted the lines between the past and the present, and more of her suppressed memories floated back in. There was no time for them now, though she'd had to give in to them sometime soon or they'd become overwhelming and strike without warning. She shivered.

"Are you sure you want to go through with this, Kate?" Miller asked.

"Now more than ever."

"You're aware of the consequences?"

Consequences of what? Parker half turned to look at Kate.

"You sure you don't want me to go?" She asked the question, but she wanted to hear this.

Kate shook her head. "Yes, I am. My chances of survival are low. We all know that, and in any other case, it doesn't matter, does it?"

Miller just shook her head. "I just wish there was more—"

"I know." Kate gave a sad smile. "I'll sign that paper if it makes you feel better."

The conversation started to make Parker itch. She didn't have the slightest clue what was going on and was bursting with questions. Between her military training and her experience as a lawyer, she'd learned there was a time for questions and a time to listen. This was the latter.

The doctor shoved her hands into her lab coat pockets. "How about Monday? And you don't have to sign that paper. We can treat some more of the symptoms, and that will help with the confusion. Monday is still in plenty of time for Thanksgiving, and you can get some more rest."

Kate tugged at Parker's hand. "Will you still be here on Monday, Parker?"

"Um, yeah, I'll be here as long as you need me."

"Then Monday will be fine, Doctor Miller," Kate said.

The doctor turned to leave. "Get some rest, Kate, you've had a rough couple of days. Give the medication a chance to do its job."

Kate patted the bed next to her. "Sit down."

Parker reached for the chair.

"Here, on the bed. There's no need for you to be so far away."

Parker settled carefully on the edge, mindful not to crowd Kate but close enough to keep their hands locked together.

"How long will you stay in town?"

Parker glanced away. "I don't know." The transfer orders had caught her off guard, but it meant she could be around for the time being. She hadn't told her mother earlier because part of her wanted to be anywhere but home. Now things had changed. She'd do everything in her power to stay as long as Kate needed her, to stay as long as it would take to make Kate better.

Chapter Six

When Parker had told Kate she'd been awake for thirty-six hours it had been a slight understatement and was closer to sixty. She was bone tired and hoped to get a few hours of dreamless sleep. The chances were slim though. The concept of good sleep had deserted her a long time ago. The only question was if her current surroundings added to the nightmares, waking and otherwise.

Her old childhood room was exactly the same way as she'd left it. There wasn't a kernel of dust, and the shelves and cabinets were still occupied by her things. The chairs and bed were the ones she'd picked out when she started high school. Even the book she'd been reading was still lying on her desk. It looked worn, like someone had picked it up over and over in her absence, but maybe her memory of its condition was sketchy. The nephrolepis exaltata plant, also known as cotton candy fern, was there on her windowsill in the same hand-painted pot Kate had given it to her in. The only change there was the size of the fern. It had flourished in her absence, overcrowding the pot it lived in. Someone had obviously tended and watered it.

Parker went to the kitchen for some juice to distract her mind from running wild. She'd spent most of her last visit in pain, but she remembered telling her mother to convert her room into whatever was convenient for them the last time she left.

"Shit." She slapped the counter. Images of a case she'd worked came to mind unbidden, where a boy's room looked exactly the same years after his abduction. The parents had never gotten over the loss. Her chest burned with every breath she took. Her mind wheeled, desperately trying to make sense of everything.

"Are you okay?"

Her mother startled her but composed herself quickly. "Yeah, do you have some OJ?"

"Sure." She went to a cupboard and got a glass. "Why don't you tell me how you are while I make dinner for the two of us?"

"What about Harry and Zoe?" Parker asked.

"Zoe has an out-of-town basketball game tonight and will be back tomorrow, and your father has dinner with a client and won't be home until late."

"Don't go through any trouble on my account. I'm not hungry, and I'm fine."

"I call nonsense on both counts. You had the same small salad for lunch I had, and I'm starving." Her mother ushered her onto a chair at the breakfast bar before she inspected the contents of the fridge. "And I won't believe for a minute that you're fine. You're my daughter I know when you're lying."

"You think so?"

"Of course, call it a mother's intuition."

Parker took a sip of OJ and enjoyed the icy liquid sliding down her throat. "So you must've known all along that I was in love with Kate."

Her mother looked away and busied herself with washing tomatoes.

"I didn't think so."

Her mother picked up the chopping knife. "That's the reason I don't believe that you're fine now. Learning that Kate is dying must have been a huge shock for you."

"Jeez, thanks, Helen, for driving that point home with a sledgehammer."

"Sorry, but I don't believe it isn't affecting you. You sit here all cool as a cucumber. You can talk to me. You know that, don't you?"

"Keeping my head under fire is kind of what I do." On the outside, that was true, but internally, it was a whole different matter. Her stomach was in knots, her heart beat entirely too fast, and she was so unbelievably cold. She couldn't tell if it was due to the weather change or the situation. But after her entire world had collapsed around her, she'd never trusted anyone enough to discuss her feelings.

The last person she'd told how she felt was Linda, who had been her sister Nicole's best friend. If someone could understand what she felt, it was her. Linda had only lost her friend when Nicole died, though Parker always suspected Linda had deeper feelings for her sister. When Parker left, she lost the love of her life and her best friend in one go. Sure, it wasn't through death, but because she wasn't good enough, it somehow felt worse.

Parker spent three days crying on Linda's couch before beginning to make sense of what had happened and what she would do with her future. They hadn't kept in close contact after Parker enlisted. Linda was already an officer, and friendships across rank were frowned upon.

They'd seen each other in the courtroom a few times over the years, usually on opposing sides. They'd made it a point to catch up over coffee when the case concluded. A few years ago, they ended up working together for a few days when they both attended the same international military simulation. They'd promised to stay in touch after the training simulation was over. Linda had returned to her assignment aboard an aircraft carrier to finish out a sea assignment, and Parker was sent back to the Middle East. They exchanged a few emails here and there, and sometimes they managed to catch up over a meal if they ended up in the same location. Even when they were busy, they checked in with each other a few times a year, mostly around birthdays and holidays.

"Where did you just go?" her mother asked as she put pasta in a pot to boil.

"I was just remembering the last time someone tried to make me talk about my feelings." Parker shrugged. "It's been a while. I've learned how to deal with things on my own since then."

Her mother slammed the lid down on the pot with more force than necessary. "But you don't have to, do you get that?"

"Apparently, I do, seeing that no one thought about telling me that Kate was this ill for months. That tells me I'm as welcome here today as I was the day I left. Why am I even here?"

"I don't know, why are you here? Not one word from you in five months and then you just show up on our doorstep out of nowhere, with all your belongings."

"So you had nothing to do with me being sent here?" Parker emptied her glass.

"No."

A strange expression crossed her mother's face, but it was gone before Parker could identify it.

"How long are you here for anyway?"

The question sounding more like an accusation than genuine interest. Every bit of the conversation made her itch. She stood up. "You know what, I can get a hotel. I don't want to inconvenience you. No need to let Harry or Zoe know that I was even here."

"Sit down, Parker."

Parker remembered her resolution in the hospital—it was time to sort out her family issues. She returned to her seat and stared at her mother.

"That's enough, honey. You've been running from us for over ten years. It's time to stop." Her mother set their bowls down and sat beside her. "Eat before it gets cold."

"I'm not running. I did what you asked me to do."

"What?" her mother asked around a mouthful of pasta.

Parker reached for her fork. "Maybe that's a question that you better ask Harry, your husband."

"He's your father. Why won't you call him that?" Her mother sighed. "But what do you mean by that?"

"Eat before it gets cold and ask him when he gets home." Parker filled her mouth to indicate she was done talking.

Colleen arrived shortly after they finished dinner. Her mother and Colleen retired to the living room with a bottle of wine. She excused herself and went to her room.

Parker lay in her bed, typed living donor liver transplant into the search engine on her cell phone and eyed the results. She opened one from a renowned medical university but realized halfway through the first paragraph that she was too tired to comprehend what she was reading and let her eyes drift shut.

She woke disoriented, drenched in cold sweat. Her heart thudded against her chest, and the scent memory of acrid burning flesh assailed her nostrils. She patted down her body until she met the unfamiliar covers draped over her legs. The soft fabric beneath her fingers pushed back the memories and brought her back to the present, her childhood room.

Slowly, she untangled her legs and got up to get a dry shirt. She turned her old Timex toward the street side window to catch enough light to see the time. She'd thought countless times about replacing it with a smart watch, but the sentimental notion that it had once been Nicole's had her hang onto it. The display showed 0345: she'd gotten five solid hours of sleep, which was rare for her. It also meant she probably wouldn't get any more.

She made her way downstairs barefoot to get some cold water and shake the remaining traces of her nightmare. The lingering mixture of brandy, cigar smoke, and her father's aftershave made her gag. He used to drink and smoke with clients outside the house. She hadn't smelled any smoke in the house when she'd first arrived, so she hoped her mother's rule remained.

The cool kitchen tiles under her feet helped lift the remaining sleep fog from her brain. She craved coffee but didn't want to chance waking everyone with the smell of a fresh brew. Besides, she had no idea how to work the high-tech monster of a coffee maker that took up half the countertop and appeared to have a cup as well as a pot mode. She poured a glass of ice water and wandered toward the living room.

In the darkness of the room, she could barely see. She stubbed her little toe on the couch and let out a small yelp. She hopped on one foot to massage her bruised toe with one hand and tried not to drop the water she held in the other.

Parker heard a soft snore from the darkness. *Who the hell was in here?* "Huh."

"I'm awake. What? I'm awake." Colleen's sleepy voice came from the sofa.

"I'm sorry." Parker instinctively reached out to steady her as she rose. "I didn't know you were sleeping down here. Go back to sleep. I'll go back to my room." She guided Colleen back to sit and began to leave.

"No, don't go." Colleen scrubbed her hands over her face. "Tell me how you are?" she asked.

Parker sighed. "Are you asking because you want to know or because Helen put you up to it?"

"Helen mentioned you were withdrawn after you came back from the hospital."

Colleen tugged Parker down on the sofa next to her. "I'm asking because I care about you, Parker. I know we haven't spoken in a long time, but I still care."

"Do you remember your last words to me?" Maybe the question wasn't fair, but she couldn't help it. Parker had never been able to forget it.

"What?"

"The last thing you said to me before I walked out of your house."

"You mean before you walked out of all our lives."

Parker didn't miss the faint trace of hurt in her voice. "If you want to phrase it like that, yes."

"You gave Kate's ring back to me and asked me to give it back to her when she was ready. I don't remember your exact words."

"That's what I said to you. But I wanted to know if you remember what *you* said to *me*." Parker took a gulp of her water, moistening her parched throat.

"Sorry, I don't."

"'It's for the better.'"

"I don't understand. Why did you ask if it's better that I don't remember?"

"That's what you said. You opened the door and said, 'It's for the better, child.'" Another memory gained momentum in her mind, but she caught it before it spiraled out of control. "Do you really think it was for the better?"

Colleen began to sob, and her entire body heaved. Something within Parker broke free, and she cradled Colleen in her arms, letting her cry herself dry. They sat like that for what felt like an eternity before Colleen struggled up from the couch. The leather squeaked and groaned when she shifted her body.

"I'm going to bed. The couch isn't a good place to sleep for old bones."

"You're going home?" Parker asked.

"No, I'll just take the guest room. Helen won't mind."

The clouds shifted, and bright moonlight streaked into the living room and illuminated the conservatory her father had built for Kate to paint in. The silvery light showed that the easel and art supplies were gone, and flowers and wicker chairs occupied the space now. Parker turned one of them to face out toward the backyard before she sat and tucked her feet under her butt. She gazed into the darkness and shook her head. How could Colleen not remember what she'd said to her? Back then, it had been like a punch to her already tender heart. Colleen's overall reaction baffled her even more. It seemed like she felt genuine regret about what had happened. If so, why had she never tried to reach out?

Chapter Seven

PARKER'S ENTIRE LIFE HAD been turned on its head in a day. She'd fallen into a state of auto-functioning and not letting any of the things happening get too close. If she had, she'd lose it before she made it to the hospital to see Kate. Everyone around her seemed so resigned to Kate's fate that she hadn't questioned it in yesterday's stupor. *Shit.* There had to be something that could be done.

Light came on in the house bordering the back yard and pulled Parker out of her musings. She'd totally missed that the darkness had receded and left the sky in a blue-gray wash with some faint pink linings on the horizon. Movement in the lit window drew her attention, and she thought she caught a glimpse of a tall blond woman in a robe. Her subconscious jumped to an image of Linda. "Yup, you're going crazy," Parker muttered.

It was time to get off her butt and busy herself before her wayward running thoughts could drive her completely crazy. She got up and sauntered toward the kitchen. Maybe she could risk giving that fancy coffee maker a go. Her body and brain craved caffeine badly.

She stopped abruptly when she saw her father at the breakfast bar, reading the morning paper. From a young age, she'd been told not to disturb him in his morning ritual. She'd find a local coffeehouse to satisfy her cravings.

"There's no reason for you to stand out there." Her father folded the paper and put it aside. "I'm sorry we missed each other last night. How are you?"

How am I? He couldn't possibly be interested in her honest answer. It had been over ten years without a single word. They were nothing more than strangers. Once or twice she'd wondered if he'd listened in when she'd Skype called them. The times her mother seemed extra tense and downright distracted. Her only reason to call was to check in on Zoe and talk to her. It wasn't her niece's fault that Parker had to leave, and she did her best to show Zoe she hadn't forgotten about her. She owed that much to her and Nicole.

In the beginning, she'd tried to make those calls every few months. She learned quickly that her mother wouldn't let her talk to Zoe alone, claiming she was afraid Parker would upset her. The time stretches between calls quickly grew as Parker settled in her new life. Ever since she left after her only home visit, Zoe refused altogether to talk to her on the phone. But it hadn't deterred her from trying to reach out. Even if all she'd gotten the past few years was a brief conversation with her mother that never ventured beyond Zoe's development.

Her father looked at her over his glasses. "Have you lost the ability to speak?"

"No, sir." She instinctively straightened her spine.

Her father examined her like she stood on a witness stand and he was searching for her weak spot. "Then answer me?"

"I'm not sure how to answer that question, sir."

"For God's sake, relax! Come in, get some coffee, and sit. I won't bite your head off."

Relax? Like she was ever encouraged to relax in his presence. Parker inhaled the aroma of fresh coffee and quietly walked toward the coffee pot. It smelled heavenly compared to what she usually got. She poured the liquid gold into her cup and stopped two inches shy of the top. "Did you want to know how I've been since we spoke last, sir? We were barely on speaking terms when I lived here. I was very much under the impression that you preferred not to know." She topped her cup off with some cold water. "Or do you want to know how I'm dealing with the fact that no one told me that Kate's health had been declining for a while? There's also the matter that I was very suddenly sent home. Did you have anything to do with that? Everyone else was surprised to see me, but you don't seem to be." She hadn't intended to say so much, and her dispassionate delivery gave her words an eerie power.

"I see. I can't really blame you for thinking that I'd rather not know, can I?" His hands closed around his coffee mug, but he didn't lift it. "Please don't call me sir. I feel like a stranger in my own daughter's life."

Her nostrils flared. "But we are strangers. We haven't seen or spoken to each other in over a decade. But I could call you Harry if you'd prefer that."

"I'd prefer Dad." He gave her a sad smile. "But I'll take Harry."

"Fine."

"And you must've known that Kate was getting worse when the transplant discussion started, and we were all tested."

The words made her fear her coffee would make a reappearance. Acid gathered in her stomach and made her gag. She couldn't be entirely sure if her last call home was before or after they had learned Kate needed a transplant. But why had no one in her family reached out to her? Or at the very least asked her to get tested when it turned out none of them was a suitable match. It surprised her that finding out they hadn't even tried to make contact bothered her so much. She thought she'd accepted a long time ago that she couldn't expect much from them.

She looked at her father, realizing how drawn he looked. He'd aged considerably in the time she was gone. His reddish-brown hair was almost completely gray and had started to thin on the top. Even his well-groomed beard showed streaks of gray.

"Are you all right? You look a little green."

"I'm fine." Parker gripped the counter and shook her head. "Okay, I'm not. What makes you think Helen told me about it? I've not talked to anyone else in years. If you don't count Zoe, who has done her best to ignore me." She heard the bitterness in her own voice.

"Helen told me not to expect you back." He got up. "So I assumed you two talked."

"Did you ever consider that she told you that because she didn't tell me?" She swallowed rapidly, thinking she might be sick.

"You really don't look so good." He reached out to her but seemed to think better of touching her and let his arm fall. "Is there anything I can do?"

Parker wanted him to answer her but wasn't sure she could handle what he might say. She tried to read his face but couldn't find anything other than concern. If it was for her or because of something else, she couldn't say. She shook her head, deciding she couldn't handle any more of this right now.

"If you change your mind, you can talk to me. But I understand if you think it's none of my business how you are." He slid a set of keys toward her on the counter. "You need a way to get around while you're here."

She examined the keys set on an old keyring of hers, two different musical clefs forming a heart. Her fingers stroked over the shape. Kate had given it to her as a good luck charm before a piano recital. She recognized the house key, the other two were a mystery to her. "What are these for?"

"Your old car."

"You kept the old Ford?"

"Yes, it's had a tune-up and is ready to go." He looked at the floor and his cheeks colored slightly. "The third is for the garage next door. You remember Madame Fourie's place?"

"Yes." She'd spent her summers doing work around the garden for their elderly neighbor. She'd always been kind to her and Kate, especially when things got complicated with her parents.

"I bought it when Madame Fourie got into some financial troubles."

"When was that?"

"The summer before Nicole got ill. It was a sound investment, and I thought maybe one day..." Her father pursed his lips.

"Yes?"

"Never mind. We're probably going to sell it at some point. I let Kate have some fun planning the ground floor renovations when her declining health no longer permitted her to work for the interior design company she's been with since college. She needed a creative outlet after she'd already given up on painting. The contractors she found did a fantastic job bringing her plans to fruition." He blushed as if he noticed he sounded like a proud father. "You should take a look sometime. Shame she won't be able to make up a plan for the upper floor." He looked away and moisture glinted in his eyes.

The keys in Parker's hand clunked and alerted her to her trembling hands. All the new puzzle pieces of information overstimulated her mind and didn't have a place to fit in her mental image of what was going on. She needed space to catch her breath and process, preferably outside the house.

Chapter Eight

PARKER ARRIVED AT THE hospital bright and early. The building was quiet, and she stopped at the nurse's station on her way to ask for Dr. Miller. Maybe she could answer some of her questions.

The nurse squinted at a computer screen. "I'm sorry. It looks like Dr. Miller isn't in right now."

"Can you tell me when she'll be here?"

The nurse tapped a few more keys. "It looks like she's off today. Can I get a hold of someone else for you?"

"Oh." Could she consult a random doctor that may not even know Kate? Parker hung her head. "No, thank you for checking."

She walked to Kate's room and hoped that she could get hold of Dr. Miller the next day. She opened the door slowly, careful not to make a sound in case Kate was sleeping. Kate was upright in her bed, brushing her hair.

"Hey, Parker." Kate dropped the hairbrush into her lap and smiled.

The tension that was a constant companion receded slightly, leaving her weak-kneed when Kate greeted her with no evident confusion in her eyes.

"Would you mind helping me? It's still uncomfortable lifting my arm after the liver biopsy."

"What was the biopsy for?" Heat crept up Parker's neck. She hadn't planned to be so direct, but all the secrets she'd been confronted with in the past day had put her on edge.

"In simple English?" Kate wrinkled her nose. "To get a better idea of how bad my liver is and put me on a higher position on the donor list. Can we not get into the *I'm dying* conversation just yet?"

Parker wanted to push but sensed that Kate was about to close off. "Okay." She swallowed the lump in her throat. There had to be some way to keep Kate alive. She needed to see if Doctor Miller would talk to her about Kate's outlook and options and to find out why they had never approached her about the transplant.

"Help me with my hair, please?" Kate asked softly.

Parker had done this hundreds of times when they were growing up and later, when they had been a couple. She'd loved the feeling of Kate's soft hair gliding through her fingers when she brushed and braided it. "I'd love to."

She gave Kate a hug and inhaled her soothing scent before she took the brush. Kate wrapped her hand around Parker's neck, and goosebumps shot down her spine. She wasn't ready for the sudden intimacy the situation created and pulled back.

"I'm so glad you came back. There are things we need to talk about now that you're here." Kate caressed Parker's face.

"Yes, there are. I have some questions too. You seem better today and not as confused."

"You mean, am I sure you're real today?" Kate gave a humorless laugh. "Yes, I am. Illusional you doesn't smell that nice. That probably should have given it away much quicker yesterday. That you were real, I mean. It was like I could sense you in the room for the first time, and your changed appearance should have been a clue too." Kate's cheeks colored.

Parker hoped Kate's blush meant she liked what she saw and not that Kate was embarrassed about what she was admitting.

"Mostly the hallucinations I get are auditory when my copper levels get out of control. I had two visual episodes, one about a year after you left—and I didn't tell anyone that I suspected my medication had stopped working—and a fairly recent one. Both times I sort of saw you, the old you, like you looked before you left, but I couldn't *feel* your presence." Kate shook her head. "I don't know how to explain it. That thing that lets me know exactly where you are." Kate's brow furrowed, like something had just occurred to her. "It always went away when they found a new drug cocktail that stabilized me for a while."

"I'm so sorry you're going through all of this." Parker ran the brush through Kate's hair, the soft strands slid over her calloused palms and made her heart clench. *God, I've missed this.* Her memories didn't do the feeling justice.

"You probably have more than a few questions."

"Probably. I'm glad we're alone." The instant connection between them unsettled her a little. She wanted to phrase her questions carefully to avoid more barriers falling or getting re-erected between them. Getting closer to Kate or being pushed away could be equally painful.

"So am I, and I'm really sorry. We should've talked a lot sooner." Kate wrapped her arms around herself. "I should've tried harder when you left."

Parker stroked over Kate's head and gently massaged her scalp, hoping she could soothe some of her growing agitation. She began to braid Kate's hair down her back when the muscles at the base of Kate's skull relaxed.

The door banged open, and a nurse with a breakfast tray in hand scowled at them. "What are you doing here? Visiting hours haven't started yet. You have to leave."

"I want her to stay," Kate said. "My mom and aunt are here outside of visiting hours all the time."

"Not on my shift. Off you go." The nurse held the door open.

Such a mundane thing as visiting hours hadn't even crossed her mind when she was in a hurry to see Kate this morning. She almost told the nurse to get lost but didn't want to make any trouble for Kate. She'd likely be the one to suffer if Parker got in the nurse's face.

Parker ignored the taunting open door and the glaring nurse. "Save the argument for when it matters, Kate. I'll be back later."

Kate looked as if she wanted to protest.

"I promise. I have questions for you." She winked at Kate.

Kate inhaled sharply. "I know." She lowered her gaze. "I'll do my best to answer them."

Parker made her way to the door. That was the best she could hope for after all the years of silence.

***

Several hours later Parker took a wrong turn and ended up taking a different route to Kate's room. The hallways and doors looked the same, and she wondered how often she would repeat this trip in the coming days. Would it be often enough that the hallways and doors stopped looking all the same? Or would she forever feel lost in the endless maze of stairways and corridors? The muted green color of the walls made her feel like they were closing in on her and left her with a strange sense of suffocation.

Her approach took longer but left her with the perfect view of Kate's room. A teenage girl with a sports bag slipped into Kate's room before she was visible to anyone from the intersecting hallway. The girl's face was foreign and yet so familiar. A faint reddish tint was visible in the dark plaited locks that hung over one shoulder. Parker's breath caught when the image sunk in. It was like the ghost of her sister had come back to haunt her. The girl looked so much like Nicole, so much like herself before she had lost her teenage roundness in her early twenties, that it could only be Zoe, her niece.

Parker pushed the door open and hovered in the entrance, but her presence in the room went unnoticed.

"Hi, Kate, how are you? We won the game." Zoe jumped and threw her arms in a victory motion. "I see Colleen did your hair today. I love it!" She walked over to the bed.

"Actually, no—"

"I tell you, school sucked big time. The stupid math test on Friday was way too complicated, and Grandma insisted I study, or she wouldn't let me go to the game. That's why I haven't visited you the last two days." Zoe sat on the edge of the bed.

Parker swallowed hard. She'd failed Zoe. She had failed Nicole, and she'd failed Kate. It was unforgivable. The emotions she'd kept in a box in her heart ever since Nicole's funeral pressed against the barriers that contained them.

"I swear it's like Grandma just doesn't get it at all. School will be there whenever. Without a miracle, I only get a few more weeks with you at most." Zoe wiped at her cheek with the back of her hand. "Really, who cares if I failed a single math test?"

Parker struggled to breathe. She needed air, but she couldn't move. It took everything she had not to lose it right there. Kate shifted, spotted Parker at the door, and motioned her over. Parker couldn't get herself to move or speak.

Zoe turned and frowned. "You're not with the hospital, are you?"

Parker shook her head. She'd hoped for recognition, but Zoe really had no idea who she was. She'd only been nine the last time she saw Parker in person.

Something registered, and Zoe threw herself at Parker, beating her fists against Parker's chest. "You have no right showing up here. You abandoned Kate when she was sick and needed you the most."

The words cut Parker deeper than any physical assault Zoe could inflict on her.

"Zoe, stop! Stop it!" Kate said.

"You left us, you left me! Why did you abandon me? All I ever wanted was to know about my mom and the sister she loved so much. But you haven't visited in years." Zoe struck Parker again. "And when you finally did show up, you barely stuck around long enough to say hello before you ran away again. Am I such a horrible person that you don't want to know me? Granddad's never home, and Grandma can hardly look at me even though she tries to hide it, and the only person that ever cared about me is dying."

It would be easy enough to stop Zoe but she'd no desire to.

She welcomed every bit of hurt Zoe could inflict physically and with words.

"Zoe, stop!" Kate climbed out of bed and shuffled toward them.

"Why couldn't she stay away and let us say our goodbyes in peace, Kate? She hurt you so much and now she's back to hurt you some more. You deserve better."

Kate reached out to Zoe. "You don't understand. I want her to be here."

Zoe's uncontrolled punches missed Kate by mere inches. It was all that Parker needed to react and hold onto Zoe's wrists. "Stop it, Zoe. You'll hurt Kate."

Zoe really looked at Parker for the first time with wide, wild eyes. Zoe tried to pull her hands free, and Parker let her.

"Get out of here." Zoe pushed Parker hard. "I don't want you here, no one does. I wish you'd died instead of my mom. I wish you were dying now instead of Kate."

The words hit her like a sledgehammer and smashed what was left of her heart. Tears welled in her eyes and blurred her vision, her throat constricted, making it difficult to breathe. It took her entire willpower to hold on to her emotions and head out the door.

"That's right, just leave. Disappearing is the only thing you're good at." Zoe glared at her.

Kate came closer. "Zoe, stop! Can't you see that you're hurting her?"

Zoe whipped around to face Kate and pointed at Parker. "She didn't care when Grandma got sick and had surgery. She didn't call once to see if she was okay before or after Grandma was in the hospital. Why didn't she stay away this time?"

Parker needed to get out of there right now before she fell apart on the spot. The revelations kept on coming. There'd been so much she'd missed. She gritted her teeth.

Her feet moved without conscious thought. Normally, she'd hit the gym and work off her emotions, but that wasn't possible right now. She wouldn't leave the hospital before she'd talked to Kate but for now, she needed a quiet space where she could give her tears permission to fall.

She moved past her mother, who stood in the hallway. Her pained expression told Parker that she'd heard enough. Her mother tried to stop her, but she kept moving. "You had surgery?" Parker didn't wait for an answer. She broke into a run and followed the signs to the hospital chapel. She wasn't much for praying, but the peace the place offered was just what she needed.

Parker sat on a bench with her eyes closed and tried to calm her thundering heart.

"May I sit?"

Parker looked up to see her mother. "Why not?" She scrubbed her hands over her face. Her tears had stopped falling a while ago, but her eyes burned, and her eyelids grated like sandpaper. She had no right to wallow in self-pity. Parker had left and not looked back because her father had told her to clear her head and get over Kate before she set foot in his house again. She'd resented her father for that impossible choice. But right now, she couldn't shake the feeling that part of the estrangement was her fault. She had to try harder for Kate's sake and for Zoe, even if it meant that she had to stay in DC and couldn't ask for a transfer somewhere else. She swallowed the hurt and looked at her mother. She had to let go of her anger toward her if they had any chance at a better relationship. "How are you?"

She gave Parker a sad smile. "I'm hanging in there. I hope you'll never have to know what it's like to lose a child. First, I had to give up my son. Then we lost your sister to leukemia, and now we're losing Kate."

Parker's head spun. She'd never considered how any of that had impacted her parents. It would be so easy to make her mother feel better by telling her Mark had found Parker and was thinking of reaching out to their mother. But she hesitated.

"I know Kate only came to live with us after her parents were killed. But I love her like she was my own and losing her will hurt as much as losing Nicole did."

"I'm sorry." Parker didn't know what else to say.

"I wished I hadn't failed my girls so terribly. I had a hard time connecting with Nicole when she was born and when she got older. When I found out I was pregnant with her, I made plans to cut back on my hours and give her the childhood I could never give my son. But after she was born, she turned into a constant reminder that my parents made me give up my first child for adoption when I was sixteen. It triggered some kind of depression that kept me from really connecting with you girls. It wasn't something that was really talked about back then."

"Do you often think about him?" She wouldn't break Mark's confidence outright. He'd asked her for time, and she'd give it to him. Maybe introducing the two at some point in the future would ease a little of her mother's sorrow.

"Almost every day, just as I think about you and Nicole. And especially on birthdays and holidays."

"Did you ever try to find him?"

"Your dad and I tried for years after we got married. We got so wrapped up in the search that we weren't there as much for Nicole as we should have been. I thought I'd done better with you but then you left without a word, never really giving us an explanation."

Parker furrowed her eyebrows. What kind of answer had her mother been looking for? She thought her actions were statement enough.

Her mother stared at the floor and wrung her hands. "And Zoe is right; I have a hard time looking at her. I do try, but then all I can see are my lost children."

Parker slung her arm around her mother's shoulders and drew her closer. "Does Zoe give you a tough time about it?"

"No, she's usually a sweet kid. But she's gotten so angry lately. I know she's having a tough time with Kate's situation. She's about to lose the only aunt she's ever known. I'm sorry she was so harsh to you." Her mother rested her head on Parker's shoulder. "She hardly remembers you. In her early teens, she obsessed over you and Nicole a lot. Kate managed to pull her out of it, but after Kate's illness became so bad, Zoe is drowning in her grief."

"Has anyone ever tried helping her with that?" Parker bit her lower lip. It wasn't her place to give advice to her mother about Zoe, especially since she herself did such a poor job handling her own emotions. But her emotions didn't affect anyone else, though coming home had opened the proverbial Pandora's box and messed with her carefully ordered life.

"We wanted her to see a professional, but Zoe refused to go. We'll have to re-evaluate the situation if Kate doesn't make it."

Parker felt her mother tense her entire body. "Are Kate's chances really that small?" There had to be a way to increase Kate's odds.

"We should always hope." Her mother sighed. "But we have to prepare ourselves. The doctors have given her a couple of weeks, at the most, unless we find a donor. She's nowhere near the top of the transplant list."

"What other options are there?"

Her mother shook her head. "We hoped living donation would give her a chance, but none of us is a close enough match. We even allowed Zoe to give blood for the initial test."

"Why?" Her throat constricted and blood rushed in her ears.

"Why what?"

She cleared her throat and tried again. "Why didn't you ask me to get tested, especially after you knew you weren't a match."

Her mother shook her head. "I can't tell you."

"What? Is there something wrong with me you don't want me to know? Because that's about the only reason I can come up with why you'd rather let Kate die than ask me for help."

"You need to talk to Kate."

So many questions ran through her mind that she didn't know which she should ask first.

Her mother pulled away. "I'll get Zoe home and give you and Kate some privacy."

"Wait." Parker reached for her mother. "What did Zoe mean when she said you had surgery?"

"They had to remove an ovarian cyst. It wasn't anything major." Her mother pulled away as if the topic was closed.

How could her mother call that nothing major? "But you're okay now?" She wanted to know if her mother would've called her if she'd deemed the situation serious. But for now just knowing she was okay was good enough.

"I'm fine." Her mother stood up. "Now let me get Zoe."

"Thanks, Helen."

"Parker, I'm here for you." She squeezed Parker's shoulder. "Harry may be my husband, and I may not know what's going on between the two of you, but I won't allow him to keep me from my child." She turned to leave.

"There wasn't anything between me and him that you and Colleen didn't agree with," Parker murmured.

Her mother turned back. "What do you mean?"

"You all hated seeing Kate and me in a relationship, and you all wanted us to separate. You got what you wanted, and I left."

"None of us meant for you to leave town."

"I knew I could never be the daughter you or Dad wanted," she whispered.

"I don't understand."

"Do you remember the morning of the day I left? We had breakfast before I went into the office with Harry for my summer internship. You said something about me needing to stop sulking over a relationship that should never have been."

"That wasn't one of my finer moments." Her mother looked away.

"Harry and I had an argument over lunch. I can't even remember what started it really. It was something stupid. But then it escalated to the point he insisted I was risking my entire future if I didn't get my head on straight. That evening, he told me to clear my head and get over Kate before I set foot in his house again." Parker shrugged.

"You know the rest."

Her mother rapidly blinked her eyes and sunk back down on the bench. "This is a bad joke." She shook Parker. "Please tell me you made that up."

Parker skirted away, needing space after she'd set those old memories free. "Don't tell me you didn't agree with him."

"I... Back then, I wanted you to get over Kate. Your infatuation wasn't healthy."

"I was in love with her, Helen. The 'My world is going to end if I lose her' kind of love. We—"

"I never wanted you to feel like you weren't welcome at home. I know we handled the situation all wrong, and I'm sorry."

They blinked at each other, seemingly stunned. Parker didn't know if she could trust her mother's lack of knowledge as to what had happened that day. It wasn't like her to be ignorant.

"I think I need some time to make sense of that." Her mother gathered herself and stood. "I'll get Zoe and go home. Give me ten minutes. I think it's better if you and Zoe don't have another run in." Her mother turned to leave but looked back over her shoulder. "I'm not going to confront your father with this right now. There are more important things going on with Kate. But be sure I'll have words with him."

Parker wanted to be offended that her mother thought this wasn't important enough to merit immediate confrontation, but she was too emotionally drained. And Kate would probably be wondering where she was. She made her way out of the chapel.

When Parker entered the hospital room, Kate sat in one of the chairs, pushing a piece of cake around on a plate. Parker had taken her time on her way back and stopped for coffee at the cart in the lobby.

"That smells like heaven." Kate looked up and frowned. "I didn't think you'd come back."

"No more running." Parker closed the door. It was time to repair what she'd damaged.

"Oh?"

Parker studied her boots. "I'll leave you alone if that's what you want, but I won't disappear again without a word." It would be hard and it would hurt, but she had to try.

"Don't you dare! Now that you're here, you aren't going anywhere." Kate pulled a chair close to her. "Come and sit. I really hope one of those is for me, or I may need to kill you." Kate pointed at the coffee cups in Parker's hand.

"I hoped I could bribe you for answers." She held one of the disposable coffee cups out to Kate.

"Not sure I'm that cheap."

"Then you won't mind if I keep both cups, will you?"

The horrified expression on Kate's face made Parker smile, and she gave her a cup.

Kate fiddled with the lid. "Did you put milk and sugar in it?"

"No, I didn't know how you liked your coffee so I left it black. I bought you these though." She placed the packets on the table beside Kate.

"I used to like my coffee the same way you did. The fancier the better, with loads of milk and hazelnut flavor or sugar. I still like it that way."

Parker laughed gently, remembering how long it used to take Kate to prepare her coffee. "My tastes may have changed a little."

"Oh, have they? So how do you take your coffee now?" Kate raised her eyebrows.

"Of all the questions you've got for me, you're starting with that one?"

Kate laughed, and it was the sweetest sound Parker had heard in a long time.

"I guess I am."

"Mostly black. There's no luxury coffee where I've been." Parker relaxed and joined Kate in her laughter.

"Where have you been?"

Parker straightened her back, saluted, and grinned. "That is need to know information, Ms. Cane."

Kate gave her an incredulous look. "Really? I don't get to know where you've been all this time?"

Parker shrugged. "I'm not exactly allowed to say where I was. I flew here from the Middle East is about all I can say."

The tension in Kate's shoulders eased a little.

"I was stationed in Afghanistan for the last three years." She took a sip of her coffee. "After bootcamp, I was stationed in California for a while. I used the time there to finish my college degree via correspondence school. After that, someone recommended me for officer candidate school and the Corps decided to send me to law school." It was a little ironic considering law was the career path her parents had wanted her to take.

"I know that much. I was so proud of you when I found out you graduated law school." Kate's eyes shone.

"How did you find that out?" She'd never told her parents what she was doing in the Corps, though she was reasonably sure that her father would have been able to read her uniform insignias. He'd served for four years after high school before he came back to marry her mother.

"Did you know the military branches have their own newspaper, and it lists accomplishments and promotions?" Kate asked and put the plate with the unwanted cake on the side table.

It was typical of Kate to find a way to keep tabs on Parker. "You checked up on me?"

"Are you mad?" Kate played with her cup and looked up at Parker from underneath her lashes.

Parker reached out and gently caressed the back of Kate's hand. "How can I possibly be mad at you?" She herself had occasionally surrendered to the need for information and had googled Kate. All she found was an old article about an art show featuring some of Kate's college work, but it became her greatest treasure.

"You didn't leave the service after your initial commitment was over. Will you stay in the Corps until you retire?" Kate asked, her expression unreadable.

A week ago, Parker's answer would have been yes without hesitation. But so many things had changed since then, and she wasn't entirely sure what her future would look like. "It's been family, you know. But who knows? Things can change." It was the best answer she had right now.

"I always wondered how you would answer that question. I practically stalked you after you left," Kate said. "I couldn't understand how you'd left all your dreams behind and joined the Marines. I asked your parents not to tell you anything about me, because I thought it would make you get in touch, and if you were going to do that, I wanted it to be your decision, not theirs."

Parker's dreams had been inextricably entwined with Kate. She didn't think she could compose music without Kate as her muse. Harvard law school had always been their parents' dream for her, and she'd been willing to go down that road to be able to support Kate and her art, especially if they'd left together like they'd planned. Parker closed her eyes and shook her head. It was a lot to take in, and she wasn't sure how she felt about the revelation. "I love that you still cared enough to check up on me. I'm more confused than anything else."

"Thank you." Kate held Parker's hand.

"Anyhow, I had questions for you, so stop interrogating me." Parker turned Kate's hand over and began to trace light circles in her palm. It was a simple gesture, but she was glad when Kate didn't pull away.

"I know. It's just easier to talk about you than me." Kate leaned back in her chair and sighed deeply. "Everyone feels so uncomfortable talking to me. They don't know what to say. I don't want you to look at me with the same expression or dance around the same elephant in the room."

The sadness displayed in Kate's face settled like a physical pain in Parker's chest. She tightened her grip on her paper coffee cup and almost crushed it. "Okay."

"I'd hoped that you'd come home to me for such a long time. Now that you're here, I won't let you go again. I lost my lover and my best friend when you left."

Parker gently turned Kate's face until her watery eyes met hers. Tears clung to her lashes, too stubborn to fall just yet. Tension radiated from Kate's body through her fingertips, making Parker's own hand tremble. "I lost the same things, Kate."

"I didn't want you to know." Kate's tears spilled over, and she sniffed. "Now that you're here, I don't want to leave this world without you being there and holding my hand."

Kate tried to move her head away again, but Parker held her chin firm. She thumbed Kate's tears away slowly, afraid that her rough fingers would mark her delicate skin. "Why didn't you tell me when it's been so important to you?"

"For the same reason we're no longer together."

She'd tried to forget the day her life had fallen apart, but she'd never been able to. She'd also never been able to make sense out of what happened that day. "I'm sorry. I don't follow."

"Maybe it's foolish. I thought if I asked Mom not to tell you anything about me when you first left for bootcamp you would eventually get in touch and ask me yourself. Maybe even come home for a visit while you're on leave so we could catch up. But months turned into years, and you never did." Kate pulled away. "I was close to giving up hope when you showed up four and a half years ago without warning. I don't really know how to explain it, but your presence woke me up in the middle of the night when you came home. I feared I was completely losing it when I saw the light come on in your room across the street. Then you moved right in front of the window and stared out into the darkness for an eternity. You laid your hand against the window like a greeting gesture, and I could have sworn you knew I was watching you from the other side of the street. You'll never know how much I wanted to run over and fall into your arms in that very moment. I wanted us to reconnect then and there in the middle of the night." Kate shook her head sadly. "But I didn't want to overwhelm you and gave you space. I was sure you would come over to talk when you were settled in. I waited for five days before mom told me you'd left again."

She sat back in her chair to allow for some space between them. "I wanted to."

"And why didn't you?"

Parker closed her eyes briefly and sucked in a deep breath. The stench of disinfectant washed over her, making the memories of the past more vivid than she'd anticipated. She looked back at Kate. "I saw you, Helen, and Zoe behind the Naval Museum the day I was on base. The day Helen told you that I'd been involved in an 'incident.' What a nice way of saying I was shot, kidnapped, and landed my ass in a hospital to repair the bullet holes before I showed up at home."

Kate flinched but didn't say a word.

"I watched the three of you for a while, and I could see that your illness was giving you trouble. You were struggling and so obviously in pain."

Kate pulled her feet up onto the chair embracing her knees. "I understand that you didn't want to deal with that."

Kate's defeated expression drove a knife straight into Parker's heart. What did it matter if she twisted it some more? "I was about to come over and meet you guys when there was a loud bang. I hit the floor. I wasn't on the base anymore. I was back in the desert with bullets whizzing past my head and burning flesh all around me. I snapped out of the flashback, but I couldn't pile my demons on top of the health issues you were dealing with. But I knew I couldn't stay away from you if I stayed in town." Parker's whole body trembled, but she made no attempt to hide it.

"What happened when you were missing?"

The simple question made the room dim around the edges and almost recede. Parker's shoulder shook with the effort to hold her self-control. She worked hard to shove the memories back in the recesses of her brain where they wouldn't do any damage. "I can't talk about it. Not yet, please," she whispered.

Kate got up and then sat on Parker's lap. "Breathe slowly, in and out with me. In, one, two. Hold it and out, two, three." Kate stroked Parker's back. "You're having a panic attack."

She stiffened. "Don't let my superiors hear that."

"Relax. No one's here except you and me."

Parker slowly came back to herself and breathed in Kate's scent. The mixture of jasmine mixed with green tea and citrus soothed her raw nerves and helped her relax. "I'm so embarrassed."

"Don't be. You're not ready to talk about it, and I won't push again." Kate yawned into Parker's neck. "The thing with Zoe drained me, I'm so tired."

Parker knew she should let go of Kate and allow her to go back to bed. She loosened her embrace, but Kate snuggled deeper into her body and buried her face in her neck. Parker's heart skipped a beat before starting off in double time.

Parker had thought she would never be this close to Kate again. She was a perfect fit against her body and the missing piece in her soul. Why had they waited for Kate to arrive on Death's doorstep to reach out to each other? It terrified her that Kate's dreadful disease could steal her away all too soon.

Chapter Nine

ZOE REFUSED TO SIT down at the same table as Parker and stomped off with a bowl of cereal, leaving Parker's mother yelling after her to come back and behave. Zoe ignored her. Her father's cellphone rang before they settled to eat, and he left the house in a hurry, leaving Parker alone with her mother and Colleen for breakfast. Her mother's stiff posture relaxed the tiniest bit after Harry's abrupt departure. She may not have confronted him but the tension between them was palpable.

They tried to watch Parker inconspicuously, making her skin prickle, and she wished she could just get up and leave like her father. The tense atmosphere ruined the little appetite she had. Even the tantalizing hot cup of coffee turned into an unappealing pool of tar.

She glanced at her watch, but it was too early to visit Kate. Parker had expected their conversation to be awkward and uncomfortable, but after she'd relaxed, it was just like old times. In the little time she'd spent with Kate, Parker had talked more about herself than she had in the last year.

With some effort, she'd managed to finish a small Greek yogurt and her coffee. She got up to clear her dishes.

"That isn't all you are having?" her mother asked.

Parker grabbed her phone off the table. It flashed another low battery warning even though she'd charged it overnight. Unfortunately, Parker hadn't managed to get a hold of Kate's doctor yesterday. So she'd continued her online research into liver transplantation and a possible donation process this morning. Her search had drained her old phone, but the things she'd found dared her to hope. She needed to find someone who could answer a few questions and maybe help her start the process before she would consider telling Kate or her family. The red battery symbol at the top of her screen taunted her like it wanted to warn her not to get her hopes up too much. "I have to run an errand." *And I need some fresh air and food that comes without being watched like a hawk.*

Parker pulled on her boots, since she didn't have any civilian footwear handy other than her battered running shoes and left the house. She jogged the few steps to the garage, got into the old Ford, and drove away. That her father had kept the car all those years stunned her, though by now, it could probably pass as vintage. The notion of him seeing it as an investment made more sense to her than him keeping it for sentimental reasons.

A wave of old memories assailed her when she adjusted the side mirror, and she half expected to see Kate in the passenger seat. They'd taken so many trips just to get out of the house and spend some alone time together that it was hard to sit in the car and not think of her. When Parker slowed down to take the turn downtown, she could almost feel Kate's warm hand settle on her thigh.

A lengthy stroll through downtown didn't provide anything that appealed to her, so she gave up and went into an electronics store to take care of her constantly dead phone battery. The salesclerk told her it wasn't worth the hassle and sold her a new iPhone and a data plan that came with a free iPad. She was still trying to wrap her head around the guy's sales pitch and how easily she'd fallen for it when she pulled into the hospital parking lot. She usually wasn't one for the latest gadget or expensive tech, but the clerk was damn good at his job and had set up the devices before she left the store.

Her father's voice filtered through the closed door when she reached Kate's room. She considering not going in, but no one knew how much time Kate had left. She'd already wasted a decade. She couldn't afford to waste another minute and opened the door.

"I don't want to be a—"

"Come."

Her father waved her in. She inhaled sharply when she registered how tired Kate looked.

He got up. "You're not a burden, Kate. I'll leave the two of you alone so you can talk before the others show up. It'll work out, you'll see."

Parker frowned but expected Kate would explain the mysterious conversation.

"If it's too complicated or expensive—"

"Stop it. If you want to come home, you'll come home. There are agencies that can send nurses or doctors to check on you at home and help with things like your medication. We'll make it work." He walked toward the door but stopped just in front of Parker. "I'm sorry I had to bail on breakfast. Kate needed me here."

"Don't worry about it." What else was she supposed to say? Kate was coming home, but she also didn't know how to feel about that. She wanted to be overjoyed. Kate would be so much happier at home, surrounded by family and friends. The immediate gratification part of her mind wanted to jump for joy that they would get to spend more time together away from the prying eyes of doctors and nurses and outside the limitation of visiting hours. But it also meant Kate was giving up, and Parker couldn't face that. She wasn't ready to hold Kate's hand and watch her fade away. Not after they'd just found each other again. If she lost Kate, Parker's soul would die right along with her, leaving her a lifeless shell.

Kate's cold fingers closed around her forearm and helped center her. Her breathing was shallow and a little too fast when she focused on Kate's concerned expression.

"You're a little pale, is everything okay?" Kate asked quietly.

Parker gave her a weak nod, not sure she could voice what was going on in her head.

"Why is it that I don't believe you?" Kate rose up on her tiptoes and kissed Parker's cheek. "You can trust me, you know."

Parker's brain short-circuited when Kate's lips connected with her skin. The world dimmed, and she sucked in a breath. Her skin still tingled where she'd made contact. *Stop it. I can't feel like this. Not again.* She bit her bottom lip until the taste of copper filled her mouth.

Kate ran her thumb lightly over Parker's lips. "Let go. You're hurting yourself."

Parker didn't move. All she wanted was to feel Kate's fingers on her skin. Everything else blurred into the background.

Kate guided her into a chair, and they sat. A comfortable silence stretched between them as she slowly came back around. Kate began to tap her foot against Parker's boot. Seeing it again made her smile. It had been one of Kate's little ticks for as long as Parker could remember. Something was on her mind, and she was getting ready to talk about it.

While Kate worked up her nerve to talk, Parker used the time to commit Kate's face to memory. Yesterday she'd struggled to see the Kate she knew, buried as she was beneath the signs of illness. Now she hardly noticed the changes the disease had made and concentrated on appreciating the woman Kate had become. It was something she couldn't put her finger on, something that radiated from within her and enthralled her still.

"I'm sorry if I crossed a line when I kissed you." Kate gripped an object that hung from her neck and was hidden beneath her sweater. A delicate silver chain pulled taut above her collar. "It's just having you here brings back all those old memories, and it's almost like you were never gone. I just couldn't help myself. This would be hard enough under normal circumstances, but nothing about this is normal. The side effects are getting worse, and sometimes I can't even tell what's real and what isn't." Kate wiped the corner of her eye. "What if all this is just a dream? If it is, I don't want it to end."

"It's okay." The past few days had been enough of a rollercoaster that she'd had trouble keeping up; how could she fault Kate for having similar problems?

"Are you sure I didn't embarrass you?"

Parker's cheeks burned. "It felt really nice."

"Oh... I know everything is different now but being around you is so familiar. It's so easy to talk to you, to be close to you. It's a little like going back to a place that made you feel safe and loved as a child—"

"Stop for a moment," Parker said softly. She didn't want Kate panicking over nothing. Experience had taught her that it wasn't easy to reach Kate once she'd gone down the rabbit hole. "You don't owe me an explanation, Kate—not for the kiss anyway. Yes, I've got tons of questions, like why didn't you try to reach out to me when you got so bad? Why didn't you consider me as a potential donor?" A smile tugged at the corner of Parker's mouth. "What have you been up to while I was gone? But you don't have to answer any of them if you don't want to. The only thing I'd like to ask of you is that you're yourself, at least while the two of us are alone. I'd be honored if you let me see you, the good, the bad, and the ugly." Parker's thigh spasmed, and she dug her fingers in to loosen it. The injury had never troubled her before but had started rather suddenly on the long plane ride home. "It would break my heart if we couldn't be real with each other."

Kate looked pensive. Whatever weighed on her mind, Parker's words hadn't eased it. Kate's foot tapping began again. Parker needed to stay patient. *I've been gone too long to assume I still know her.* The realization wrapped another length of barbed wire around her heart and tightened.

Kate looked up at her, her expression seemingly shy. "Will you tell your wife?"

"What?" Why the hell would Kate think she was married?

"That I kissed you. I don't want to cause you any trouble."

"I don't have a wife," Parker said.

"Oh." Kate's cheeks flushed, resulting in a slightly orangey hue on her skin that looked very unhealthy. "Husband?" She nibbled her bottom lip.

"What makes you think I'm married?"

"That." Kate tapped the gold band on Parker's left ring finger.

Parker looked down and saw that her ring was turned around, hiding its red stone. She turned it back around. "It's not a wedding band. It's my Marine Corps ring."

Kate took her hand and studied the ring. "It's beautiful, not at all what I remember my dad's military class ring looking like."

"It's not a typical one. The band is much thinner and the stone smaller, and so are the designs on the side. I had it made after I finished law school. It has the eagle, globe, and anchor design on one side and the scales of justice on the other to hold the stone setting."

"Do you have someone back where you've been stationed?" Kate played with Parker's ring turning it this way and that.

Parker's ears grew hot. "The Middle East isn't the best place for a lesbian relationship."

"That's not an answer."

"Nobody steady. I find relief when I need it." That sounded so bad out loud. What she meant was that she took care of herself quietly in her own quarters. She'd turned not making a sound while she got herself off into an art form. It had been different after she got back from her first assignment. They'd just repealed Don't Ask, Don't Tell. Back then, she'd hit the bars hard and behaved like a sex-crazed teenager for a while. That quickly lost its appeal when nothing could seem to fill the void where her heart used to be, and her wild child days ended the day she shipped out again.

Kate let go of Parker's hand and fidgeted in her chair. "How many women have you been with since we broke up?"

She didn't want to answer *that* question. She crossed her arms and leaned back.

"Sorry, that was an awfully personal question." Kate studied her feet. "Forget I asked."

"How about I'll answer your question if you answer one of mine."

"Okay, but you go first," Kate said.

"What exactly did you want to know? How many relationships

I've had or how many women I've had sex with?" They'd had lots of intimate conversations as teenagers, but she hadn't talked with anyone about her sex life since she'd left. Kate seemed eager to ignore the distance between them or maybe break it down by being so candid.

"The last thing—no, the first one." Kate looked a bit embarrassed. "Both?"

Parker sighed. "No steady relationships. My life doesn't have room for one."

"Oh." Kate looked away and nibbled on her lower lip. "And the other?"

Parker felt the heat rising in her neck crawling up onto her cheeks. "Let's just say there's been a few."

"How has that worked? Did you spend a few days with someone you picked up and then moved on? Or are we talking one-night stands?"

"That's a second question." Parker grinned.

Kate raised her eyebrow in silent challenge.

Parker shook her head but gave in anyway. "I took women to a hotel mostly, never home. Military housing and one-night stands don't go so well together. Then I started taking care of my needs at the club and would leave alone when I was done."

Kate's eyes grew comically wide, but she didn't comment nor ask another question.

"How about you, Kate? Anyone in your life?" Parker held her breath. She hadn't seen anyone at the hospital, but that didn't have to mean anything. She hoped that Kate kissing her earlier meant there wasn't anyone else holding her heart.

"That's on the top of your list of questions?"

"You started it."

Kate suddenly looked very sad and shook her head. "Not many girlfriends sign up to be a nursemaid. Even friends tend to forget about you when you get seriously ill."

"That's not true." Parker's anger rose, and she fought to pull it back. If she'd had her druthers, she would have been at Kate's side all this time. But her job had given her an insight into how many marriages didn't make it due to the physical and psychological effects of war. Her own mental state had been what made her run away before anybody could reject her the last time she'd been here. "Maybe."

"That wasn't really on your list of questions, was it?"

"No, I want to know what Harry was talking about when I came in, about you coming home."

"I want to come home to the house we grew up in. I want to spend the time I have left with you, Mom, Dad, Zoe, and Aunt Colleen."

Parker wondered when Kate had started to refer to her mother and father as Mom and Dad again. She'd done it in her early teens but had stopped when she'd moved in with Colleen at sixteen. A lot of things had changed.

"I'm sick of the sterile hospital rooms," Kate said. "I want to spend the remaining time where I feel most at peace, with the people I love. I want to have time with you away from this." Kate gestured around them. "I want you to make memories you can think back to when I'm gone. I couldn't bear it if the only thing you had to look back on was this room, with me dwarfed by all the machines that are supposed to keep me alive long enough for the doctors to find a miracle." Kate shook her head. "You and I both know there are no miracles. If there were, we—"

There was a short knock on the door and a nurse came in with an infusion bag in her hand. Parker cursed the nurse's timing. *If there were miracles, then what? We would have been able to stay together.* Kate got up and went over to sit on the bed where the nurse set up the infusion and connected it to a line in Kate's hand.

"Doctor Miller will be in shortly. Try to stay awake until then." The nurse left and closed the door behind her.

"Can you come over here, please?" Kate patted her bed.

Kate linked their hands as if to reaffirm their connection. "I'm sorry, but I'm going to fall asleep on you and won't be good company for the rest of the day. Promise me you'll do something nice rather than spending the entire time sitting next to my bed."

"But—"

"No buts. This will help me with the pain and confusion for the next couple of days." Kate pointed to the bag the nurse had just hung. Her eyes fluttered close and her breathing settled.

Parker hoped she had a chance to ask Dr. Miller a few questions when she came to check on Kate. First and foremost, why they had never considered her as a donor candidate for Kate.

Colleen came in just as Kate had drifted off and Parker was tucking her in. They exchanged a few words quietly before Colleen settled into a chair and began knitting. The soft clicking sound of her knitting needles combined with the faint dripping of Kate's IV created a monotone background noise and almost lulled Parker to sleep. She'd spent most of the night awake, reading articles about liver transplantation online and staring up at her ceiling. She never slept much, and only if she had to, and that had gotten worse after she'd been injured. She never told anyone she had debilitating nightmares when she slept too much, sure that if she did, she'd end up on a desk somewhere out of the way.

Parker abruptly stood when a yawn struck her. She needed fresh air. "I have to go, Colleen. I'll see you later." Parker hurried out the door and ran straight into Dr. Miller.

"How are you holding on, Ms. Snow?" Dr. Miller asked.

What a stupid question.

"Ms. Snow?"

She'd stayed silent too long and probably stared through her. "Hanging in there, I guess." She pulled a face. "It's Parker, please. Mrs. Snow is my mother, and I can't stand the all the Ms. And Miss stuff, you know what I mean."

"Yes, ma'am, I know exactly what you mean."

Parker inclined her head toward Kate's room. "How is she?"

"You know I can't say much, but she's holding on better than we expected."

"Would a transplant make her well again?"

"Even if Kate received a transplant today, we couldn't be sure that she would make a full recovery. Some of the side effects of her disease can leave permanent damage, especially the high copper levels in her blood. We can't know how much permanent damage it has done to her brain at this point."

"So the sooner she gets a transplant, the better?"

Dr. Miller gestured toward a couple of chairs in the hallway and sat down. "Yes, it would be, but the severity of the illness determines how high the patient's name is on the transplant list. And even if you're on the top of that list, you can only receive an organ that matches. The only exception to where you're placed on the waiting list is if a relative or friend donates part of their liver through the living donation process specifically to her."

Parker studied the doctor's face. She couldn't read what was going on behind the mask of professionalism. "But the people who got tested didn't match."

"Unfortunately, no."

"Is there a reason I was never tested?" Parker needed to know if they had already ruled her out as a possibility.

Dr. Miller frowned. "Haven't you refused to get tested?"

"No!" Parker's voice shot through an octave. *Where had the levelheaded side of her gone?*

"Maybe they didn't want to ask or already knew you wouldn't be a match for Kate. Some feel it's too big an ask of a loved one."

"That's bullshit." Parker's reaction was instinctive, and she tried to reel in her temper. "My apologies, ma'am."

"I've heard far worse, believe me."

"What if I want to get tested now?"

"You would have an initial blood test to see if you have a matching blood type and a physical to rule out anything that would exclude you straight away. If the results match up there would be more extensive tests and a mental health screening. Not everyone is fit to serve as a living donor. In your case there may be additional concern since you have been out of the country and just recently returned. You would also need the military's permission."

"So, we start with blood type. That should be easy enough; Kate and I should have the same, at least according to that test you do in high school biology. Besides, the internet said that general blood donors have an increased likelihood of a match. Wait, what do you mean by I need the military's permission?"

"Careful with what you read on the internet." Dr. Miller squeezed her arm. "You're an active service member, so in a way, the military gets to say what happens to your body. They're usually quite reasonable, but there are protocols and a chain of command to follow."

Parker tried to swallow the sudden lump in her throat, but it wouldn't budge. The little hope she'd held onto since learning all the details of Kate's current condition tried to wriggle out of her fingers.

Doctor Miller got up.

"Wait." Parker jumped up too. "I want to get tested. I heard what you said, but I have to try."

"Let me get you some information to read," Dr. Miller said. "I'll be back in a moment."

Parker paced the hallway, barely able to contain her nervous energy. When time dragged on, she worried the doctor wasn't coming back. It took at least ten minutes before Dr. Miller reappeared.

"These are for you." She held out a few booklets. "You're sure that you'd go through with this, even if it means you wash out of the Corps or land permanent desk duty?"

"Yes." Parker had subconsciously risen to her full height and looked directly into Miller's brown eyes. Her heart was racing, and she could hear the drum of her own heartbeat in her ears.

"Be here tomorrow at 0800 sharp. I'll arrange for someone to take you through the testing process." The doctor started to leave.

Parker's heart skipped a couple of beats. The smallest seed of hope had been planted and she would see to it that it would grow. "Who do I need to contact about that permission?" Parker asked before the doctor had taken two steps.

"Don't worry about that yet, if we get to that stage there will be people who can help you with all that. They can explain what consequences it may have to your career and walk you through the permission process. If it makes you feel better, I could see if I can get in touch with a former colleague that works over at Walter Reed Hospital."

There was the confirmation that Dr. Miller had a military background. Parker felt smug until all feeling disappeared from her left leg, and she sat back down hard. It started to annoy her. What was going on with it?

"Are you okay, Parker?" Miller sounded alarmed.

Parker waved it off. "Just a lot of information, don't worry. Please get in touch with your colleague at Walter Reed. The sooner this gets rolling the better, right?"

Chapter Ten

PARKER WISHED SHE'D BEEN more successful avoiding her mother when she made it home. From the moment she walked through the door, her mother roped her into helping out in the house. She folded laundry, cleaned the dining room, vacuumed the living room, and started chopping veggies for dinner.

Parker avoided conversation because she didn't want to discuss any of her thoughts with her mother. All she wanted to think about was the feel of Kate's lips on her skin, her hand in hers. And she didn't want to think about the reason they hadn't asked her about possible donation. What if it wasn't because they knew it wouldn't go anywhere but because someone was afraid they *were* a match. Her skin crawled and felt much too tight. The house made her claustrophobic, and she missed her usual outlet. Normally, she was in the gym every day until her body hurt. It unsettled her that she didn't have an opportunity to physically exhaust herself since she'd been back. She yearned for the pain that kept her centered. She considered slipping the knife she was using to cut the onions to accidentally nick herself. She understood Kate's reasoning behind the secrecy when she'd left for bootcamp. Still, she couldn't shake the feeling that there was more. Why didn't anyone break the silence months ago? Surely, they wanted Kate to live as much as she did.

"What are you thinking?" her mother asked when she placed another peeled onion next to the cutting board for her to chop.

"Nothing." There was no way she'd admit to thinking about hurting herself to control her emotions. If she wanted to care for Kate, she needed a healthy way to tend to her own well-being.

"I seriously doubt that," her mother said. "You look like you've got the weight of the world on your shoulders."

Parker was grateful when the doorbell rang so that she could avoid the inquisition.

"Can you check who that is?" her mother asked.

Parker opened the door to a pregnant woman and—could it be? "Linda? Or is it Lieutenant Commander?"

"Look what the tide washed up." Linda enveloped Parker in a hug.

"How did you know?"

"Scuttlebutt around the watercooler has it that you were coming to work for us. I wasn't quite sure it was true though, considering you're a Marine." Linda took the other woman's hand and pulled her closer. "This is my wife, Suzan. I don't think you've met before."

Parker shook her hand. "Nice to meet you, Suzan. This one couldn't stop talking about you for weeks after you ran that simulation together." She laughed and looked back to Linda. "Scuttlebutt is correct. I was reassigned to work with Navy JAG on a case a few years back. The Marines have either forgotten all about me or they don't want me back." The continued reassignment irked her, but it wasn't her place to question it.

"Who would want your ugly mug back?" Linda bumped her shoulder.

"Screw you." Their banter made her feel more at ease than she'd been in days.

"Who is it?" her mother called from the kitchen.

Parker stepped aside. "Come in."

Suzan motioned at a bouquet of flowers. "These are for Helen."

For Helen? Since when did they have such a good relationship with Parker's mother?

"Hi, Mrs. Snow, how are you today?" Linda asked when they reached the kitchen.

Her mother pulled her pot off the stove before walking to Linda and Suzan. "I almost forgot what day today is. There's so much going on this year." She accepted the flowers from Suzan. "Thank you, that's so kind of you. I don't think even my husband remembered Nicole's birthday today."

Oh, shit. How could I forget my sister's birthday? Parker had the sudden urge to bang her head against the wall. Her mind had been so singularly focused on Kate, she'd forgotten everything around her.

"Are you okay? You're shaking," Linda whispered.

"Do you know a gym around here that allows military personnel without having to take out a full membership?" She tried to take even long breaths to calm herself. Things had slipped through her fingers, and she hated the out-of-control feeling.

Linda leaned in closer. "How about the two of us sneak off to the Navy base gym and let those two catch up for a while. They like to gossip, and Suzan can walk home when she needs to rest. We live next door when you count touching backyards."

"Since when?"

"For close to a year now. I wanted a stable place to start our family. My father moved us around so much, I never felt at home anywhere except for the time I spent at this house with Nicole. When we started to look for a house of our own, Suzan suggested we look for something in the area, and we got lucky."

"Really?" She'd known that Linda liked to spend time at their house with Nicole. But she'd always expected it to be more about Nicole as Linda's best friend than feeling at home in their house, especially since she had trouble considering it home.

"Yep, she's really great that way." Linda knitted her brows together. "Is it weird that we're practically neighbors now?"

Parker shook her head. "I don't live here, and Helen seems to like it."

"I think she's pleased. She and Suzan really hit it off. I catch them talking across the fence all the time." Linda shrugged. "I think Helen hopes to get news about you when she talks to Suzan."

"Do they know how big the military is?" Parker rolled her eyes.

"I think they do." Linda looked sheepish. "But I may have said that it was my fault that you joined in the first place."

"I don't think they blame anybody but me for that, and if they do, I'm very sorry."

"They're very proud of you, all of them. Sometimes I can't tell who is proudest, Helen or Kate. Last time I saw Kate, she had a picture of you in uniform as a lock screen on her tablet. How is she doing?"

Parker swallowed hard. Everybody knew but her. "Not very well, but she wants to come home. I wonder how Kate got a picture of me. I never sent one home." She needed to get out of the house and burn off some of her negative energy. "Anyway, let's hit the gym."

Parker offered to drive but Linda had waved her off. Linda's SUV was parked out front since they'd picked up the flowers on the way over and her workout gear was already in the trunk. The promise of exercise and time spent with Linda was enough to let Parker relax into the soft leather seat. Her usually calm under pressure demeanor started to come back to her.

She was thankful the gym was practically empty. She slid the weight plate in place on the barbell and secured the clip. Linda did the same on the opposite side.

"How about the spotter catches the other up on what's going on in their lives?" Linda placed a towel on the bench.

"Sounds good to me," Parker said. "Do you want to start?"

"Honestly, you look like you need the exercise more than I do."

Parker gave Linda a playful punch on the arm. "I meant talking, you know I'm not big on words. The blubbering teenager on your couch should've been proof enough of that."

When Linda had been friends with Nicole, Parker had little to do with her. Linda and Nicole weren't interested in the younger siblings. And Parker wasn't all that interested in Nicole—she had Kate to focus on. After Linda moved out of town, she'd stayed in contact with Nicole and spent most vacations with them. Only after Nicole died did Linda and Parker bond over their shared grief. And it had been Linda she'd run to when her life in Washington had fallen apart.

"Hey, daydreamer, are you getting on the bench or not?" Linda stood behind the barbell, waiting.

Parker lay down and wriggled into the right position. She saw Linda's gold wedding band. "When did you get married? And you're going to be parents. That's exciting."

She said it because that's what was expected, but surprisingly, she actually meant it. She *was* excited for them, but also sad for Kate, who'd always dreamed of the white picket fence, the kids, and the family dog. She'd never get her fantasy life.

Linda gave her a goofy smile when she helped her take the bar off its stand and guided her first repetition. "The parenting thing scares the shit out of me. They're so tiny when they're born, and you can do so many things wrong. We got married four years ago when we decided we wanted to have a baby. I needed to know Suzan and our kid would have security if anything ever happened to me. But the ceremony was nothing fancy. We went to city hall with two friends as our witnesses. You'd just shipped out again after you recovered from your injury otherwise I would've asked you."

It saddened Parker that Linda hadn't even told her after the fact. But since she was the only one who knew Kate's and Parker's whole story, it wouldn't have surprised her if Linda had tried to protect her feelings. Parker rested the barbell across her chest. "I never took you for the marrying kind."

"It wasn't on the cards for any of us for a long time. But when Suzan and I knew it would be forever, same sex marriage was still illegal in most States, and Don't Ask, Don't Tell was still very much alive in the military. Neither of us needed a piece of paper to prove we loved each other." Linda shrugged. "What we did was dangerous enough. If someone had found out about us, I would've been booted out. No one would've cared that my service record had been exemplary up to that point."

They were silent for a few reps, and Parker concentrated on the first slow burn in her chest. Dr. Miller flashed in Parker's mind and made her wonder. Just because she was androgynous, it didn't mean she was a lesbian, but Parker's gaydar had tickled her senses. "When did you get back to Washington DC?" Parker asked.

"I finished a sea assignment about a week ago, so I'm on leave but I'm staying to work at Navy JAG headquarters. I'm hoping to get to see my kid grow up for the first few months, maybe years. How long have you been back?"

"Since Friday." Parker extended her arms fully, and Linda guided the barbell onto the stand. "I was sent here with no notice. I think someone may have pulled a few strings because of Kate, but I don't know who yet. I'm supposed to report to Admiral Pike at JAG in two weeks."

"So, we may end up working together." Linda sounded excited.

"It's possible. If so, it's back to me addressing you as Lieutenant Commander."

"No way I outrank you."

Parker got up. "Yep, you've got three years on me." She pointed toward the bench. "It's your turn."

"But you graduated high school early and had your college degree finished when you joined."

"I'm still a captain." Parker grinned. "I didn't start out as an officer, remember. And my degree was only almost finished when I joined."

"To be honest, I forgot. Besides you earned a Medal of Honor. I wouldn't be surprised if that promotion comes sooner than you think." Linda settled down on the bench. "Would you have imagined me married and with a child on the way ten years ago when you hid on my couch?"

"Nearly eleven years." She didn't want to think about how much time had passed.

"Time flies."

Parker placed her hands beneath the bar as Linda lifted. "And I could hardly think past my own misery when I was bawling my eyes out on your couch, much less envision a future for me or anyone around me."

"And now?" Linda's voice strained under the exercise. "Is there someone you're thinking about settling down with? Are you seeing someone? You aren't getting any younger, my friend."

She knew Linda didn't mean any offense, but the emptiness the whole conversation left in her chest was very real. There'd been only one person she'd imagined getting old with, and she'd lost that chance. With Kate, Parker had been able to imagine the house and the kids playing in the backyard. But she'd woken from that dream a long time ago.

"Parker?"

"No, there isn't anyone." She wanted to lighten the mood. "There definitely won't be a boyfriend. Could you imagine two people with the need to be on top?" She shivered.

Linda gave a hearty laugh. "Point taken. That never was a question for me either. Hell, even the two of us has never been an option. You're a beautiful woman, but you're not my type at all."

Parker blushed. "No, we both like our women on the femme side, and besides, you already had Suzan back then."

"It's always been Suzan for me. But I bet you've been with a few women since Kate."

Parker's heart gave an odd little flutter against her ribcage before it felt like someone had tightened iron shackles around it. "No, not really." She looked across the gym floor. "I went crazy for a little while after it was safe for my job to set foot in a gay bar. The shiny feeling of freedom wore off after a few dozen women who rarely stuck around after sunrise. There was no one even remotely serious though."

Linda sat up and pulled Parker down next to her. "I'm sorry for stirring up your painful memories. The entire Kate situation can't be easy for you."

She just nodded, needing the rest of her composure to hold the tears at bay that she felt welling up in her eyes again.

"You don't have to tell me anything. Just know that me and my couch are there if you need someone to listen. From the little I caught being your parents' neighbor, things between you and Kate are still complicated."

"That's the understatement of the decade."

Linda's expression fell. "I was convinced that you and Kate would get back together eventually. Maybe I should have encouraged you to work it out with her when you came back from basic training, rather than agree to not mention her again in your presence."

"Maybe that would have been a good thing. Instead, I avoided her." Parker hated herself for that now. Why had she waited for Kate to make the first move? And Kate had done the same thing:

"I still can't believe you only went home once and that wasn't even voluntary. What the hell, Parker? I think you could've used some tough love instead of me coddling you. Do you regret it at all?" Linda sounded incredulous.

Parker nodded and headed to the cable machine. She yearned for her muscles to hurt and take her mind off her emotional agony.

Linda followed and squeezed her arm. "Sorry, I didn't mean to go off on you. It feels like there's more to the story you told me so far. Why don't we finish our workout with some free sparring and maybe catch a drink after? You can talk about it or not. Whatever works for you."

They'd spend the rest of the workout in silence and Parker had reached the contented state where her body had the right amount of exhaustion and physical pain to quiet her mind. If Linda was willing to be her sounding board, she could start to work through some things.

Chapter Eleven

PARKER PLACED THE COLD beer in front of Linda as she slid into the opposite booth with her glass of iced water. The bar Linda had picked had lots of small booths for privacy. The Mexican food on the menu looked great, but her stomach was in too many knots to contemplate eating.

"You feel like talking?" Linda asked.

"No." Parker lifted her glass and clinked it to Linda's beer. "But this might help. I don't know." She hadn't made the effort to really connect with anyone in so long that she really didn't know if it would help her process things or make it worse.

"What happened after your first visit home, Parker?"

"First and last." Parker laughed humorlessly. "Before the entire ordeal that got me shipped home, I was actually thinking about a voluntary visit, you know? And I mean thinking about it as in looking at dates, not a runaway thought when I felt sorry for myself and couldn't sleep. Only took me close to seven years to reach a place where I thought I could face them in person." She took a mouth full of the ice-cold liquid to soothe her suddenly dry throat, and for the first time in a long time, wished she had something stronger for liquid courage. "Before I had a chance to solidify any of my plans, a team was tasked to protect a political asset. I was ordered along to make sure the evidence was handled the right way. The building we were holed up in was attacked, and I was shot and captured. By the time I got sent home on medical leave, I'd acquired a shitload of new baggage than I hadn't bargained for or knew what to do with. All my progress was blown to smithereens, and I wasn't ready at all to face them."

"Bullet to the thigh? I saw the scar when you changed."

"Yeah. I was very lucky it went through without damaging anything vital. I got some muscle damage, and it took some time for it to be the same. A bullet grazed my left side in the same incident but that didn't even need stitches by the time I saw a doctor." There'd been no point after ten days. Her captors had been kind enough to keep her wounds clean even though they'd added their fair share of bruises. She knew now that the nomads that took her had seen her as a trade commodity and couldn't risk her catching an infection. But it hadn't made being strapped to a table naked for hours on end with a blindfold over her eyes while someone poked her wounds any more pleasant. Nor was standing with her wrists bound above her head for hours.

"And Kate couldn't handle it?"

"I didn't even talk to her." Parker gulped some of her ice water to make her dry throat work. "I saw her at the base from afar, and it was clear she had her own problems. I couldn't bring myself to pile my issues on top of it."

"But you just said your injuries weren't so bad." Linda frowned.

"The physical ones weren't." She fell silent. Linda had heard her out before and been nothing but comforting. Maybe it was time to share a little of her experience with someone she'd always trusted. "It didn't leave me in a good place for a while, and I didn't want to come home. But that's what they do after something like that. They send you home."

"I understand where you're coming from. But you should've given Kate the opportunity to make her own choice. You made the decision for her and for your parents." Linda played with the label on her bottle. "I know what your parents did was shit. But don't you think it could have been an opportunity for all of you? They might have changed their stance when confronted with your mortality. I can't imagine Kate wouldn't have made an effort, especially with her own knowledge of how valuable support can be."

"If I couldn't be the kind of support Kate needed, I had no

business being there and making things harder for her. I didn't want my parents to feel obligated."

Linda stared at her, wide-eyed. "I've done the exact same thing in different circumstances." She shrugged. "You remember that Suzan's parents disowned her when she came out?"

Parker nodded when Linda looked at her.

"Early in my career I worked a case where a high-ranking officer was accused of being involved in his son's death after they had an altercation when the officer found him in bed with his boyfriend. The father claimed he'd kicked his son and his partner out and never saw them again. But the civilian legal system started a witch hunt, and my superiors wanted the mess to go away. That case really did a number on me, not only mentally but physically. I couldn't eat or sleep, and because of Suzan's history, I refused to let her in. I pulled away so much I moved into a hotel. After a week, she'd had enough and followed me when I left work. She stormed into my hotel room and demanded to know what was going on. She was on fire thinking I was having an affair. When I told her what was really going on, she was hurt and angry that I didn't trust her enough to make the right decision for herself. It has been the only real fight I ever had with Suzan, and she was right to give me hell. It's not for me to decide what she can or cannot handle. Life isn't always easy, especially military life. It will destroy every relationship you have if you don't trust the person you're with to know what they can handle and what they can't."

"But we weren't in a relationship. We weren't even friends. Not since the day Kate told me that she wouldn't leave with me." Parker clenched her jaw to hide her trembling chin. The memory came fast and without warning. Standing in Colleen's house, Kate had looked deep into Parker's eyes. She thought Kate was going to kiss her, but instead, her words ripped Parker's soul into shreds: *"I can't leave town with you, Parker. Colleen and your parents are right, it will pass."*

"Parker?" Linda squeezed her hand. "I want you to tell me what happened when you and Kate split up. You never really said, only that it was over. Now you say you aren't even friends, yet you are here when she's in the hospital."

"Kate is dying." Her voice was flat and every inch of her body tensed, waiting for a battle that wouldn't come.

"That can't be. What are you talking about?" Linda's raised voice caused a few patrons to look their way. "That's not fair."

Seeing Linda's reaction, Parker wondered if hers had been entirely too muted. She hadn't raised her voice or argued at all. She was mad as hell but had kept quiet. She'd been defeated before the battle had even started.

"Parker, you can't drop that kind of a bombshell and go all quiet on me, what the heck is going on?" Linda clicked her fingers in front of Parker's face. "Does this have anything to do with the thing that was going on with Kate when you left?"

"You sure know how to make me feel like a jerk," Parker muttered.

"Right?"

"If you mean the Wilson's disease Kate has, then yes."

Linda kneaded the back of her neck. "But I thought you said it wasn't that bad."

"Well, it's not something that goes away. With medication, most people can lead a normal life with a few restrictions. I was under the impression she was on the right medication, and that they had a good handle on it."

The waitress showed up to check on them and made it clear she was interested in Parker. Linda cleared her throat and glared at her until she took the hint and left them.

"Talk to me, Parker."

She gave Linda a basic rundown of what she'd learned over the past couple of days and fought against her tears. Everything blurred in front of her.

"Please look at me." Linda stilled Parker's hand running lines over the table. "I don't need you to tell me how you feel about Kate, it's written all over your face. This must be hell for you."

Parker swallowed hard and averted her gaze. Her water was almost finished, and for the first time in ages, she considered ordering alcohol and wanted little more than to get hammered.

Linda stood and startled her out of her reverie. "I'm getting another beer. Do you want another water or something stronger?"

"I'm getting tested."

"What?" Linda asked.

It took Parker a second to realize she hadn't answered Linda's question. "Just water. You know I don't drink." Right now, Parker wished she could abandon her self-imposed rules on alcohol, but with her upcoming appointment tomorrow, getting wasted was out of the question.

"What do you mean you're getting tested? For what?"

"I want to find out if I could be a donor match for Kate. I talked to her doctor about it earlier today," Parker said.

"Please tell me you aren't going to do something stupid." Linda sank onto the seat and took hold of Parker's hand in a vice-like grip. "Like kill yourself."

"Are you crazy? Who do you think I am?" Parker tried to pull her hand free but couldn't. "I want to help Kate, not kill myself. What's wrong with you?"

"Um." Linda's cheeks flushed. "Don't you have to be dead to be an organ donor?"

Parker's eyes grew wide. "No. Not for liver donation. Much like you can donate one of your kidneys to someone, you can donate part of your liver."

"I didn't know that," Linda said.

Parker exhaled. "I want to get tested and see if I might be a match for Kate. She's on the national waiting list but they fear she won't last long enough to make it to the top."

"And you're okay with giving part of your liver to her after all that's happened?"

She didn't have to think about her answer. "Yes, I would."

"I don't know what to say."

"You don't have to say a thing." Parker pushed her empty glass toward Linda. "I'll have another water. I want whiskey, but I haven't touched that stuff in ages, and it'd screw my head."

"I get it." Linda headed to the bar.

No temporary relief alcohol could offer was worth sacrificing the clarity she'd gained from her workout and by talking to Linda. With all the things that were going on in her life right now, she needed it, especially if she wanted to help Kate in the way she hoped to.

Chapter Twelve

IT WAS HALF PAST seven in the morning when Parker stuck her head into Kate's room. She started to pull back when she saw the nurse.

"Come in. Raul won't bite your head off." Kate lifted her hand. "He'll free me of this." She pointed to the cannula stuck in the back of her hand.

She walked in and waited near the door. She'd come to say good morning and check on Kate before going to the appointment Dr. Miller had arranged for her. She hadn't told anyone about what she's planning to do apart from Linda. Linda had encouraged her to tell Kate and her parents, but she hadn't. There was no point getting their hopes up if it turned out Parker wasn't a match after all these tests.

Kate grimaced when the cannula came free, and Raul pressed a gauze pad onto the back of her hand.

"See, it didn't really hurt," he said.

"Tell my brain that." Kate rubbed at her hand.

"I'll help you with your hair before I go. Another nurse will come with your discharge papers and some medication later, and then you'll be good to go." Raul reached for the brush on the side table. "Is someone coming to get you?"

"I think she may already be here." Kate looked over at Parker questioningly. "No need to do my hair though. I can manage."

Parker smiled. Same old stubborn Kate. "Sorry, I've got an appointment. I won't be able to take you home, but Helen and Colleen are coming."

Kate took the brush from the nurse. "Thank you, Raul, for everything."

"I hope to see you back here for a transplant," he said and left.

Kate began to brush her own hair, but her discomfort was clear when she lifted her right arm over her head.

"Why don't you let me help you?" Parker held out her hand.

"You don't have to do that."

"I know, but I want to." Parker settled on the edge of the bed.

Kate held out the brush but pulled back when Parker reached for it. "Only if you tell me what appointment is keeping you from taking me home."

"What if I can't tell you?"

Kate looked hurt. "The last time you said that, you ended up packing your bags and disappearing again."

Parker let out a noisy breath. "I'm sure I didn't say that to you."

"No, you didn't even bother to come talk to me. I had to hear that from Mom."

"I promise I'm not going anywhere."

"How can I be sure?" Kate folded her arms across her chest.

Parker looked at the dark circles under Kate's eyes and guilt engulfed her. It wasn't her intention to stress Kate, but she didn't want to tell her what she was up to until she knew one way or the other. The tightness in her chest had lessened some after she'd exhausted herself at the gym, but it slowly started to creep back the more she stayed silent.

Kate watched Parker the same way Parker watched Kate, like they both tried to see past the barriers they'd erected, guessing at what would make the other talk or stop asking.

Parker fidgeted and pulled back a little. "I'm having a physical." She supposed it was close enough to the truth, but it still grated on her resolve not to tell them.

Kate's expression went from curious to alarmed in an instant. "Are you okay? Is that why you came back?"

"I'm fine."

Kate tossed the brush to her. "Don't baby me. I'm capable of handling the truth. I'm so sick of everyone keeping things from me."

"What do you mean by that?"

"I'm fed up with everyone tiptoeing around me." Kate threw her blanket back and kicked it down with her feet, forcing Parker to move. "I'm sick, not weak. There's a big difference, you know."

Parker wrapped her arms around Kate. "You're the strongest person I know," she whispered into Kate's ear. She felt the anger slowly leave Kate's body as she relaxed into her embrace.

"I'm sorry," Kate mumbled into her neck.

"Hey, there's nothing to apologize for." She stroked over Kate's tangled hair. "I bet I would've lost my temper a long time ago if our roles were reversed." She suppressed a bitter laugh. She'd already lost her wits a couple of times, as it was.

"You're not sick?" Kate asked.

"No, I'm just taking care of myself."

Kate pulled out of her arms and searched her face as if to divine whether or not Parker was lying before she turned so that Parker could brush her hair.

Ten minutes later, Parker made her way to the nurses' station to ask where she could find Dr. Miller and spotted Kid's sister. "Good morning, Jazmin."

She turned around and scowled at Parker. "Can't you see I'm busy, and it's Dr. Callahan to you."

Christ, what had Parker done to deserve that? Parker made a mental note to text Kid later and check in with him, all part of her new plan to make an effort with the people in her life.

"Excuse me, you're in my way." Jazmin shouldered past her. "I have to talk some sense into one of my patients." Jazmin walked off into the direction she had just come from.

Dr. Miller came around the corner with a woman in a Naval Commander's uniform.

Parker saluted. "Good morning, ma'am."

"Captain." The woman saluted and scanned Parker from head to toe.

How did the stranger know her rank? She'd found some

old clothes in her closet that still fit her well enough. She'd been surprised to find everything there exactly as she'd left it.

"Good morning," Dr. Miller said. "This is Commander Hazelwood. She's the doctor I told you about. I'd hoped someone here could do the initial tests but with Thanksgiving coming up, we're a little short-staffed. If you don't have any objections, I'll be doing it. But since I'm also Kate's doctor, I thought it wise to have the commander observe to avoid any conflict of interest, if that's all right with you."

"Yes, of course," Parker said without hesitation. Whatever it took, she was prepared to do it all.

"I also asked Commander Hazelwood to bring your medical records." Dr. Miller continued. "If you're okay for me to review them, I need you to sign a release."

"Sure, no problem." Parker's heartbeat increased. She knew what the records held and even after all these years, she wasn't comfortable with someone reading through the papers that detailed the physical and emotional wounds of her time as a prisoner.

Parker was poked and prodded by a nurse that tried to find a vein, stripped naked, X-rayed, and asked a bunch of invasive questions. She had given straight answers and done as she was directed. There was no point in making the ordeal any more unpleasant or complicated.

Dr. Miller handed her a bunch of paper towels to clean off the warmed ultrasound gel from her torso. The doctor went on to examine the scar that was located two fingers above her right hipbone.

"You're lucky the bullet missed your tattoo," Dr. Miller said. "Your lady justice looks a lot like Kate."

Parker's muscles tensed under the doctor's fingers. "That's because it is Kate."

"Honor, duty, respect, family," Dr. Miller read what was written in one half of the justice scale. "Balanced out by an eagle, globe, and anchor. It's thoughtful."

Dr. Hazelwood stepped closer. "The image looks familiar."

"I doubt it. Unless you follow the college art scene." Parker had gotten the inspiration for her tattoo from Kate's graduation piece. She sat up and rubbed her thigh to soothe the sudden twinge. "But that's not why we're here, so can we move on, please?"

"I'm sorry." Dr. Miller's cheeks turned pink, and she busied herself with Parker's medical file.

"How long has your thigh injury been giving you trouble?" Dr. Hazelwood asked. "I've seen you massaging it twice, and I've only met you this morning."

Parker crossed her arms and took a breath.

Dr. Hazelwood raised her hand. "Before you tell me it's none of my business, I'm only concerned about your well-being. I didn't see any mention about lasting side effects from your injury when I reviewed your file."

Parker exhaled, letting go of the tension. "About three days." That was when Colleen had stilled her hand. She hadn't even noticed at the time.

"So this is not only a recent development, but it also started after you learned about Kate's condition?"

"I think so." Parker was amazed that Dr. Hazelwood was so well informed. It seemed like Dr. Miller was right to involve her.

"Are you worried?" Dr. Miller asked while she still perused the file.

"No," Dr. Hazelwood said. "My guess is that it's psychosomatic."

"What?" Parker's eyes went wide.

"A manifestation of the added emotional stress. I expect it to disappear when the situation resolves." Dr. Hazelwood handed Parker her shirt.

Dr. Miller looked up from the file. "There's a record of two HIV tests a couple of years ago."

Parker's blood ran cold, and she winced. From the moment she'd signed the release form, she'd been dreading this conversation. The tests had been routine after what she'd gone through, and they'd all been clean, but she wasn't eager to revisit that part of her past.

"There should have been a one-year follow-up, but I can't see any record of it."

"It's been done, and it was clean like all the ones before," she said, trying to keep her voice cold and flat while she clung onto the present with every bit of her willpower.

"Why were they ordered?"

"Isn't that in the file?" She looked at the floor to avoid the looks of pity and shame. "I was captured and held for several days. When I was returned, they ordered those tests and a boatload of others." Her stomach lurched. Her stay at the hospital after she had been released had been almost worse than her time spend in captivity. They'd poked, prodded, and evaluated her until it was decided she was fit for duty after her leg had healed.

"Since the last HIV test results aren't in here, I'd like to do another one just to be on the safe side." Dr. Miller typed something into her tablet.

Parker's demons circled closer and closer like vultures. She needed this to be over with, and soon. "Do whatever you have to do."

"Okay, I think that's all we need for today. Anything you'd like to add, Commander Hazelwood?"

"No. For now I have everything I need." Hazelwood stepped closer. "Unless the captain has any more questions?"

"Uh, not a question per se, more a general bit of information. I'm sensitive to most pain medication. They make me fuzzy, even in low doses, and I go to sleep if I need to take something stronger. You haven't mentioned it, but it should be in my file. When I had surgery to repair the damage to my leg, it took me a long time to come out of the post-op drug haze."

"I saw nothing about it. It's not as relevant right now, but it will be for any kind of pain management post op. If that is where this goes."

Dr. Miller closed her medical records and handed them back to Commander Hazelwood.

Parker swallowed the lump in her throat. Dr. Miller's seemingly easy dismissal of her concern worried her. The sleepy, fuzzy mess she'd been after her leg surgery wasn't anything she was eager to repeat. This was about Kate, however, and for her, she would endure just about anything.

Chapter Thirteen

AFTER PARKER LEFT THE hospital, she took a detour on her way home to clear her head. The need to see Kate and make sure she was settled in and okay was strong. But she was of little use in her current, frazzled state.

The results would take a couple of days, and the hospital would be in touch when they had any answers for her. Parker still wasn't telling anyone about what she'd been doing. Hopefully, she could tell them good news when it came.

She took a small bouquet of flowers to Arlington cemetery. It had been a very long time since she had visited the grave of Kate's parents. After she placed the flowers into a small vase near the headstone, she settled onto the same bench Kate had loved to sit on to draw.

They'd snuck out in the early morning hours more than once so Kate could sketch the sunrise over the cemetery. She'd said it made her feel closer to her mother. Parker had kissed Kate for the first time on this bench when she was fifteen. The memory tingled in her tummy and spread warmth through her body. She could almost taste Kate's sweet lip-gloss. She could see Kate's face before her eyes like it was yesterday. Her rosy cheeks had been cold when Parker had cupped her face. She had fallen right into those soulful blue eyes, and everything around them had disappeared. The stress with her parents and the pressure of school had no longer mattered. Kate's eyes and smile made her feel safe and loved long before any of them ever dared to say the words.

The sun had slowly risen over the horizon and bathed Kate in a golden light that made her look like she was wearing a halo.

The light reflecting in Kate's eyes was the first time Parker had noticed changes. She'd asked Kate several times what was going on but had stopped asking when Kate assured her nothing was wrong. Parker blamed herself for not asking more questions and not telling her parents. She'd often wondered if anything would've been different if Kate's disease had been diagnosed earlier and if she'd gotten her on medication sooner.

She ran her fingers over the metal engravings on the bench's armrest. What ifs were of no use to anyone. She couldn't change the past. "But I'll try my best to give Kate a chance at a future."

"Can you help me with the dinner preparations?" her mother asked when Parker walked into the house.

Parker had no desire to help with the cooking again, but the stern look she received when she started to make excuses had her washing her hands in the kitchen sink.

"Don't look like you prefer to be anywhere else but here." Her mother pointed toward the fridge. "Get the steaks out, please."

Parker did as she was told. "That's not it. I don't mind being back. I just feel like I'm a nuisance."

"You're not a nuisance," her mother said.

"I didn't mean to you in particular." She busied herself wrapping large potatoes in foil. "Zoe can't stand being in the same room with me. Harry runs out every chance he gets. And you're constantly afraid I'll disappear again, so you don't want to let me out of your sight. I'm disrupting everyone's lives."

"You're wrong."

"Am I?"

"Maybe not about me." Helen sounded defeated. "I just don't want you to leave and stay away for another five years. The last time you went for an appointment, you packed up and left the next day. I just hoped if you felt more like part of the family, you might like to stay. Or at least, to come back more often."

"Kate didn't tell you where I went?"

"She didn't talk much to us when we got her home." Helen

shook her head. "I think she resents us for trying to protect her from what will come. What coming home most likely means. I know she is an adult and the doctors probably explained it to her. It's just like it's not happening until we say it."

"Kate knows that without a miracle, she's not got long left." Parker turned away so her mother couldn't see her face and muttered. "When you're faced with your own mortality, platitudes become awfully meaningless. You'd much rather spent your time and energy on the memories and things that are important to you." She clenched her fist on the kitchen surface, and the smell of cooking meat brought back memories of her own.

"You aren't talking hypotheticals, are you?" Her mother took Parker by her shoulders and turned her to face her. "You know?"

"I can't blame Kate that she wanted to keep her medical struggles secret after I left her. After all this time, I don't have the right to presume what's important to her. But you should have told me regardless of her wishes when things got out of control." Parker carried on like she hadn't heard her mother for a moment. "I've been close enough to know how much things can change. I've just been lucky enough to get a second chance." *And I've been wasting it all those years.*

Her mother made a face. "When?"

"I'm not important here." Parker turned away.

"Is that it? You decided that we weren't worth your effort?" Her mother raised her voice.

"You have no idea what happened, and you never will, not because it's none of your business but because you're my mother, and I want to protect you from the ugliness." She wiped her hands on a dish towel and stormed out the kitchen, yelling over her shoulder, "I left last time so you didn't have to witness the ugliness of the aftermath."

It didn't take long for her mother to follow her into the living room and settle beside her on the piano bench in silence. The baby grand had once been Parker's, but she hadn't really played since she'd left. She'd found a public piano here or there. There are instruments set up in public places, either temporary or permanently, that anyone who wanted to could play for a little while. Some were in great shape, but others hadn't been tuned in ages or had strings or hammers missing.

Her fingers trailed over the thick padding over the keys, protecting the precious instrument that lay slumbering beneath.

"Do you still play?" her mother asked.

"Not really."

"You left everything behind when you walked out," her mother said, the sadness obvious.

"Not many pianos around where I've been," Parker said.

"This is a perfectly good one that misses your capable touch."

Parker looked at the pictures that decorated the piano lid. Family shots and high school pictures placed chronologically. The most recent picture of her was the one her mother took the day she graduated high school—or had been kicked out of high school, depending on how you choose to look at it. The school hadn't been too understanding when they caught her and Kate kissing under the bleachers. It'd been such a cliché. The school gave her a choice: expand her course work to complete her credits and graduate that summer, a year ahead of her peers, or get kicked out of school. They made it clear there wouldn't be any consequences for Kate if Parker graduated early, so that's what she'd done.

Placed right next to a picture of Nicole, the family resemblance was obvious. Nicole was holding Zoe just a few hours after she'd been born. Nicole's face was pale and her eyes bruised. The leukemia had riddled her fragile body beyond recognition.

"What are you thinking about?" her mother asked.

"The pictures." She turned to face her mother.

Her mother smiled. "Are you the same on the job?"

Parker frowned. "What do you mean?"

"Your answers are so perfectly vague, you may as well not say anything at all. Perhaps you could have a lucrative career as a politician instead of a lawyer and soldier."

She wanted to roll her eyes at her mother but thought better of it. "I thought you'd be happy with me being a lawyer. The Corps thought it was a good idea even though I tried to escape that fate."

"Why didn't you tell us that you hated the idea so much?" Her mother couldn't hide the hurt in her voice. "We only wanted you to be happy."

She hated to see her mother like this, but she wasn't able to soften the hurt. There were things that needed to be said. "That's hard to believe. If that's all you ever wanted, why didn't you let me and Kate be together?"

A myriad of feelings crossed over her mother's face, each gone too fast for Parker to identify before she settled on a stoic expression that revealed nothing. "You were teenagers, hardly old enough to understand the consequences."

"Yeah, that's pretty much what I expected," Parker said. "But you apologized for it when I arrived. Did you mean it or not?"

"Why would you think I didn't?"

"Well, you don't want me to leave, but you're not ready to accept me for the woman I am."

"That's not true. I don't have a problem with you being a lesbian."

"You don't?" She wished she could believe her. She hadn't as a teenager. Now she wanted to see actions to back up her mother's words and so far, she hadn't. For the sake of all their futures, she hoped she would.

"No."

"So, you wouldn't mind me bringing a woman home to meet you all?"

"Of course not."

"A random stranger isn't a problem but being in love with my best friend is?" Parker took in a sharp breath when her error registered. By the fleeting confusion on her mother's face, she'd caught it too.

Her mother straightened her back and exhaled. "She's your

sister."

"Not by blood." Parker ran her hand through her hair. "Kate and I met in kindergarten. She came to live with us because her parents died, and the court wouldn't let Colleen take her in because she's a lesbian and never cared to hide it. The judge who made that decision was a homophobic old-timer, just like her grandparents who would've done anything to not let Kate live with her aunt."

"Parker."

"What?" Parker stood up and started pacing.

"We're your parents, but that doesn't mean we're infallible. We made mistakes, and we have to live with them." Her mother hunched her shoulders and looked at the floor.

"Look at me." Parker stood in front of her mother. "Yes, you're human and you make mistakes, but that doesn't keep you from trying to make it right."

Her mother shrank back, and Parker realized that she was being too aggressive. She calmed herself. "I've been reassigned to JAG HQ, so I'll be here a while if you want to try to make up for the past. I'll start apartment hunting tomorrow. Neither of us want me moving back home."

"Wait," her mother said as Parker reached the doorway. "You mean it, you're staying?"

"For now," she said. "I don't know how long they'll keep me here."

Her mother jumped up from the piano stool and crossed the room. She threw her arms around Parker and held tight.

"Don't keep us at arm's length, I want us to really try. You could talk to your dad about a place to live. We have an apartment downtown, and there's the house next door."

What had her father called the neighboring house? An investment. No doubt the apartment downtown was more of the same. Her mother mentioning it though was her version of an olive branch. Parker needed time to think about it. She wanted to repair the rift between them, but she wasn't quite ready to ask her father for a place to stay. Besides, as long as Kate was staying in this house, so was she.

Chapter Fourteen

PARKER WOKE AT MIDNIGHT and headed to the kitchen. A faint creaking caught her attention. She went through to the living room when she spotted the faint glow of light from the adjoining sunroom. When she reached the doorway, she froze. Kate sat on the two-seat wicker chair, wrapped in a fleece blanket nursing a steaming cup in her hands. She looked lost in thought.

Parker leaned her head against the doorjamb and watched, silently caressing Kate with her gaze. Backlit by the hidden lamp behind her mother's plants, Kate looked almost angelic.

Kate lifted her right hand and grunted before she grasped her mug with both hands again. Parker's heart grew heavy, knowing that she had no right to stand there and spy on Kate. She tried willing herself to back away before she disturbed her.

"How long do you want to stand there before you join me," Kate asked softly.

Parker bit her lower lip. She was caught and had no good excuse to be there.

"Are you coming or not?" Kate placed the cup on the small side table.

Parker stepped back. "I didn't want to disturb you. I'm sorry." She wondered briefly how Kate had known she was there, but Kate had always known when she was close.

"Nonsense, get your ass over here."

Parker walked in and sat in a chair opposite. "What gave me away?"

"Would you believe me if I said I felt your presence? Even if I couldn't feel, I can smell you. I've missed that scent." Kate opened the blanket wrapped around her. "Will you come over here already? You'll freeze your butt off dressed like that."

"What's wrong with what I'm wearing?" Parker looked down at the gray Marine Corps T-shirt and old sweatpants cut off above her knee.

"Nothing, but humor me, please?" Kate waved the corner of her blanket.

Parker got up and sat beside Kate. She tucked her feet under her ass to keep them warm. The low light in the room prohibited her from seeing anything beyond the windows, so she searched for something else to stop her from staring at Kate.

Kate shuffled sideways to look at Parker. "You were quiet and withdrawn tonight. How did your check-up go?

"Why would you say that?"

"You didn't say anything at dinner, not even when Zoe had another go at you. And now you're only speaking because I'm asking you questions."

"Zoe seems to be happiest if she doesn't have to see me. I guess I can't really blame her."

"I need you to do me a favor." Kate fidgeted. "I need you to try harder with her. She needs someone in her life she can trust. Currently that's me, but I won't always be there for her." Kate pulled Parker close and wrapped the rest of the blanket around her.

"What do you expect me to do?" Parker fiddled with the soft fleece to occupy her hands and stop them straying onto Kate's body.

"Show her that she can survive her grief. She was too young when her mother died, and the rest of us didn't cope well. That left Zoe with issues no one ever fully understood. Now she's grieving over me before I've even gone." Kate looked at her, almost ashamed. "That grief will be something the two of you will share. You can use it to connect with her and show her that she can survive it and be stronger on the other side."

Parker fought the urge to jump up and run. She'd never dealt with her grief. She'd taken it, shoved it into a box, and locked it before burying it in the most forlorn place in her heart. She stayed silent for a long while and played with some loose wicker on their chair. "I don't think I'm the right person for that."

"Yes, you are. You're kind-hearted, funny, and loving, and you can give her all the things I won't be able to. And most important, she'll see that it does get better."

"You give me too much credit." Why did everyone think she was over Kate and wouldn't feel a deep sense of loss if she died?

"No, I don't."

"You do." She turned in her seat toward Kate. "I'm good at letting people see what I want them to see. I've not been too good at that since I got back, but I'm working on that. I'm a survivor, yes, and hopefully, I'll get through this. But I won't be better or stronger for it." Parker shook her head. "Underneath all this armor is the same lovesick, heartbroken teenager that left here all those years ago. I've never been able to fit those pieces back together."

"Parker," Kate touched her hand, but she pulled it away. "I don't know what to say."

"You don't have to say anything." Parker put as much space between them as the small two-seater wicker chair allowed.

Kate's eyes glistened with tears. "Why are you pulling away?"

"I don't want to make you uncomfortable." And it was too hard, being so close and not being able to touch Kate, to caress her skin just as she used to when they were alone in this same chair years ago.

"I enjoy having you close to me." Kate wiped at the corner of her eye. "I just don't understand why you never came back."

"How could I know that you wanted me to? I did what you asked me to do."

"What I asked you to do?" Kate buried her face in her hands. "I wanted you to follow your dreams without me holding you back. I always hoped you'd come back to me one day."

Parker frowned. "You hoped I'd come back? After I abandoned

you here to deal with my family, threw all our plans away, and joined the military, an institution you never wanted to be a part of after your parents died. You wanted me home?"

"Always." Kate lifted her head.

"We're quite the pair."

Kate shivered and burrow deeper into the blanket.

"Are you cold?" Parker asked.

"I never seem to get warm these days." Kate rubbed over her arms. "It's the same with sleep. When I want to stay awake, I'm exhausted and fall asleep all the time, and when I actually want to sleep, my body is wide awake. Even valerian tea doesn't help."

Parker opened her arms. "Do you want to snuggle against a human toaster oven?"

Kate hesitated for a moment before she grinned and moved in. "Definitely."

Parker pulled the blanket tight and rubbed her back. "Are you comfortable?"

Kate sighed softly. "Very."

"Can I ask you something?"

"Hmm."

"Why did you never ask me to get tested?" Parker regretted the words as soon as they had left her mouth. Kate stiffened in her arms. Parker rubbed slow circles on her back hoping she would relax again. "You don't have to tell me."

It was a while before Kate loosened in Parker's arms.

"I never asked anyone else. They volunteered. I still have a hard time wrapping my head around the fact that they did."

"Why? They all love you."

Kate shrugged against Parker's chest. "I don't know how to explain it. It's like I passed the burden to save my life onto them. Don't get me wrong, I'm extremely grateful for what they did. But how could I ask them to choose my life over theirs? What if there are complications or they get ill themselves?"

Parker pulled Kate in but couldn't get her close enough.

"Helen asked if she could tell you when I got worse again, but I wouldn't let her, and she gave me her word. It was selfish and maybe foolish. I didn't want you to get in touch for the wrong reasons. And I didn't want to risk being a distraction in case you were somewhere dangerous."

Again? That meant it wasn't the first time Kate had problems with her illness and the medication she took. Parker swallowed hard. "She kept her promise. She never spoke of you in our calls."

"Never?" Kate's body tensed again. "I secretly hoped she would at least tell you about the good things."

Parker smiled. "I asked a couple of times in the beginning when I called for Zoe, but she wouldn't tell me anything. Eventually I stopped asking about you. I let her know that I was okay and would spend the rest of the call with Zoe, if she talked to me, that is. In the past years, I've been catching up with Zoe's progress through Helen." Parker inhaled Kate's citrusy shampoo. *God, I've missed being this close to you.* "She once asked me why I always asked about you. I think she was trying to tell me that I should talk to you directly."

Kate trailed patterns over Parker's arm. "Why didn't you try to talk to me?"

"Back when Mom suggested it, I wasn't ready."

"I'm glad you're ready now."

Kate's fingers found the small circular scar on her upper thigh. She trailed over the spot, her fingers barely touching Parker's skin. Her thigh tensed at the contact.

"Does it hurt when I touch it?" Kate asked.

The scar was almost numb, but Kate's touch strangely sensitized it. A hot trail of sensation ran over her thigh and up her leg, settling in her center. Parker held her breath. She should be in better control of herself. Her cheeks flushed hot, and she was thankful for the muted lighting.

"I'm sorry. I didn't mean to hurt you." Kate pulled back but Parker held her hand in place.

"You're not hurting me." Parker drew small circles on the back of Kate's hand. "It's just that no one has touched it except the doctors."

"Oh. I didn't want to make you feel uncomfortable."

"You're not. It just feels a bit strange." Parker let out a long breath. "The same incident that gave me that scar also left me with some emotional stuff to deal with. I was sent home to recover from my injuries."

"Did your parents know?"

"I think they knew some of it. They were informed about the incident—"

"That isn't what I mean. Did you tell them about what happened to you?"

"No, Mom knew I was injured, but she doesn't know any details. I avoided talking to her about it. Harry was out of town most of the time, and Zoe was too young to understand what was going on."

"I wish I'd known what was going on. I would've been there for you." Kate pulled her hand free and squeezed Parker's. "Just like I wish I'd let you know about me, so you could've been here sooner...if you'd wanted to."

They both went silent, and Parker hoped Kate would go to sleep, though she was much too wired to even contemplate any shuteye tonight. She played with Kate's hair, soothing herself with the repetitive motion. She turned Kate's last words over and over in her mind.

"I wish it hadn't taken us this long to figure out we were wrong," Kate said after a while.

"Me too." Parker kissed the top of Kate's head softly and decided to see what Kate would say to what she was already doing. "I'd like to get tested too."

Kate sat up abruptly. "No."

"Why not?"

"What if you are a match, and you decided to do it? Your life would change forever. I wouldn't ask that of you, not after everything you've already been through. You haven't thought about how it might affect your career."

"You didn't ask." Parker gently tugged on Kate's arm, and she settled back against her. Kate yawned, and Parker pulled the blanket tighter around them. "Don't worry about it now. Get some sleep."

It didn't take long until gentle puffs came from Kate to indicate she'd fallen asleep. Her reaction to the testing made Parker glad she hadn't led with the fact that she'd already started the testing process. If she was a match, Parker would face that battle then.

Chapter Fifteen

THE COLD NOVEMBER AIR did little to cool Parker's bad mood when she followed Zoe out of the school building. Her mother had asked if Parker could get Zoe since she was due in court and couldn't make it. Zoe had gotten into a fight and the school was sending her home. Her mother had said that it was entirely possible that Zoe had acted out so she could stay home the rest of the week with Kate.

"It wasn't my fault," Zoe said when she stomped toward the car.

Parker didn't respond and waited for Zoe to climb in. She started the car and pulled out of the parking lot. She'd been looking forward to a quiet morning with Kate after the conversation they had the previous night.

It wasn't Parker's intention to get in her parents' way on how to raise Zoe, but this seemed like a good way to see if she could come through on what she and Kate had talked about last night.

"This isn't the way home," Zoe said as Parker took a turn out of town.

"No, it's not." She drove in silence for a while. "If you hoped to get home early today, you're going to be disappointed."

Zoe folded her arms. "I have homework to do."

"You would have had the same homework when you got home after school. And since they don't want you back for the rest of the week, you've got plenty of time to do it. A few hours aren't gonna hurt you. That is what you keep on saying, isn't it?"

Zoe glared at her but didn't comment. Parker hadn't ever really had an adult conversation with Zoe, and she got the distinct feeling that Zoe wasn't interested. Parker concentrated when she turned from the country road into the forest. It'd been ages since she'd been here, and she wasn't even sure if the lake between the trees was still accessible. When she'd been Zoe's age, she and Kate tagged along when the older students drove out here after school in the summers.

"Oh, wow!" Zoe said as Parker rolled to a stop between the trees that ringed a small pond.

Zoe unbuckled and was out of the car before Parker switched the engine off. She leaned against the hood of the car and watched Zoe run to the water's edge. The place was deserted except for a few birds in the surrounding trees, and they complained loudly about their quiet being interrupted. The air was crisp and clean just as Parker remembered.

After a while, Zoe came back and leaned on the hood of the car beside Parker. "Why did you bring me here? And has anyone ever told you that your car is ancient?"

"Is it?"

Zoe gave her an incredulous look. "You can't even connect a phone to the radio. Central locking, anyone? You literally have to walk around and unlock every single door."

Parker couldn't hold back her laugh. "You know this was your mother's car, right?"

"What?" Zoe jumped off the hood and turned to look at it. "This was my mom's?"

"Yeah. Your grandad gave it to me when I got my license, but it was Nicole's first. She used to take us out here in summer. Her and Linda would meet up with the boys from school, and me and Kate would bug her for a ride. We usually wandered off over there." Parker pointed across the pond into the woods. "There was a small table someone had made from fallen trees. Kate loved to sit there for hours and sketch."

"What did Mom do out here?"

"Apart from swimming and hanging out with her friends, I don't really know. Spending time with her younger sister wasn't cool.

You could ask Linda."

"Sometimes I'd rather not know," Zoe said.

Parker rubbed at a speck of dirt on the hood. "Why?"

Zoe sighed. "I don't know that it would help me understand who I am if I knew who my parents were but they're not here, so what good will it do me?"

She had to give it to Zoe, her reasoning was mature for her age. She wandered off again, and Parker got a sweater from the car.

"I hate seeing you in this." Zoe returned and pulled at the sleeve of Parker's top.

"Why?"

"You in uniform means you'll leave again."

"I thought that's what you wanted," Parker said.

"Yes. No." Zoe pulled at her hair. "I don't know. I don't know what's going on with me. I'm angry all the time." She sank onto the hood again and hung her head.

"Is that what happened in school today?" Parker asked softly.

Zoe nibbled on her lower lip. "Some of the boys made fun of my friend Melody and me. They said we're going out, and because she has two moms, she has to be the same." Zoe looked away. "I just lost it and punched one of them in the face."

Parker didn't know if she should be angry on Zoe's behalf or be proud of her for punching the bully in the face. She suspected neither reaction was the right one and searched for something more responsible. "You know punching someone isn't the answer, right? I'm not saying that they shouldn't be spoken to, but violence isn't the answer."

"Like anyone in that school ever will," Zoe said. "But yes, I know punching someone isn't right. And Grandma is wrong if she thinks that I did it just to be sent home. I just lost it. Usually, I can control my temper, but it's just so hard lately."

"When did that start? You being angry all the time."

"During summer maybe?" Zoe shrugged. "There was so much

going on with Kate that I didn't pay much attention to myself. It's like, first, I couldn't believe what was going on, and when I thought I eventually had my head wrapped around everything, the smallest thing sets me off."

"Have you seen anyone about that?" Parker asked.

"You mean like a shrink?"

Parker nodded. "Like a shrink."

"No." Zoe shifted sideways and put more space between them. "I don't want to see a doctor that screws around with my head."

"They don't screw with your head. They can really help you."

Zoe looked at her. "Have you seen one?"

"The military makes us see one when they think it's needed. Like when we have been away for a really long time or something happened. So yes, I have been a few times. But I talk about work stuff. I've never seen one to deal with my private matters like losing your mom." She let her head fall back and stared up into the trees. "Have you tried to work some of your anger off with sports?"

"Basketball helps a bit, but it's a non-contact sport, so I can't get too rough, or I get pulled up."

Parker smiled. She'd always avoided sports where she couldn't just slam into someone. "Maybe we can try something else to help."

Zoe cocked her head. "Like what?"

"I'm going to show you what I do to deal with my anger. We'll need to make a stop on our way home." Parker got off the hood to walk toward the driver's side and smiled when she spotted the tree where Kate had kissed her.

"What are you smiling at?"

"An old memory. Get your butt in the car."

Zoe looked in the same direction and zeroed in. "That looks like the one in Kate's paintings."

"That's because it is." Parker remembered Kate making the first sketches that would later turn into the painting known as "Lovers under the tree."

"She sold the original several years ago, but she still makes prints of them. Kate gave me a small one for my tenth birthday because I loved it so much. I put it over my bed."

Parker had a hard time keeping a straight face when she thought of the painting, safely tucked away in her storage facility. It had taken some doing to buy it from the art gallery while she was out of the country, and none of the family had known. It had been their place, hers and Kate's. No one had ever tried to keep them apart at the pond, their little safe haven. Kate had done the painting to commemorate their love and connection. When she'd spotted the painting for sale years later, it had shattered what was left of her heart. She was convinced that Kate would only have let go of it because she was over Parker. But *she* hadn't been able to let go of their connection, not then, and she would do everything to rebuild it now.

They got in the car and drove to a sporting goods store. Parker went straight for the boxing section to look at the punching bags. They had pre-filled ones and empty bags to fill yourself to choose from. Parker inspected the materials of the punching bags that were for self-filling.

"Why are we doing this, Parker?"

Parker sat down on one of the benches, holding one of the bags. "I have a problem with anger too. But I don't want a doctor poking around in my head. Boxing really helps me."

Zoe looked at her like she was an insect under a microscope. "You really mean that?"

"Oh yeah, I punch the shit out of a bag on a regular basis."

"Okay. So what are we doing?" Zoe seemed a little more interested.

After a little discussion, they decided on a medium-weight, pre-filled bag. It took a little while to find gloves that Zoe liked enough to wear. A salesman had first presented Zoe with a pretty pink pair that she declared she wouldn't be caught dead in.

"Why don't you get gloves?" Zoe asked. "You just said they were super important so I wouldn't get injured. I want you to show me how it's done."

Parker smiled at the seemingly small progress they were making. "I have a perfectly good pair in my storage unit."

"But how will you show me?"

"I've been doing this a long time. I'll just wrap my hands. I'll get the rest of my gear out of storage when I find an apartment."

"You're staying?"

Parker nodded. "For now."

Zoe squealed and wrapped her arms around Parker's neck. Her first instinct was to distance herself, but she remembered Kate's request. *I'm making progress. Don't ruin it.*

Zoe picked out a beautiful black and blue patterned hand wrap and insisted that Parker buy it to keep her hands safe until she got her gloves. She had hand wraps in her luggage—she never went anywhere without them—but she got these since it seemed to make Zoe happy.

They hung the bag in the two-bay garage that housed the old Ford. The space clearly wasn't used for anything else, and it was a great size for a home gym. After the bag was secured on one of the ceiling beams, Zoe couldn't wait to get her first go at it.

They changed and worked out for almost an hour. Parker showed Zoe where to place her feet, how to hold her upper body, and all the different punches. She demonstrated technique and corrected Zoe's posture. When Parker noticed Zoe's arms droop, she brought an end to the workout for the day. She didn't want Zoe getting into the same bad habits of over-training that she'd fallen into. Zoe gave her a sweaty hug before going off to shower.

Parker heard voices coming from the ground floor, guest room Kate had moved into so that she didn't have to climb the stairs.

By the time Parker had come up from putting her sweaty clothes and some other stuff into the laundry, it was silent. She closed the basement door and turned to face Jazmin Callahan. "What are you doing here?" Parker asked.

"I could ask you the same thing," Jazmin said.

"I live here."

"I don't think so. You haven't shown your face here in years."
Jazmin glared at her. "It would've been better if you stayed out of
this."

"What's that supposed to mean?" Parker asked and clenched
her jaw. What the hell was her problem?

"You know damn well what I mean."

"I really don't." She straightened to her full height and stepped
into Jazmin's personal space. "Why are you here?"

"To check on my patient."

"Your patient? Dr. Miller is responsible for Kate. The plan was to
hire a private care agency. Are you moonlighting instead of being
on vacation with your brother?"

"Someone has to talk some sense into Kate! She belongs in
a hospital with constant care. This is suicide." Jazmin lowered her
voice. "Don't think you know anything about me just because you
work with my brother."

"And by talking sense, you mean yelling at her? Dr. Miller
agreed to discharge Kate, and *she's* her doctor." Parker registered
the expression on Jazmin's face and the pain in her eyes. It was the
same one that had stared at her in her reflection day after day when
she'd left home. Parker realized this was much more complicated
than she'd thought. But she needed to know. "Are you one of Kate's
doctors or are you something more?"

"Can't I be both?" Jazmin slammed her fist into the wall she'd
backed up against.

"Apparently not if you're not able to stay impartial."

"I've known Kate for a long time."

"As what?"

Jazmin said nothing and averted her gaze. The front door
opened, and Parker backed away.

"What's going on here?" her mother asked as she and Colleen
came inside.

"I was leaving," Jazmin said. "Parker was walking me out."

"That's nice." Her mother put her briefcase on the floor and took off her heels. "What are your plans for Thanksgiving, Dr. Callahan?"

Jazmin turned back from the door. "Usually, I'd spend it with my parents, but they're on a cruise this year, so it's just me and my brother, who's on leave. No plans yet, Mrs. Snow."

"I didn't know you had a brother," her mother said.

Jazmin blushed. "Yes, he works with Parker."

Her mother looked at Parker. "Is that so?"

"Yeah. Lieutenant Callahan is my legal aid until he finishes law school. He's a lovely guy." *Unlike his sister.*

"That's so nice." Her mother seemed oblivious to the tension. "Would you like to join us for the holiday if you don't have any other plans. I'm sure Kate would like to have her friend here."

Parker didn't like how this conversation had developed at all. But it made it clear that the family saw Jazmin as a friend and not as Kate's doctor. Parker wanted to know how Kate saw their relationship. If they were more than just friends, where did that leave Parker?

Chapter Sixteen

PARKER HAD KNOCKED THREE times and was about to turn away.

"Come in if you must."

She stuck her head through the door. "I just wanted to see if you were okay. I can leave."

"No." Kate waved at her, clearly a little sleepy. "I thought you were someone else. Please come in."

Parker looked around. "Where's all your stuff?"

"In my room." Kate gave her a weak smile.

She raised an eyebrow, wanting to ask why she hadn't had everything brought down. But it looked like the discussion with Jazmin had taken a lot out of Kate.

"This isn't my room," Kate said. "I've got a room upstairs and one at Colleen's. I should have my own place, but I don't, so I had to move back in here." Kate yawned.

"If you need to rest, I'll leave. I can come back later."

"Stay, please." Kate rolled onto her side and looked at Parker. "The pain meds make me sleepy, but I'd love to have some company, if you don't mind that I'll probably fall asleep on you at some point."

"Are you in a lot of pain?" Parker didn't want to imagine how much pain Kate was in. She wished she could lay her hands on her and pull it from her body. Maybe if the tests were a match, that's what she'd be doing.

Kate pushed herself up to a half-seated position. "Why don't you come sit with me for a while?" She pointed to a chair in a corner. "Jazmin gave me an injection for the pain. It's the only kind that seems to do the trick these days."

If she really wanted to know what the business with Jazmin was about, this was her opening. But did she actually want to know? Wouldn't it just hurt her all over again?

"Penny for your thoughts?" Kate asked.

"Who is Dr. Callahan to you?"

"I met her during a medical trial a little over two years after you left. She was working on the trial together with two other doctors. Back then, Jazmin was still a resident." Kate nibbled her lower lip. "I was the youngest person in the trial and had little in common with the other participants. Jazmin and I were similar ages so we ended up talking a lot, not only about trial related things, but personal stuff, our dreams and goals in life."

Parker pushed her fists between her thighs to hide them. This wasn't what she wanted to hear. Kate and Jazmin had known each other for almost the entire time she'd been gone. How could it not have turned into something deeper?

"I went back to see my old specialist after the trial ended. I saw Jazmin there, and she asked me out for coffee. She was no longer my doctor and I'd always enjoyed talking with her, so I said yes."

Parker closed her eyes and slowly inhaled. "And then what? A few coffees turned into dinner and a date, and the rest is history?"

Kate whipped her head around and stared at Parker. "What makes you think that we're more than friends? I told you I was single. We're just friends. She listened when I needed to vent because everyone else is wrapping me in cotton wool. I was sick of being told what was best for me by everyone else. I haven't seen her as a friend since she started working with Dr. Miller because of the potential conflict."

Kate was clearly oblivious to Jazmin's interest, which made Parker feel a little better. "I don't know what it's like, you're right, and I apologize for making an assumption."

"How could you know? You haven't been the one with overbearing family who went insane with worry every time I got a cold." Kate let out a breath. "But Jazmin has been there to make sure I have everything I need, and she explains things to me in plain English."

"Jazmin never makes any medical decisions for your care or tells you what decisions you should make?" The mere idea made her protective instincts come out in full force.

"Why are you asking that, Parker?"

"There's a reason why doctors aren't supposed to treat family members. It's a question of ethics. I think it should extend to close friends."

"We're not close. We've had dinner a couple of times, but we haven't done that in ages."

"She never invited you to her place?"

"A couple of times." Kate glared at her. "If there's something you want to know, ask already."

"Have you ever slept with her?"

"Not that it's any of your business who I may or may not have slept with, but no, I've never slept with Jazmin. She isn't even a lesbian." Kate blushed. "Sorry, that's not fair after all the things I asked you."

"Jazmin likes women, I guarantee you that." Parker mentally kicked herself. She had all the tact of a bull in a china shop.

"There's nothing going on you need to be concerned about, ethically or otherwise." Kate pulled her blanket up. "I told you before, no one's interested in having a sick girlfriend. When everyone else wants to go out to a party and get drunk, I want to crawl onto my couch with a soft blanket, a cup of hot chocolate, and a good book."

"What's so wrong with that?"

"Nothing, but it gets old real fast when you're young and hungry for life."

Parker frowned. "You're talking like this has happened to you." She'd hoped to cheer Kate up, but their conversation had started badly and gone downhill from there.

"You're forgetting, Parker, I've lived with this disease for years.

There's just been no point even trying."

Parker shook her head, stunned that Kate hadn't clocked Jazmin's interest. "You haven't seen what's right in front of you."

"What do you mean?"

"You really think that no one has been interested in you since I left?"

Kate crossed her arms over her chest. "Can you at least look at me when you're talking to me?"

When Parker met Kate's gaze, the hurt she saw in her face hit her hard.

"I certainly didn't have the opportunity to sleep around," Kate said sharply.

Maybe the jibe was justified, but Parker clenched her jaw to keep from responding harshly. She regretted being so open with Kate about it, but that chapter of her life was over.

"There was one girl I thought was interested in me when I went to college. We were in a study group together and after a few months, she asked me out on a date." Kate bit her lower lip and slowly let go. "After the second date, she wanted to come up to my room for a drink. She was nothing like you, and not what I hoped for in a partner. But one drink turned into two, and she got hot and heavy." Kate's face pinched together.

Parker closed her hands around the edge of her seat she was sitting on, hoping this story wasn't going the way she thought it might.

"You can relax and stop looking like you want to murder someone." Kate patted her leg. "Nothing happened. I told her I wasn't ready to sleep with her and wanted to wait. She told me that I wasn't worth waiting around for and that I was uptight and boring, so I showed her the door and looked for another study group the next day. I didn't speak to her again."

There were so many things Parker wanted to say, but she couldn't find a place to start and all she could do was stare at Kate. Admiring the woman Kate had become was so easy, it scared her.

Parker was proud that Kate hadn't succumbed to pressure from anyone and had done what was right for her. But Kate hadn't seen how interested Jazmin was.

"After that, I decided that dating wasn't for me while I was in college." Kate shrugged. "By the time I finished, most of our friends had decided that spending time with me came with too many sacrifices. They figured I wasn't worth the hassle. It made sense that no woman would want it either."

Parker's heart convulsed. How did Kate not understand what a wonderful woman she was, and that anyone would be lucky to have her in their life? "That's not true. You're worth more than you could ever know." She took Kate's hand. "Someone who truly cares for you wouldn't think it was a sacrifice to cuddle up on a couch with such a gorgeous woman and read a book or watch TV instead of going out to a party. They'd simply be honored to spend time with you and share the same space. They'd wait for the day you were ready."

"Thank you, Parker, that's really sweet of you to say."

"Why do I have the feeling you don't believe me?"

Kate looked away. "Because it's hard for me."

"Why?"

"I don't deserve it." Kate's eyes became glassy, and she shifted in her bed.

The admission that Kate thought she didn't deserve to have someone in her life that made her happy broke Parker's heart. She wanted to show her that she did...but it wasn't Parker's place to show Kate. She'd lost that when she'd stayed away. But maybe it wasn't too late for Kate. "Jazmin is in love with you, Kate, and she has been for a while."

"Don't be silly."

"She cancelled the vacation plans she had with her brother and her entire family so that she could be at the hospital and spend your last weeks with you." Parker choked. "That's not something people do just out of friendship."

"You have to be wrong," Kate said, and her tears fell.

Parker moved away to give Kate the space she thought she might need. "I wish I were, but it takes one to know one." She inhaled sharply at her admission.

"But I'm not in love with Jazmin." Kate slapped her palms on her comforter.

"I never said you were."

"My heart belongs to someone else," Kate said. "It always has."

"Who?" she whispered. Parker needed to hear the words before she could dare to let her heart hope for more. But the possibility also scared her shitless. Their stakes were already so high with Kate's life in the balance. Could she add to it by telling Kate that she wasn't alone? Her fingers cramped from the tight hold she had on the chair. Before she could decide what to say, Kate's eyelids fluttered shut and her breathing evened out.

Parker watched her. Even in sleep, her brows seem to knit together in pain. The tightness to her lips had softened, and a small smile played around the edges. There was no way to deny it: her heart belonged to Kate.

Chapter Seventeen

PARKER WOKE IN THE middle of the night in cold sweat, the distant screams still ringing in her ears. She dragged herself into a hot shower to wash away some of the ghosts that still clung to her skin. It helped clear her head and she had no desire to go back to bed. Instead, she headed to the living room with her iPad. She wrote a quick email to Mark about being unexpectedly sent to DC for a family matter. She didn't go into more details other than it had something to do with Kate and that he didn't need to worry about their parents. She signed off with a promise that they should meet before she left town again.

The punching bag called to her from the garage. Her workout session with Zoe the previous day had a calming effect even though she hadn't exhausted herself. It was tempting but she wanted to break her bad habits, be kinder to herself, and set a better example for her niece.

She donned her running shoes instead and pounded the pavement. The nightmare lingered in the background, keeping her brain busy. Kate's revelation that she was in love with Parker added another layer to her pent-up emotions. She ran like the devil was after her, as if each mile would bring her closer to the results of her transplant suitability test. Her lungs burned and her fingers tingled from the lack of oxygen in her blood. If Kate still loved her, that changed everything. Parker would put everything on the line for a future together.

When the morning traffic around her started to pick up, Parker returned to the house. She'd done a good six miles, and it left her a lot more clear-headed than when she'd started.

She was about to prepare her third cup of coffee for the day when her mother and Colleen entered the kitchen.

"Make a pot, if you don't mind. We'd like some too." Her mother pointed to a blue can. "Use those beans. I want a treat this morning."

Her mother looked like she'd spent an equally restless night. She was dressed for work but had taken the rest of the week off. If Parker thought about it, she couldn't recall her mother dressing casual much even when she lived at home.

Parker prepared the beans and slid the pot into place and waited. When it had brewed, Parker was tempted to steal away with her cup while her mother and Colleen were distracted making breakfast. It seemed like Colleen had temporarily moved into the other guestroom, which made sense since everyone wanted to spend as much time with Kate as they could before—

Parker shook off the thought. There was still hope, and she wasn't about to put Kate in her grave just yet.

"Where are you going?" her mother asked as Parker headed to the living room. "Would you stay? We need to talk."

Parker flinched at the phrase she didn't want to hear from anyone. She turned around and sat at the breakfast bar. Colleen scrutinized her in silence. "What?" Parker fidgeted on the chair.

"Are you okay?" Colleen asked. "You look a little pale."

"I'm fine." She took another gulp of coffee. "I just didn't sleep very well last night."

"Are you sure you're okay?" her mother asked.

"I think the jetlag is catching up on me, that's all." She wasn't ready to tell her mother that she was haunted by nightmares that robbed her of sleep, and the only way she ever got rest was to push her body to exhaustion.

"I hope you'll settle back in soon. But that wasn't what I wanted to talk about." Her mother sat beside her. "We wanted to talk to you about Zoe. We didn't have the time to talk last night, but Zoe told me what you did together after you picked her up from school."

Parker knew it'd been a bad idea not to tell her mother about the punch bag last night, but they just hadn't managed to connect. Now she'd probably think Parker had interfered, and she didn't like it.

"I appreciate what you've done for Zoe. She seems less angry this morning. I'm not sure if your trip or the boxing did the trick. It was a nice idea to buy a punching bag for her so she can use it when she needs it. Where else did you take her? She didn't know a name for the place you went to."

"The old lake where we used to hang out in summer," Parker said.

"We know it's our fault that she didn't get help to deal with the loss of Nicole." Her mother played with her coffee cup. "Every time we or the school tried, she pushed us away and closed off. But this morning, when I looked at her, I could see part of the sweet girl she used to be."

"I think part of what's going on is puberty, Mom."

Her mother smiled, teary-eyed. "You called me Mom." Her mother sniffed and reached out to her but let her hand drop to the counter when Parker pulled back.

"Anyway," Parker said, uncomfortable with her mother's unexpected show of emotion. "For now, Zoe shouldn't work out alone, not until she's had a few more sessions with me. And you probably want her to do her schoolwork and chores first."

"Don't do this, please."

Parker rolled her neck. "Do what?"

"Pull away again." Her mother took Parker's hand.

She shook her head, not able to voice what was going on in her own head. Her mother let go of her and looked away, perhaps to hide her disappointment.

"I'm going to see how Kate's doing."

Her mother nodded. "Okay. After we've had breakfast, we're going to get the turkey for tomorrow. Let me know if you want to come."

Parker hurried out of the kitchen and found Kate in the sunroom, reading a book. She settled into a chair opposite Kate so she could look at her without disturbing her. She wanted to talk about last night, and about what it meant for them both, but she wasn't sure where to begin.

She cleared her throat to speak, but Kate raised a hand to stop her without looking up from her book. Interested, Parker studied the cover of Kate's book. A pair embraced under the full moon, their torsos bare. A wolf's head seemed to come out of the woman's skin, as if she was howling at the moon.

A frantic turn of the page and a slight quickening of Kate's breath told Parker that the scene was captivating. Kate's pupils dilated.

"I thought you didn't do straight romance. Didn't you say it was unpleasant to read?" She couldn't stay silent any longer.

Kate blinked at her like a spell had been broken. "There are lesbian romances, you know. I found them by accident browsing the library."

"I didn't know that." When it came to books, her time allowed for little leisure reading. Most of it was job related.

"What did you want to say when you came in? I don't think discussing lesbian romances is what you had in mind."

"I didn't know you liked fantasy romance books." Parker bet she looked a little sheepish. How would she have known? A lot of her own preferences had changed and matured. It was only natural to expect that the same was true for Kate.

"Don't look so shocked." Kate laughed at her. "I can lend you one of mine if you like."

"Thanks, I think I'll pass."

"Well, you'll miss a guaranteed happy ending." Kate closed the book and put it on the small table. "Too bad you don't get them in real life." Kate patted the space alongside her. "Why don't you come over here? I wanted to talk to you about the thing you mentioned the other night."

Parker rose and sat beside Kate. She took her hand and

caressed her gently. "We've talked a lot lately. Which thing in particular?" Parker tried to stem the rush of excitement that they could possibly talk of a future together. Damn those tests for taking so long. She wanted to share it with Kate now.

Kate's eyes bore into her. "I wanted to talk to you about the test. I don't want you to do it."

Oh, crap. Parker didn't want this conversation. It was one thing not to mention it to Kate, but to lie outright was another entirely. "Why not?" Parker stood. "If you got a transplant from the waiting list, you wouldn't know who the other person was. What difference does it make if that person is me?"

"A huge difference. A dead person doesn't need their organs anymore. You're alive. You have your entire life ahead of you. You shouldn't do anything to risk that."

"I risk my life every day in my job. Why shouldn't I do the same thing for the woman I love?"

"Get away from me." Kate grabbed her book and stood.

Parker wanted to claw her words back. She hadn't meant for them to come out this way. So eerily similar to the sentence that shattered their relationship.

"Leave me alone." Kate fled the room.

Her words punched Parker square in the chest. Tears sprang unbidden to her eyes and rolled down her cheeks before she could do anything to stop them. She'd laid her heart bare and once again, had been rejected. It hadn't been her plan to overwhelm Kate with her feelings, but it had happened anyway.

The urge to pack her stuff was almost crippling, but she fought it. She contemplated going to the garage to work the bag, but that was too little physical space between her and Kate. She grabbed her running shoes in the hallway, pulled them on, and sprinted out of the house. And just like before, she didn't look back.

Chapter Eighteen

PARKER AIMLESSLY WANDERED THROUGH the neighborhood. A light drizzle had turned to a downpour, and her hoodie was soaked through. A rivulet of water trickled down her spine and soaked into her sweatpants. A dark sedan rolled to a stop in front of her, and the passenger side window opened to reveal Linda.

Parker opened her mouth to speak but closed it, not sure what she was supposed to say. One look at Linda told her she had seen Parker's tears before she'd even stopped the car.

"I'm afraid to ask how bad it is since you're still crying. I drove past you half an hour ago to drop Suzan at a friend's house, and you were already wiping at your tears." Linda reached over and opened the passenger side door. "Hop in."

Without words, Parker got into the car and buckled in. Linda shifted the car into gear and drove on. She wasn't ready to go home, but she didn't know how to ask Linda not to drop her on her parents' doorstep. Linda turned a corner and pulled into the driveway of a house close by.

Linda turned off the engine. "Come in. You can have coffee and dry out some. Give me your wet clothes, and I'll throw them in the dryer for you."

Parker's body couldn't handle any more coffee today. "Juice?" Her words came out in a croak. The silent tears had strained her vocal chords more than she had thought possible. It'd been so long since she'd cried this much, she'd almost forgotten how it felt. But the present and the past now ran together in her mind and distorted reality.

Linda had her change into a dry t-shirt and led her into the kitchen, where she sat on a chair and watched Linda make coffee and pour some fresh orange juice.

"Are you hungry?" Linda opened the refrigerator. "I know it's late for lunch and too early for dinner, but I haven't eaten since breakfast."

Food was the last thing on her mind. "No, I'm fine."

"When was the last time you ate?"

Parker hadn't had lunch before she stormed out, and her breakfast had been three coffees.

Linda seemed to have decided that she'd taken too long to answer. "Not today, I take it. How about some scrambled eggs and toast?"

"I'm really not hungry." Parker's protest was weak, even though her stomach gave a low rumble.

Linda glared at her and pulled a carton of eggs from the fridge. She broke three eggs into a bowl and began to whisk.

Parker nodded. "Eggs and toast sound good." She got up and reached for the juice Linda had placed on the counter for her. A sheet of paper stuck to the bottom of the glass and fluttered to the ground when she picked it up. The paper was a schematic drawing that made no sense to her. Parker held it out. "You probably still need this."

Linda looked and then backed away. "Theoretically, I do, but I swear those are the worst instructions I've ever seen. I'll probably have better luck assembling it without any help at all."

"What is it?"

"The instructions on how to put the baby crib together."

Parker eyed the sheet more closely. It took her preoccupied brain a while to realize that she was holding the piece of paper upside down. After she turned it around, it made marginally more sense, but Linda was right. Whoever created it had failed at their job.

"If you have some insight let me know," Linda said.

Linda held out a plate with two golden brown toast slices

topped with fluffy scrambled eggs. Parker shrugged and refolded the paper until a specific square landed on top. "Do you want some help with that?" She pointed at the paper.

Linda smiled at her. "That would be great, but food first."

Common sense told her she should eat something, so she scarfed the food down as fast as she had when she was in basic training and they had less than three minutes to refuel between the grueling sessions.

Linda led her upstairs to the baby's room. It was decked out in creams and light blues with silhouetted mountains and trees. Several furniture boxes leaned against another wall. A bigger box lay open in the middle of the blue rug, with a couple of the larger parts already spread out across the floor.

Parker sat cross-legged next to the box and quickly scanned the pieces on the floor before rifling through the box.

"It looks like you know what you're doing," Linda said.

Parker didn't respond until she found a small box that rattled and held it up. "I was looking for this."

"What's that?"

"The first piece of the puzzle."

Linda sunk to the floor next to her, still holding her coffee cup. "I don't follow."

She looked at Linda and saw the dark circles under her eyes and worry lines around her mouth. Parker's own misery had distracted her so much that she hadn't noticed the tight set of Linda's shoulders. "You can talk to me too, you know."

Linda exhaled slowly. "Suzan had a checkup yesterday."

Parker could see the wheels turning in Linda's head and waited for her to carry on.

"The doctor's really worried about her high blood pressure. It could really hurt the baby. I have the feeling she isn't taking it seriously enough. She's known for a while that her blood pressure is an issue, but she hadn't told me. I had to hear it from the doctor."

"And now you're worried and angry all at the same time?" It was a lot like she'd felt a couple of days ago.

Linda nodded and reached for the cardboard box that still sat on Parker's leg. "I don't want to be, but I am."

"Have you asked her why she didn't tell you?"

Linda opened the box. "No, I was too angry."

"Maybe you should. Maybe she didn't tell you because she didn't want to distract you from what you were doing while you were away?" Parker fished another paper out of the box Linda had opened and studied it. "I haven't had a relationship since I signed up, but I don't imagine that it's easy for someone who loves you to cope with the danger we face every day."

Linda didn't respond but looked like she was contemplating something. Parker left her to her thoughts and began to screw the metal connectors into the wood. It felt good to do some manual labor, and it helped her to quiet her own mind down.

"You must think I'm an idiot for not being able to figure this out." Linda gestured toward the box.

Parker shook her head. "No, I don't. I guess you started this yesterday after you came back from Suzan's appointment?"

Linda nodded before she reached for the next part they needed.

"It's clear that your mind was somewhere else when you started this. It's okay to not see the woods for the trees sometimes. You shouldn't be so hard on yourself. You're only human." Parker swallowed audibly. "You love each other; that's such a beautiful gift. And now you're having a baby together. That's amazing."

"You're right, of course. I should've asked Suzan why she didn't tell me. I just freaked out on her." Linda sniffed and wiped at the corner of her eye. "That's why she didn't want me around today when she went to the baby shower for one of the friends she's made in Lamaze classes."

"I'm sorry, Linda. It's a stressful time for both of you." Parker stood up to rearrange the bigger parts of the crib, ready to attach the sides to the headboard.

"It's starting to look like it might go together properly." Linda too got off the floor and held onto one of the sides so that Parker could screw them together. "But enough about me, what's up with you?"

"Kate doesn't want me to get tested, so I had to tell her I was already doing it. I couldn't lie to her after she told me outright."

"And it didn't go so well?"

"That's an understatement." Parker looked away. "I also told her I loved her—but she'd said I still had her heart too."

"If Kate hadn't figured that out, I don't think anyone can help her." Linda gently turned Parker's shoulders so she faced her. "It's so obvious."

"I thought I'd learned to hide it better. Can you lift your piece a little further?"

With joint effort, they managed to attach the head and footboard with the sides.

"Can you help me move it into place?" Linda pointed to an empty corner of the room.

"Of course."

They moved the bed and got rid of the empty packaging. Wordlessly, they started on the next piece of furniture that needed assembling. Parker enjoyed the silent work routine and in no time, they had the changing table put together.

"You still haven't told me why you were crying." Linda came back into the room with a chilled bottle of water.

"Being told to leave kind of does that to me." Parker emptied half the bottle in one go. "I know I don't have much to offer, and Kate's priorities are somewhere else. Shit, I made everything more complicated. I wish those words had never left my mouth. I honestly have no idea what I was thinking."

"Looks like you're human too."

"Never said I wasn't. I'm pretty faulty though."

"Come on, don't say that." Linda flicked a piece of balled up paper at her. "You're a good woman and a great friend, even though we only get to see each other every other year."

"You know more about my past than most. Tell me who would want all that baggage?"

"Everyone has it, Parker. Baggage is life." Linda pulled her into a hug. "You deserve to be loved."

"I'm pretty sure Kate doesn't want to see me around. She said so herself." Parker's shoulders slumped. She really hoped Kate's harsh words had been triggered by old ghosts, and she would calm and realize it wasn't the same situation. "I'm worried that she'll refuse the transplant if I'm a match."

"You don't have the results yet?"

"No, they said it would take a few days. And if I'm a match, I need permission from my CO. So, it's complicated."

"Let me know if you need help with that."

Someone knocking interrupted their conversation. Linda went downstairs and Parker followed.

Linda opened the door to find no one was outside. "What the hell?" The knocking continued. "Ah, the back door."

"I need to use the bathroom," Parker said.

Linda walked to the back of the house. "How can I help you?" Linda asked.

"Is Suzan home?"

Parker's heart almost stopped when she heard Kate's voice.

"No, I'm sorry. She's at a friend's house."

Kate sighed. "I'm sorry that I disturbed you."

Parker peeked around the corner.

Kate drew the thin cardigan tighter around her. "You know Parker, don't you?"

"Yes."

Parker moved back around the corner. Why did she keep ending up eavesdropping on Kate?

"Would you happen to know where she might go to be alone?" Kate asked, sounding hopeful.

Parker closed her eyes. It seemed the moment of truth had arrived, and she wasn't the least bit ready.

"I think you may want to come in," Linda said. "Parker, come in here, please!"

Parker couldn't make her legs move. It was like someone had glued her feet to the floor. She heard the patio door close and the rustle of fabric after Linda asked Kate to sit down.

A moment later, Linda stood in front of her and gently shook her. "Your girl is sitting in my living room looking for you. You better get in there and talk to her. I'll give you some privacy."

Parker composed herself and went into the room. She heard Linda's footsteps recede on the stairs. Kate was curled up on the couch. She pulled the cardigan tighter around her, and her entire body shook violently.

"Why are you shaking?" She sank to her knees in front of Kate. "Are you cold?"

"You left," Kate whispered.

Parker shook her head. "But I didn't run away. I just needed some air. Linda found me wandering around the streets."

"You were no longer in the house when I looked for you," Kate said.

She carefully loosened Kate's clenched fist and held her hands. "You told me to get out. And I needed some space."

Tears brimmed over and rolled down Kate's cheeks. "You overwhelmed me. You're so prepared to give up a part of you to save me. I don't know how to deal with that. It's just like when you were so ready to give up your dream of becoming a pianist for a job that could provide stability in case you needed to take care of me. You were eighteen; you were supposed to be chasing your dream."

Parker rubbed Kate's ice-cold fingers to warm them up. "I understand that the whole transplant topic is hard for you to talk about—"

Linda came in and tossed Parker's now dry sweater and shirt at her. "I'm really sorry I have to disturb you, but Suzan called, and she needs me."

"Of course." Parker got up and draped her clothes over her shoulder. Kate pushed herself up from the couch, wobbled when she took her first step, and lost her balance. Parker wrapped her arm around Kate's waist and steadied her. "Careful."

"Thanks. I'm feeling a little dizzy."

Linda looked between the two and toyed with the car keys in her hand. "Do you want me to drop you off?"

Parker shook her head. Suzan needed Linda, and that should be her priority. "No, that's okay. We'll cut through your backyard."

"Sure." Linda opened the patio door for them.

Kate leaned hard into Parker. "I'm not sure I can make it back now."

"What are you, ninety-five pounds soaking wet?" Parker asked.

Kate rocked against Parker. "You should know better than to ask a woman her weight."

"Your chariot awaits." She scooped Kate up like a bride in her arms. She was lighter than Parker had expected, and it made her worry yet again about Kate's illness.

"Call me later," Linda said.

"Sure thing." Parker focused on Kate after Linda closed the door behind them. "Can you put your arm around my neck, or will it hurt you too much?"

"It'll be a little uncomfortable, but I can do it."

Parker made her way down the patio stairs. "Don't if it hurts. I couldn't bear making you worse."

Kate gave her a faint smile. "You won't make me worse. My right side's tender. The biopsy they had to do didn't help. Sometimes it's uncomfortable to lift my right arm, but I don't have to the way you're holding me." Kate slung her left arm around Parker's neck and leaned into her.

Kate's intoxicating scent swirled around her and did all kind of unspeakable things to her body. Her nipples stiffened, and she couldn't be sure if it was the cold air or the proximity to Kate in her arms. She knew Kate had seen the evidence when she blushed and averted her eyes.

"I'm sorry," Parker said. She couldn't believe she was aroused, considering the situation, but there was always something special about carrying a woman in her arms, especially Kate.

"Are you apologizing because it's cold?" Kate shivered violently.

"You're freezing. I should've put my sweat top on you."

"Sorry, I should have brought a jacket."

"Take the pullover from my shoulder and try to cover yourself. We'll be home soon."

Parker's phone started buzzing shortly before they reached the house, but she ignored it. Kate was still shivering even with Parker's top over her, and she'd only get colder the longer they stayed outside.

"You're buzzing," Kate said.

"I noticed. My hands are kinda full though." Parker grinned and hoped that it was the hospital calling with the results. Her phone stopped buzzing but even before she reached the back door, it started buzzing again. Someone was in a big hurry to get a hold of her. They reached the back door as her phone started going off again.

"Don't you want to get that? It seems urgent." Kate tensed in anticipation to be set down.

"If you can open the door, we'll soon be inside, and I can set you down on the sofa."

Kate reached for the door handle, but it wouldn't open. "I didn't lock it."

"I didn't bring my key."

Kate bit her lower lip and shook her head. "I haven't got mine either."

"Since when can't you open the door from the outside if it's not locked?"

Kate shrugged. "It should be open."

Parker walked around the house so they could ring the front doorbell.

"Can you let me down now? I don't want Zoe or anyone else seeing me like this." Kate turned her head and looked in the direction of Parker's mother's car.

Parker did as she was asked and went to ring the doorbell.

The door flew open, and her mother glared at them. "What were you thinking? We came home, and you were gone. You can't just run around outside with Kate."

Jazmin crowded in beside Parker's mother and started talking as well. The words washed together when Colleen joined in. Kate was still shivering, and now that she wasn't in Parker's arms anymore, the shivering had gotten worse.

She tried to get a word in, but the three women didn't stop berating them for their stupidity and her irresponsibility. She moved them aside and led Kate inside the house with a steadying arm around her waist. The dull thud of the door closing made Kate stiffen in her arm and step away. Her entire posture became rigid, and she stared back at the three women still mainly yelling at Parker.

"Can you all just shut up!"

They just continued to run over each other. Jazmin inserted herself between Kate and Parker and tried to lead Kate away.

"Stop it!" Kate yanked her arm free from Jazmin's grasp. "What makes you think it was Parker's idea to drag me out or that it's her fault that I'm cold? She wasn't even here when I left the house. God, I'm so sick of you all treating me like I'll drop dead the second I leave the safety of the house." Kate stepped away from all of them. "My body is shutting down on me. That won't change, so why not enjoy nature and fresh air while I still can?"

"You need to go back to the hospital," Jazmin said.

Kate turned to Jazmin. "I appreciate that you care, but please find it within yourself to respect my decision to be at home. There's very little the hospital can do for me except manage my pain. I chose to spend this time at home with my family and friends, and I'd hoped you were one of them. If you can't do that, please don't come here anymore."

Kate walked away, and Parker's mother honed in on her again. "Where have you been? Why weren't you here to keep Kate from leaving the house?"

"I met with Linda to help her put up the baby crib. I didn't realize I was Kate's designated babysitter. Maybe you should've told me that." Parker began to walk after Kate to make sure she was okay.

"You should've been here. What if Kate had been unwell?"

Parker turned back to look at her mother. "With all due respect, *Helen*, I'm not Kate's keeper and neither are you. She's an adult, and if she wants to leave the house, she can. She's not your prisoner." A big part of her knew they were just concerned, and rightly so. Kate had only walked a few hundred yards, and it had wiped her out. But she had the right to make that decision, even if it ended up being a bad one. Wasn't that what being an adult was all about?

Chapter Nineteen

PARKER WENT INTO HER bathroom to get the hot water bottle she'd discovered in a drawer then headed to the kitchen to boil water. She hoped that a hot cup of tea and the hot water bottle would warm Kate up a little bit. The last thing any of them needed was for Kate to get a cold. She found the tea Kate used to like in one of the kitchen cupboards and made a pot so they could share.

"Kate refuses to see any of us." Jazmin stood at the entrance of the kitchen. "She wants to know if you're okay or if we made you run."

"Why wouldn't I be? It's not the first time someone yelled at me."

Jazmin came a few steps into the kitchen. "You told her, didn't you?"

She screwed the filled water bottle closed and laid it on the countertop.

"All those years, and Kate didn't have a clue. When she looked at me today, I could see in her eyes that she knew." Jazmin came far enough into the room to put a pill bottle onto the counter. "Can you give those to Kate, please?"

"Sure." She reached for the bottle and put it on the tray. "I hoped that Kate would find someone who completed her." She took the tray and walked past Jazmin. "I'm sorry it hasn't been you. She said you've been a good friend to her."

Parker balanced the tray precariously with one hand and knocked. The tea slipped and the entire thing threatened to topple over, so she opened the door before she got an answer. Kate was curled up in a ball on her bed, shivering under her blanket.

"Who is it?" Kate asked.

"It's me." She walked in and set the tray down on the small nightstand next to Kate's bed. "I brought you some hot tea and this." She slid the hot water bottle under Kate's blanket until it hit her feet. "I hope it's not too hot."

"Hm. Thank you, that's great." Kate shivered a little less.

Parker took a cup of hot tea and carefully settled on Kate's bedside. She stroked the top of Kate's head since that was all that peeked out under the blanket. "If you can sit up, I have some warm tea for you. It may help."

Kate mustered the energy to sit up and take the cup. "Thanks."

She held it in her hands and didn't drink, but Parker was glad the warmth from the ceramic mug would seep into Kate's still-cold fingers. "Is there anything I can do for you?" Parker asked.

"Stay. I don't want to be alone." Kate slowly took the first sip of the tea. "Mm, my favorite."

Parker was thankful for small gifts these days, and the dreamy look Kate had when she sniffed the tea was one of them.

"Who tried to call you?"

With all the turmoil when they came in, Parker had totally forgotten about the phone calls she'd missed. She fished her phone out of her pocket to see that all the calls had been from her mother, and there were two texts about Kate being missing. "Mom wanted to know where we were." Before she could lock her phone, Kate tugged at her wrist and looked at her screen.

"That's the picture that is sitting on your desk upstairs, isn't it?"

"Yeah, it's the only one I've got. A screenshot or two from Mom and Zoe when I called them." She shrugged. It hadn't passed her by that taking selfies and taking pictures of everything from food to friends was normal, but she'd never gotten into that. It was one more sign on how truly out of touch she was with the outside world.

Kate took Parker's phone and opened the photo app. The guy at the electronics store had transferred all her pictures to her new phone, but there weren't many. On the rare occasion she'd been out with fellow Marines and sailors, she'd taken a snap or two only when someone had asked.

"Why don't you have any pictures of us on your phone? Except those very old ones?" Kate asked.

"How could I? I wasn't around to take any, and Mom never sent me one." She took her phone back.

"Never? Why not?"

"I don't know. Probably because I never asked, and no one ever volunteered." She slipped her phone back into her pocket. "Besides, my previous phone was ancient, and photos didn't look great on it."

Parker reached for the chair now that Kate had stopped shivering and some color started to come back into her cheeks.

"Please sit with me." Kate wiggled to one side and padded the space next to her on the bed. "There's enough space for two."

The proximity was inviting, but Parker questioned her sanity when she eased up next to Kate. Her body responded, and this time she couldn't blame it on the temperature. A low electrical sound signaled the raising of the head of the bed to provide them with a nice backrest. Parker reached for her own cup of tea, and the familiar taste of the first sip brought back pleasant memories.

She remembered Kate and herself sitting on a sofa in her aunt's house talking about their future long after Colleen had gone to sleep. There'd been many evenings and nights like that, and they had talked about everything and nothing. Her heart grew heavy at the realization that years had gone by without having her best friend, and she'd missed out on all those talks by her side.

"Where did you go?" Kate leaned against her.

Parker lowered her cup and balanced it on one thigh. "This tea is powerful stuff. I was remembering us drinking it while we talked about our future, way back when." Parker felt Kate's body sagged beside her. "It wasn't a criticism. I repressed a lot of those memories after I left. Doing that was the thing that got me through the days without falling apart." Who was she kidding? She was still in pieces every minute of every single day.

Kate cleared her throat and took Parker's hand but said nothing. She knew by the way Kate played with her fingers that she was trying to find words, most likely for an apology.

"You don't owe me any apology, and I don't want one. We all made mistakes. We should let them rest and move on." The aroma of the tea made her warm and fuzzy inside. She gently squeezed Kate's hand and leaned her head against Kate's.

"But I do." Kate leaned closer into her. "I freaked out on you twice when I should have fallen around your neck and thanked you. I bit your head off both times without giving you a reason."

"Dr. Miller explained that the whole transplant situation is a huge thing and I understand it's hard for you to ask for that kind of help. But have you ever thought about what you would do if the roles were reversed? Let's say for the sake of argument Zoe needed a new liver. Would you get tested?" Parker put her empty cup back on the tray. "Besides the results aren't back yet, I may not be a match like the others."

"Harry was prohibited from the donation process for medical reasons. They didn't complete the tests but until then, he was a promising candidate."

"What? Is Harry ill, too?"

"I'm not even supposed to know that. I heard a doctor talk to my transplant coordinator when they thought I was asleep. They didn't elaborate on the medical reasons, so I don't know why he hasn't said anything. But maybe they're just trying to spare me more worry."

The news hit Parker harder than she thought possible. Would that increase her chances, or could she have some congenital condition passed down from her father?

"Everyone wants to do what's best for me. But how can they if I don't know what that is myself?" Kate half-turned and rested her head on Parker's shoulder. "I'm scared, Parker."

She shifted and drew Kate into her arms. Kate still fit into the side of her body like they were two perfect puzzle pieces. Kate burrowed in deeper, like she wanted to crawl up inside Parker, and all Parker wanted to do was protect her from the world.

"Do you remember back when Nicole got diagnosed with leukemia and needed a bone marrow transplant?" Kate whispered. "It didn't take them long to find a match, but her body rejected it."

The memories of her older sister made Parker break out in a cold sweat that ran down her spine and made her shiver violently. After Nicole's body was already depleted from cancer and pregnancy, she'd barely made it through the chemo and radiation treatment. When her body rejected the marrow transplant, there'd been very little the doctors could do. The family spent day after day at Nicole's bedside, holding her hand while she slowly and very painfully faded.

"You're freezing." Kate pulled the duvet up to cover Parker.

"I'm not cold. It's just a weird reaction I get when I think back to those days. It made Nicole so weak."

"The same thing could happen to me. I know it's not likely, but the thought terrifies me." Kate wrapped her arm around Parker's waist. "I don't want to die, I really don't. But I don't want to risk killing us both."

"I don't understand. There are some risks, sure. There are with all operations, but I wouldn't die." Parker frowned.

"When Nicole's transplant failed, you were destroyed. You stopped eating, going to after school activities, enjoying life. You just existed." Kate fell silent.

The words hit home. She had done exactly that. After Nicole had died, Parker lost touch with herself and everything around her. Kate's love had eventually brought her back to life, which also strengthened their bond even more and led her to realize that Kate was the one who held her heart in her hands.

"If I did get a transplant and my body rejected it, I most likely wouldn't survive it," Kate said softly. "I still know you even though we haven't seen or talked to each other in a decade. I'm worried that it'll destroy you if it didn't work."

Parker almost joked that it wouldn't surprise her if Kate's body rejected her, just as her heart had. "Don't you think I'll be devastated if you don't even try and die anyway?" Parker realized how surreal all of this was. They had no influence over or control of the outcome. They were talking about something that may not even be possible.

"That's why I never wanted you to find out," Kate whispered. "If you didn't know, it couldn't hurt you. You forget how well I know you. You're the most honorable person I know, and I knew you'd want to help because of what we shared. I knew you couldn't resist."

Kate began to cry softly, and Parker's heart sank. For a while, they stayed silent in each other's arms.

Kate took a deep breath. "All I ever wanted was to see you again, to talk to you one more time. But I was too afraid that you'd find out how ill I was, and I couldn't risk it. Now you're here, I'm so grateful for every embrace, for every time I get to smell your scent or hear your voice. All of that is a bigger gift than you'll ever know."

Words wouldn't come so Parker hugged Kate closer and pressed a kiss into her soft hair, closed her eyes, and breathed Kate's scent in, committing it to memory. She had a pretty good idea how much of a gift this moment and their connection was to Kate, because it was the same for her. There *had* to be a way she could get Kate to understand that her life was worth all the risks in the world.

Chapter Twenty

Sleep wouldn't come for Parker as she rolled onto her side and pulled her knees up. The bed in Kate's room was far better than many of the holes she'd slept in over the years, but it wasn't the comfort that stopped her sleeping. She hadn't planned on staying, but she couldn't make herself get up and leave.

Kate had drifted off hours ago. Her peaceful sleep became more fitful by the minute, and Parker contemplated waking her. But fitful sleep was probably better than none at all. The moon slowly crept past the clouds and cast the room in dull silver light. It highlighted the sweat on Kate's face and the damp strands of hair stuck to her pillow.

The moon was almost full. Parker wondered if Kate still looked at it from time to time. Watching the full moon had been their thing after Kate had come to live with them. It had been an attempt to make Kate feel closer to her dead mom.

A painful sounding moan escaped Kate's lips, and Parker immediately sat up, her sluggishness gone in an instant.

"No, please don't." Kate's arms flailed.

"What is it, Kate?"

Kate didn't respond. Her eyes were closed, but her body contorted under the sheets.

"Blood. Everywhere blood. Not Parker. No!"

Parker caressed Kate's face. "Kate, wake up." She grasped her shoulders and gently shook her when Kate started to thrash again.

Kate's eyes blinked open, confusion written all over her face. "Parker?" She paused, clearly becoming more lucid. "Parker!"

Kate's hands flew up and touched Parker's face before they

glided down over her neck and shoulders. Then she checked over her ribcage down to her hips.

"Are you okay?"

Parker nodded. "I'm fine, Kate. Relax. You were having a nightmare."

"Are you really okay?" Kate's eyes became hazy again. "I saw you bleeding all over, lying in a moving steel box."

"You had a bad dream, that's all." Parker drew Kate into her arms and rocked her gently.

They settled back down under the covers with Parker spooning Kate from behind. "I'm here for you." She carefully wrapped her arm around Kate's waist to pull her closer.

Kate sighed heavily. "It's a recurring nightmare. I'm somewhere in a desert, and everything around me is chaos. People are screaming, but I don't understand the words. I'm running and carrying something, but I never know what, and then a white light comes, and I'm suddenly floating inches above you, outside the metal box you're lying in. It's rocking your body from side to side, and blood is running down your face and neck. Your shirt's soaked in blood, and I call for you, but you can't hear me."

"Shh." Parker stroked gentle circles over Kate's back to soothe her. "I'm here, and I'm okay. You don't have to worry."

"Sometimes I stop floating and stand right next to you. Then I can see that you're restrained on something, but I don't know what." Kate choked. "Your eyes are closed, and blood's dripping off your head onto the desert sand beneath you."

All Parker could do was rock them both. Some of Kate's description hit too close to home. "When did those dreams start?"

"They're nightmares," Kate said, her voice still shaking with fear. "They started after you left for boot camp, but they weren't that bad. I think they reflected my worry for you. They were more about general injury, not so vivid. They got worse with time."

"Did they get worse with time or after you learned that I had been injured?" Parker asked in a whisper not sure she could stand the answer.

Silence stretched heavily between them when Kate eventually shook her head against the pillow. "I don't know. I don't think it was sudden. Maybe they got bloodier after I found out you'd been injured in the line of duty. Before that, it was more a *sense* of you being injured." Kate inched closer to her. "When I learned you'd come home, I was so relieved. I thought I would be able to see you, touch you, and finally put those nightmares to rest."

"And I ran before you ever saw me," Parker said, once again plagued by regret.

Kate nodded and grasped Parker's hand. "And my fears spiraled out of control even faster. I saw you dead or close to it in my dreams and blood everywhere. I so wish I'd come over that first night and touched you then, stroked your skin and made sure you were whole."

She wanted to tell Kate that she too wished that she had just come over that night. Maybe things could have been different. She wondered if it could have changed things for Kate. Would it have made things better or worse for her? If she stayed now, would Kate be able to go back to sleep if they just lay there silent for a while?

"The night I saw you standing in front of your window looking out. You were wearing a sports bra, and you peeled a big white bandage from around your waist."

"I took it off to take a shower." She swallowed hard. "My captors didn't care much for my injuries while they had us."

Kate rose to look at her in the faint moonlight. "You were captured?"

"Sort of."

"How can you be sort of captured?" Kate asked.

"More like taken hostage for money. The important thing is that I'm okay, and all of that is in the past."

"How can you be sure?" Kate clutched the hem of Parker's T-shirt. "You could still get injured when you go back...or worse."

"That's the risk I take being a Marine. I knew that when I signed up."

"I want to know what happened. Will you tell me?"

Parker took a deep breath and let it out slowly. She closed her eyes for a moment and when she opened them, the need for answers in Kate's expression was clear. Maybe talking about it with the person she loved most in the world would make it smaller for both of them. "We were protecting a political asset when the building was attacked. We managed to escape and hid in a bombed-out school building. They sent two helicopters to rescue us, but the enemy shot one of them down." She swallowed hard, fighting the images of the dead soldiers in the crashed helicopter. "While I was helping rescue soldiers from the wreckage, I got shot in the leg. A jagged piece of hot metal sliced my upper arm as I fell. But I pulled two soldiers from the wreckage. I carried one of them to the other helicopter, to safety. I went back for the pilot but before I could get a good hold of him to carry him out, I was hit by something and knocked out. I don't know how I got the injury on my side." Parker paused and looked at Kate, and her eyes were fixed on Parker.

"Go on."

"I vaguely remember coming around while being dragged through the sand before I passed out again. Then a jolt of pain jerked me awake, and I was in the bed of an old pickup, I guessed someone threw me in. I was later told by the leader of a nomadic tribe that he'd been hiding nearby. He saw me go down and thought we were worth something to someone. He hoped to trade us for medical aid for his child and took us deep into the desert." Parker's breathing became shallow and fast, but she couldn't control it.

Kate came closer and pressed her forehead to Parker's. "How badly were you hurt?" Kate pulled on Parker's shirt.

A slow shaky breath escaped Parker. There was no way she would elaborate on what had happened after they reached the nomad's camp. "When I woke again, I was still in the truck. The adrenaline from the fight had long gone, and it was like my whole body was on fire. I was restrained and couldn't move, and I had a head wound and probably a concussion from whatever had hit me. I also had the bullet wound in my leg and another caught me just under where my vest ended."

"Vest?" Kate whispered.

"I was wearing a bulletproof vest. Good thing given the bruising I discovered later on my chest."

A short glimpse of moonlight shone in Kate's glistening eyes. Parker felt bad for adding to Kate's emotional pain and bringing up her past looked like it had hurt them both more than it was worth. She wanted to move back to give Kate some space, but Kate held her tightly.

"Sorry, I can't shake the sight of blood. I know it shouldn't be there, but I still see it." Kate gently touched Parker's forehead. "I know light would help shake off the lingering dream, but I can't bear the thought of you getting up to turn it on."

Parker had the sinking feeling that words wouldn't be enough to help Kate, and she didn't have the slightest idea what she could say to make it better. She took Kate's hand from her forehead and intertwined their fingers. She slowly guided their hands into her hair and settled Kate's fingers over the scar the headwound had left. "See. It's all healed now."

She watched Kate's face carefully for changes while Kate timidly explored the scar tissue.

The tension lessoned around Kate's eyes and mouth. "Did you get stitches for this?" Kate circled around the scar.

"Eventually someone cleaned my wounds and stitched the ones on my head, shoulder, and side."

Soft moonlight filtered through the clouds again. "Can I see the others too?" Kate asked then she shook her head. "Sorry, that's probably awkward for you. Forget I asked."

"It's okay." Parker guided Kate's hand to her left shoulder. Her T-shirt covered the spot, but she pulled her sleeve far enough up to expose it. Kate half sat up to look at the exposed skin and slid her hand free to tenderly inspect every part of it. She knew the exact moment Kate had found the slightly raised and hardened line of skin. The scar was barely visible, but it was easy enough to feel when you touched it.

"Does this injury restrict you in any way?"

"No, it was just a flesh wound."

Kate settled her head back on the pillow. The worry and tension hadn't seemed to have entirely left Kate, but it had lessoned considerably.

"This really is helping. Thank you."

Kate's touch had sensitized Parker's body, and she was afraid that Kate touching more of her was a bad idea, but she couldn't ignore that it was helping Kate, and that's all she wanted to do. She took Kate's hand again, guided it under her shirt, settled it flat over the ragged scar on her side and released her. Her stomach muscles clenched involuntarily when Kate started exploring. Kate's soft touch drove her almost insane. This scar was super sensitive, and Kate's light touch seemed to enhance the sensitivity. Her skin flared hot and felt too tight to allow her to breathe. Parker bit her lower lip and closed her eyes. It was the only way she could let Kate explore without interfering.

Parker's breath caught in her throat when Kate's hand crept even higher. She could tell the exact moment when her fingers had found the beginning of the tattoo. With the same care she had with her healed injuries, Kate's fingers explored the lower edge of the tattooed skin.

"What's this? It doesn't feel like another scar."

"It's a tattoo."

"I want to see it, but it's too dark to make anything out."

Words deserted her. The tattoo was an integral part of her, but she didn't know if it was good for Kate to see it, not after how she reacted to Parker's declaration of love. Instead of exploring it further, Kate's fingers started to slide down again. She ventured lower and stroked over the top of Parker's shorts. The fiery trail

Kate left on her skin seeped into her belly and slowly sank deeper. Her lips parted to suck in fresh air and took in the scent of Kate's sweet skin. Her entire body became a live wire, and the urge to kiss Kate, with her lips so close to hers, was nearly overwhelming.

"What's this?" Kate asked when she ran her hand over the pocket of Parker's sweatpants and the contents crinkled noisily.

The question was like a bucket of ice water being dumped over her. Parker gulped air and tried to orient herself. "It is my 'in-case' letter. We write it in case we don't come back. Mine was always addressed to you, so I wanted you to have it." An owl hooting in the distance was the only sound between them. Kate pulled out the folded and well-worn envelope from her pocket. It had been in her wallet since the day she left boot camp.

"I have one too," Kate said, her voice trembling. "It's on the desk in my room. Promise me you'll get it tomorrow." Kate placed Parker's envelope on her nightstand and turned back around. "Can I snuggle closer?"

In a silent invitation Parker turned on her back and waited for Kate to settle her head on her shoulder and curl her body against hers. Her letter to Kate was as much a letter about love as it was absolution. When she had put pen to paper that day, she still had so many swirling emotions for Kate. She'd channeled all her love into her words and told her that Kate was not to blame for Parker's decisions and actions. She'd pleaded with her to remember their good times together and find someone that she could love as much as Parker loved her, someone that loved her back with the same intensity. She'd asked Kate to let her go, embrace her future with open arms, and live a full happy life. Parker swallowed the sudden lump in her throat. What would Kate's letter say? Would it be similar to her own?

Chapter Twenty-One

AFTER PARKER CLIMBED UNDER the dining room table, she managed to figure out how to pull out the table extension. Her mother had tasked her to set it for the Thanksgiving dinner and with Colleen, Jazmin, and Kid being there as well they needed extra room at the table.

"Parker, can you help Grandma in the kitchen?" Zoe stood holding a kitchen knife. "She's driving me insane."

Her mother had given them all very specific chores, ramping up the tension Parker already had from the previous night with Kate. However, after Zoe and Parker's morning sparring session with the bag, Parker had been able to work some of that off. With Zoe there, it had been much easier to stop while it was still healthy and before she exhausted herself.

The moment she stepped into the kitchen, she knew why Zoe had bailed. There were several onions sitting on the cutting board while her mother was kneading dough.

"Zoe was supposed to be doing these." Her mother wiped her forehead with the back of her hand, leaving a streak of flour.

Parker washed her hands in the sink. "If you want those onions peeled and chopped today…"

"She'll never learn if she doesn't do it."

"I think she knows how. I just don't think she likes how they make her cry." Parker took care of the onions quickly. "I'll be out of your hair soon, so there'll be one less kid for you to take care of."

"What do you mean?" Her mother sprinkled salt into the mixing bowl.

"I'm looking at a few apartments tomorrow. I'm hoping to get something to move into soon."

"You're moving out?" Kate asked as she walked into the kitchen with her empty cup. "Why didn't you tell me?"

"Did you all expect me to move back in permanently? I'm thirty years old."

Kate slid onto a stool at the breakfast bar. "No, but I hoped to have more time with you."

"You have all the time you want. I'm not leaving town."

"Can we not talk about leaving? I'm already missing two of my children at the table tonight." Her mother turned and looked at Kate and Parker. "And this may be the last Thanksgiving we have with Kate here."

Those words hit Parker deeply. She still hadn't heard anything from the hospital, but she had the urge to tell her mother about the tests, and that there might be hope yet. Her mother wiped the corner of one eye on the back of her sleeve before she turned away.

"I've never asked," Kate said after a period of silence, "but have you ever tried to find your son?"

Parker swallowed hard. She knew who and where Mark was, and it was becoming harder and harder not to tell her. But she hadn't heard back from him since her last email, and she didn't want to give her mother any false hope.

"The last time we tried was when Nicole got ill, and she needed a bone marrow transplant. But with a closed adoption, we had little chance of ever finding him. We hired a private investigator, but they had no luck either." Her mother leaned against the counter and looked at Kate with unfocused eyes. "I never saw him before the nurse took him away. I only remember hearing him cry. I was in too much pain to remember much else. My mother never told me what she put on the adoption papers, so I don't know if he could find me—if he wanted to."

"It sounds like you miss him very much," Kate said softly.

"A mother never stops loving her child, no matter if they're with them or not. The love never goes away."

Kate looked forlorn. Parker's mother came around the bar and drew her into a hug. "I love you like my own."

Kate inhaled sharply but didn't respond. Something Parker's mother had said hit a nerve, but she'd clearly thought better of saying something. Emotions were already running high, and maybe she didn't want to add to them.

"We all made very poor decisions when we learned that you and Parker were in a relationship," her mother said. "I wish we could turn back time and do it over again, but we can't."

"We all wish we could do that week over," Kate said in a shaky voice before she slid off the chair and left the room.

Parker started chopping the rest of the vegetables sitting on the counter. "Why did you never talk about your son when Nicole and I were younger?"

"It wrecked me when my mother made me give him up. But I didn't want you two to feel mine and your father's loss."

"I thought you met Dad in college?" Parker asked.

"No, we went to high school together. He was two years older than me and the only man I ever loved. Actually, the only man I have ever been with."

That was a tidbit Parker hadn't known and one she probably didn't want to know. The doorbell ringing gave her the perfect excuse to get away from the uncomfortable conversation. She opened the door to Jazmin, who explained that she'd arrived early to check in on Kate and make sure she had everything she needed to be comfortable throughout Thanksgiving dinner. Parker took her through to the living room to Kate.

"I think it would be a good idea if you got ready for the evening before I give you a quick checkup. That way you could take some medication for the pain and wouldn't have to worry about not getting ready in time because they made you wobbly again."

Kate whipped her head around and squinted at Jazmin as if she wasn't happy with the way things were going. Parker suspected that Kate saw Jazmin's actions with different eyes after she'd told Kate about Jazmin's feelings for her. The abrupt movement had Kate lose her balance, and she grabbed hold of the armchair.

"Careful, Kate," Jazmin said and reached out to steady her. "We don't want you to fall."

Kate moved out of Jazmin's reach. "I'm fine."

Parker watched the unfolding disagreement and wondered if she should help Kate to the sofa since she was so unsteady on her feet. No, if Kate wanted her help, she would ask for it.

"Since everyone seems busy with Thanksgiving preparations, I can give you a hand. You're obviously dizzy, so you shouldn't be in the shower alone," Jazmin said.

Kate plopped down on the wicker chair in the sunroom and folded her arms. "There's no way you're helping me get showered."

"Someone has to. You're having trouble walking in a straight line. It would be irresponsible if you'd be all alone in the bathroom. What if you slipped and fell?" Jazmin followed her into the room.

"Fine, Parker can help me," Kate said and pointed right at her.

Parker felt the heat rising in her cheeks at the thought of seeing Kate naked. Her throat went dry, and she had to swallow a couple of times to get it working again. "What?"

Kate struggled off the chair. "You can help me get a shower. Come on."

"Um." She hurried after Kate, who was heading up the stairs while clinging to the railing. "Does the downstairs guest room not have a shower?" she asked.

"It does, but it feels and smells like a hospital bathroom. It's sterile with hand holds and smells of disinfectant. I want to relax in a nice room with the products I love. I want to really feel and smell like myself for a change."

Parker shrugged and wrapped her arm around Kate's waist to make the ascent easier. "If that's what you want."

It took a few minutes to get up the stairs, but they made it, and Kate pushed her bedroom door open. She pointed to an envelope on her bedside table. "Hey, I wanted you to have that."

Parker took it and looked at her name on the envelope in Kate's neat script. A cold shiver ran down her spine. Parker didn't really want to know what was written in the letter. Because it would mean that she'd failed to save Kate. She slid it into the front pocket of the black hoodie she'd picked out of her teenage wardrobe this morning.

"You should take off your watch and leave your phone out here," Kate said. "They'll get wet in the bathroom."

Parker placed her valuables on Kate's desk, stripped off her hoodie, and hung it over the back of the desk chair before she followed Kate into the en-suite bathroom. She sat on the closed toilet lid and tried not to watch Kate go into the shower and occupied herself by following the pattern of the bathroom tiles. Anything to distract her from Kate's naked body on the other side of the shower stall door.

Kate said something, but Parker couldn't hear it over the sound of the shower.

"What?" She tried not to think about the hot water running down Kate's naked body.

"What are you doing?"

I'm trying very hard not to look at you. "Nothing. Just waiting." The fresh citrusy scent that constantly seemed to surround Kate intensified in the shower steam and lulled her into a contented daydream.

"Ouch, shit," Kate said loudly over the running water.

Parker jumped up to see Kate still standing with her hands braced against the wall. "Are you okay?" She went a few steps closer to the shower but didn't attempt to open the door.

Kate moved away from the wall and immediately another string of curse words escaped her. "I can't wash my hair."

She hadn't considered that this would be a problem even though she should have thought of it. The past couple of days either Colleen or she had helped Kate brush and braid her hair in the morning.

"Could you come in here and help me?" Kate opened the door a crack and stuck her head out.

"Sure." Blood pounded in Parker's ears when she stripped off her socks and sweatpants, but she kept her boy shorts and tank top on.

"Are you coming?" Kate asked.

"I'm here." Parker opened the door and entered. Her white tank dampened with the trapped steam and turned half translucent. Now she felt stupid for leaving it on. It wasn't like she hadn't had enough showers with other people, particularly in the Marines, but the thought of Kate seeing her half-naked unsettled her.

She took the shampoo from Kate and massaged it first into Kate's hair and scalp. Kate moaned when she reached the base of her neck, so Parker began to work Kate's shoulders. The knots she'd found slowly loosened under her touch, and she smiled when Kate leaned back into her.

"More, that is so good," Kate said.

"No, darling." Parker stopped. What was she doing? Taking advantage of Kate when she needed her? "You're getting cold," she whispered, her voice thick with arousal, and reached to open the shower door.

Kate stopped her by holding onto her wrist. "You can't leave. I need your help to wash it out and with the conditioner too."

Kate was so close, Parker could feel her radiating body heat. Her lower belly tightened, and her nipples stood erect. She couldn't explain them away with any notion of being cold since the water coming was way too hot. Kate trailed her fingers on Parker's bicep, stroking her skin. The warm water did nothing to hide the trail of goosebumps Kate's fingers caused.

"When did you get that?" Kate turned her arm to get a better look at the rose and wing tattoo with Nicole's name, her birthday, and the day Nicole took her last breath.

"Right before I left home the first time." She gently pulled her arm back and shifted so she could wash the soap out.

Kate held out another bottle. "Don't forget to condition it."

Dutifully, she massaged the conditioner in.

"It needs to stay in for a few minutes." Kate sat on the built-in shower bench to rest.

When Parker noticed where Kate's eyes had gone, she bit her lower lip. Her tank had ridden up, baring her midriff. Her scar and the bottom part of another tattoo were exposed.

Kate's soft fingers connected with Parker's skin, and she traced over the ragged scar before moving up. Kate slid her fingers beneath it and pushed it further up to uncover the rest of Parker's inked skin.

Parker froze in place and held her breath. Kate continued her exploration but said nothing. Parker became more unsure with every passing minute.

"How is this possible?"

Parker wasn't sure what exactly Kate was asking so she remained silent and simply stared at Kate's fingers moving over the lines that formed the face of the lady justice tattoo, the lines that formed Kate's face on her body.

Kate stared up at her, full of questions. "Who did this?"

"Masao, a guy I served with, inked it." She stilled Kate's fingers. "I found a photograph of your original when you had that gallery showing on the internet."

Kate shook her head. "The original shows you, I started it after I found out you'd become a lawyer after all. It was my graduation piece."

"I know, but you're my guardian angel." She turned away, not ready to see the anger in Kate's face that was surely to come with the rest of her confession. "My art skills are terrible, but with an old photo and a little help, I got it altered enough for Masao to be able to tattoo it." Parker pulled down the wet fabric and avoided Kate's gaze. "Let me wash your hair out." She helped Kate back to her feet.

Kate stayed silent while she rinsed her hair for the second time, and Parker made no attempt at conversation either. She was sure Kate would only tolerate her for as long as she had to, so she worked as fast as she could without missing a spot or pulling Kate's hair. When she was sure Kate's hair was clean and the rest of the soap gone from her body, she turned off the water and pulled the towel down that hung over the door. Without a word, she held it open and waited for Kate to step into it.

As soon as Kate held onto the towel, she turned and retreated toward the shower stall door. She was soaking wet, but she'd dry off in her own room.

"Wait," Kate said softly.

She took the hem of Parker's tank top and pulled it up as far as she could move without hurting herself. "Take it off. You can't go out there dripping wet."

Parker did as she was told, her back turned to Kate. She held onto her wet top like a comfort blanket. Kate tugged it free and tossed it to the ground, where it landed with a wet splash.

"These need to go too." Kate hooked the fingers into Parker's shorts and slowly slid them over her hips. She trembled from head to toe, and every single nerve cell stood at attention waiting for Kate's soft touch.

Kate pressed her body against Parker's back and slipped her slender arms around her waist. "It's beautiful, thank you for letting me see it."

"You aren't mad?"

"Why should I be? Silly," Kate whispered, her hot breath on Parker's neck.

Her body went into overdrive. If she didn't defuse the situation, Kate might regret where it would lead. "I think we need to get ready, or someone will start banging on the door." Her voice was low with desire, and her body thrummed with arousal. But she couldn't do anything now with a houseful of people waiting to celebrate the holiday. And especially not without knowing, truly knowing, that coming together again was really what Kate wanted.

Chapter Twenty-Two

THE ENTIRE HOUSE SMELLED of delicious food cooking in the kitchen as they made their way downstairs. After she'd changed into dry clothes, Parker had helped Kate do her hair, and time had flown. The doorbell rang and Colleen opened it to Kid, a potted plant in one hand and a bottle of wine in the other.

He held them out to Colleen, who took the gifts and thanked him.

"Good evening, ma'am, I'm Caleb Callahan."

"It's a pleasure, but please don't call me ma'am. I'm Colleen."

As Kid stepped inside, Parker saw the car parked on the opposite side of the street, and Mark stood outside the passenger side door looking over the roof directly at her. She was out the door and halfway across the street before she even realized she was barefoot.

"You look good, little sister."

"Thanks." She hesitated. Should they hug?

He looked past her to the house. "Was that Helen, our mother?"

She shook her head. "That was Colleen, Kate's aunt. But you should come in, I know she'd really like to meet you."

"I don't think that's a good idea." Mark said. "It looks like you have a full house with the holiday and all. Me going in would attract all their attention and take away from you being here."

"I don't mind about that. Besides, they'd be devastated if they found out you were this close, and they didn't get to meet you."

Parker saw her parents coming out of the house out of the corner of her eye. They seemed to argue, and her father got in the car and drove off. She had no idea where her mother had gone since her focus was on Mark.

"We already have plans for the evening." Mark looked past her and stiffened.

"Parker," her mother looked from Mark to her and back. "Who is this?"

Her mother's face showed that she had a damn good idea who Mark was but couldn't quite believe it.

Mark looked like a deer in headlights and didn't say a word.

"Parker?" Helen asked and gripped Parker's arm painfully hard.

"Yes, Helen, it's him." Parker loosened her mother's grip on her arm.

"But how?" Helen reached out as if she wanted to touch him to make sure he was real.

Mark hadn't said a word, and he looked like he wanted to flee. Parker took pity on her brother and tried to move them along a little.

"Mark, may I introduce you to Helen, your biological mother." Parker motioned to her mother. "Mom." She caught her mother's eye and motioned toward her brother. "This is Mark, your son."

"It's nice to meet you, Helen."

Mark held his hand out, but Helen pulled him into an embrace. Tears rolled down her mother's face. "Welcome home," Helen said, her voice thick with tears. "Please come in and spend Thanksgiving with us."

Mark pulled back. "I'm sorry, I can't." He looked over his shoulder to the car where a man sat behind the wheel and watched them. "Ben and I are expected for dinner at my in-laws."

"You're married?" Helen asked.

"I am." Mark said. He looked at the car again, not seeming all that comfortable with the direction the conversation had taken.

The man exited the car and joined them. "Hello, I'm Ben, his husband." He held his hand out to Helen, and they shook.

"Please, you must come in. Your father would be over the moon to see you. He'll be back in a few minutes, I'm sure. I only sent him to the store to buy some more bread." Helen motioned to the house.

"Didn't you and Colleen buy enough food yesterday?" Parker asked.

Helen waved her question away. "Please come in. We could have some coffee while we wait."

"I think Mom will forgive us if we're a little late," Ben said and rested his hand in the small of Mark's back. "We can go in for a few minutes, if you like."

"We can't stay more than fifteen minutes. The traffic is awful today. It seems like the whole of DC is on the road, and we have to drive up all the way to Baltimore."

Parker trailed behind when they walked back to the house. Mark and Ben seemed to have an easy-going connection. She wondered how long they'd been together. Mark had mentioned that he was gay and in a committed relationship in one of his letters after she'd come out to him in one of hers. *Could that have been her and Kate if they had stayed together?*

They made their way into the kitchen that was surprisingly empty. Colleen's and Kid's voices were audible from the living room. She wanted to see where Kate and Jazmin had gone, but when she moved to the kitchen door, her mother looked at her and mouthed, *Don't leave me alone.*

"Coffee, tea, water?" Helen asked.

"No, thank you." Mark said and took one of the stools at the kitchen counter. "I think your saucepan needs looking after."

Parker looked at the stove and saw it was in danger of spilling over.

Helen laughed while rescuing the pan. "I must've forgotten to turn it down." She turned off the stovetop. "I don't know where my head's at today."

Mark looked around, seemingly uncomfortable, while Helen looked like she was having a hard time containing her joy about having her long-lost son and his husband in the house. She fired questions at both of them but didn't leave either of them enough time to answer.

"You look so much like your father when he was your age." Helen sighed, reached out, and trailed her fingers over Mark's cheek. "I have no idea what's taking him so long. He should've been back by now. He'll be so overjoyed."

Mark looked at his phone. "I'm sorry, Helen, but we really need to get going, or we'll miss our own dinner."

"Are you sure?" Helen held onto Mark's arm.

Mark took a business card out of his leather phone case and gave it to her. A timer went off in the kitchen as Helen and Mark finished their goodbyes.

Parker escorted them back to the front door and hugged them both. "Happy Thanksgiving and thank you for stopping by. When I told you I was in town, I didn't think you'd just come by."

"It was a bit of an impulsive decision when we got in the car," Mark said. "I had the sudden need to see that you were okay."

"I'm fine." Parker ushered them out. Now that she'd been in the same room with her brother, she wanted to tell him about Kate and pick his brain. As a doctor, he might be able to give her a different perspective on things. She would reach out to him tomorrow and ask if he had time.

Helen called for help, so Parker made her way back to the kitchen to help with the remaining dinner preparations. She would have much rather checked in on Kate and visited with Kid, but no one else seemed to volunteer. Harry made it back just in time to carve the turkey.

Parker was the last to enter the dining room with the bowl of mashed potatoes. The chairs either side of Kate had been claimed by Zoe and Jazmin. Parker took the only empty seat on the other side of the table. Her parents sat like they always had, at opposite ends of the table.

When Parker's eyes met Kate's, she didn't seem particularly happy about the seating arrangements. Parker shrugged and frowned in Jazmin's direction and hoped her silent "What can I do, and what is going on there?" message reached Kate.

Kate closed her eyes and shook her head.

"Are you two having silent conversations again?" Colleen asked. "You did that all the time as kids. It was like the two of you had your own language."

Parker smiled at Colleen. They'd done that a lot, but after all those years she wasn't sure Kate still understood her silent messages. "I hope you like the food," Parker said.

Appreciative noises went around the table, and they all ate in relative silence for a while.

"I think this is the first Thanksgiving I can remember with you, Parker." Zoe reached for seconds. "Why haven't you come home before?

"That's a really good question, Zoe. Why haven't you ever been back, Parker?" Jazmin asked. "I'm sure Kate would have loved to see you every once in a while."

Kid shook his head at his sister as if to shut her up, but she looked at Kate and paid no attention. She whispered something to Kate that Parker couldn't hear.

"So would I," her mother said.

What was her mother doing? They'd already had that conversation. Her mother had to know that it could only lead to disaster. Parker exhaled slowly and pushed her plate away, her appetite gone. "Let's not talk about that today. It's Thanksgiving. We all have a lot to be thankful for tonight, don't you think?" She looked at her mother and raised her eyebrows, willing her to take the hint that she was talking about her meeting with Mark earlier. "That we're sharing this meal together, for one."

"Who was the man that came to the house earlier?" Zoe asked. "Did he tell you that you have to leave us again, Parker?"

Parker hadn't seen her around when Mark and Ben were in the house. "How—"

"I saw you talking to him when I looked out of my window." Zoe reached for her soda.

"No, honey, he didn't come here for Parker. That was your uncle, Mark," her mother said.

"Excuse me?" asked Harry.

The activity around the table stopped and even Kid, who had been enjoying the food like he hadn't eaten in days, put down his cutlery.

"Our son came to the house earlier when you were out. They couldn't stay."

"Why didn't you tell me that the second I came back?" Harry asked.

"I wanted to know how it felt to keep something so fundamental from the person I love." The happy expression slowly faded from Helen's face. "How could you, Harry?"

Her father frowned as if he had no clue what she was talking about.

Helen turned to Parker. "And don't think for a moment I didn't realize that you and Mark had met before. How long have the two of you been in contact?"

"Helen," Colleen reached out to her, "maybe you want to check on dessert."

"Don't Helen me," her mother said and turned her attention back to Parker. "How could you lie to me?"

"Why didn't you tell us?" Harry chimed in.

"I didn't lie to your face. I didn't tell you what I knew. There's a difference," Parker said.

The situation was spinning out of control. Parker thought her mother was happy about meeting Mark at last; how was it they were having an argument now? Dinner sat like a cinderblock in her stomach, and Kid fidgeted on his chair, clearly uncomfortable and probably wishing he'd never come.

"You should have told me anyway," Helen said.

Parker shook her head. "It wasn't my story to tell. I gave Mark your information when I was sure who he was. He has your address, email, and phone number. The rest wasn't up to me."

"You could have called me when you found him."

Parker tried to control her raising anger. Was she the only one who saw the double standard? "The same way you should have told me about Kate?" She shook her head. "It wasn't my story to tell, period. I don't want to fight tonight. Can we please get back to dinner? If not, I'll just leave."

"Maybe you should," Jazmin said under her breath but in the sudden silence, her words almost rang through the room.

"What?" Parker asked and kicked herself for rising to the bait.

Kate stared open mouthed at Jazmin, who seemed not to notice. Everyone else around the table seemed too perplexed to say anything at all.

"Leave," Jazmin said. "Your presence is disrupting everything, and all this chaos," Jazmin gestured around the table, "isn't good for Kate. You're telling everyone that it wasn't your place to tell them about some lost brother. But you know what? It would've been your place to tell Kate and your family that you were leaving town to join the military. Heck, maybe even tell Kate that you weren't interested in her before you left. So her heart had a chance to heal and eventually fall in love again."

"Jazmin, stop it," Kate said, her cheeks flaming red.

"Was a sick girlfriend not good enough for you, Parker?" Jazmin asked.

Parker's blood boiled, and it took everything not to physically remove Jazmin from the room. She was seemingly oblivious to the stress *she* was causing Kate.

"Enough, Jazmin!" Kid's tone left no room for argument. "Maybe it's time for us to go."

Jazmin didn't move. The silence in the room was deafening.

"Is it true you left Kate because she was ill?" Zoe asked and looked confused. "That would be so not cool."

Parker wanted to answer, but her throat was too dry to croak any words out, and she searched for her glass of soda.

"No, it's not true," Kate said.

"Maybe," Colleen said, "but it would have been nice to have some warning that she was going to leave town. Her disappearing act really did a number on you, Kate. I suppose I should have known after she tried to give you the ring back."

"What ring?" Helen, Zoe, and Jazmin asked together.

"Were you two, like, engaged?" Zoe asked.

Parker inhaled. Oh, how she wished they had been. Zoe had been far too young to be able to remember anything from back then. "No."

"Yes," Kate said at almost the same time.

She and Kate stared at one another. The other people in the room were instantly unimportant. *What was happening here?*

"You put the Claddagh ring on your left hand," Kate said softly.

Her words where almost drowned out by the turmoil around the table. Parker tried to remember she'd moved the ring from her right to her left ring finger.

"What the hell?" Helen asked and was echoed with similar versions of the same thing by Harry.

"Wow. You were an idiot for leaving." Zoe threw her balled-up napkin at Parker. "Sorry for the language, grandma."

Parker closed her eyes. *When did we stop listening to what's being said and just start accusing each other?* She'd stay silent until they were ready to listen to her. If she said anything now, it would only spiral further out of control.

"You're an even bigger jerk than I thought," Jazmin said, her voice the only one penetrating Parker's mind. "I would never have walked away from a woman like Kate. She deserves someone better than you, Parker."

Parker heard Kid's sharp inhale of breath. She was sure he would drag his sister out by the collar any second now.

"Shut up!" Kate yelled.

Parker's eyes flew open, and she saw Kate try to stand.

"You don't know a thing about what happened. I broke up with

Parker, not the other way around." Kate closed her eyes briefly. "Breaking up with the woman that I love with all my heart was the hardest thing I ever did. But I couldn't bear the thought of holding her back. I couldn't bear the thought she would one day wake up and regret her life." Kate looked around the table. "So leave her alone. It's not her fault. She begged me not to do it."

Parker shook her head. "It's okay, Kate, I can take being the bad girl."

Kate shook her head and glared at Colleen and Parker's mother. "It was more important to you what society thought than what Parker and I felt. None of you supported our relationship. I wanted to spare her more of this; I set her free. If anyone broke anybody's heart, it was me breaking hers." Kate pushed away from the table. "And my own." She walked out of the room.

Parker stood up and looked at her mother and then at her father. "Just to make sure we're all on the same page, I didn't leave because Kate broke my heart. I left because I was told I wasn't welcome in this house as long as I had feelings for Kate." She turned and followed Kate.

"That's what I meant, Harry," her mother said as Parker walked away. "How could you not have told me what you said to her? Speak up," Helen yelled.

Parker heard a dull thud of something crashing before she saw Kate sitting halfway up the stairs, her head buried in her hands. "Hey, are you all right?"

Kate looked up at her with wide eyes. "Did I really just do that?"

"Yes, you did." She nodded and sat next to her. "You didn't need to tell them. That was always between me and you. They didn't want us together, but they also couldn't handle their broken-hearted kids. I needed them to be there for you since I couldn't, even if it meant drawing their frustration over our misery and not being able to heal your heartache on me."

"I couldn't take it any longer. They're always poking at you for breaking my heart when it's not true. I hurt you so much that you left town and changed the entire course of your life."

"That wasn't your fault. Harry told me to get out and not come back home until I stopped loving you."

Kate's eyes widened. "That's why you never came back?"

"Yeah, basically, it is. I still go out and look at the full moon every time I can and talk to you." She felt the blush creep up her face.

"Like you did with me after my parents died? I remember all the times you listened while I talked to my mom, and you held me until I cried myself dry." Kate leaned into her.

"There's a full moon tonight, you know?"

"Let's go," Kate said.

Her grin filled Parker with a light so powerful, it almost pulled her off her feet. She held out her hand, and when Kate took it, she saw what their future could be like...if only Parker was a match, and if only Kate would let Parker do what she most desired—to take care of her for the rest of her life.

Chapter Twenty-Three

THE BALCONY LOOKING OUT over the backyard provided them with the perfect view of the full moon. The fluffy clouds framing the moon added a romantic feel. The soft rustle of trees in the background belied the fact that it was already fall. It was the perfect little escape from the insanity of dinner.

Kate's room had always been smaller than the other bedrooms, but it came with its own balcony which they had often taken advantage of. On their way out, Parker grabbed the patchwork blanket from the foot of Kate's bed and put it around her shoulders.

After a little while, Kate began to shiver.

"You're getting cold. We should go in," Parker said.

"But this is so beautiful. I don't want to leave it just yet," Kate said. "The view takes my breath away."

"Hmm." It was Kate who took Parker's breath away. Next to her, the full moon paled.

"I'm so happy to be here with you," Kate said through chattering teeth.

"We really need to get you inside and warmed up."

"You can warm me up." Kate held open the blanket and beckoned her in.

Parker snuggled up behind Kate and drew the quilt around them both.

Kate pulled Parker's arms tighter around herself. "This is how you keep someone warm." She laid her head back onto Parker's shoulder. "God, I've missed this."

"Haven't you done this since I left?"

"I did, but it isn't the same without you. I often stood out here and begged my mom to keep you safe while you were out there. Silly, isn't it?"

"No." Parker was warmed by Kate's confession. "I talked to you a lot. There was hardly a full moon when I didn't take a moment to look up and think of you."

"Really?"

Parker smiled. "Really."

For a while, they stood there silently, lost in their own thoughts. In the distance, a dog barked and a car honked. A window rattled downstairs and muted voices drifted up.

"Let's go inside, I don't want to listen to them any longer." Parker's main concern was that Kate was still cold, but she probably wouldn't respond to that argument any better now than she had before. Besides she really didn't want to listen to their family arguing tonight.

"Of course." Kate stepped closer and brushed her lips over Parker's cheek. She took the blanket from Parker and dropped it onto the trunk that stood at the end of her bed. When Kate turned back to fully look at her, she nibbled at her lower lip. "There's something I wanted to try."

Kate's eyes hooded, and she slowly rose on her tiptoes. Kate's soft lips brushed Parker's and left a sweet fruity taste behind when Kate pulled away. Parker's lips tingled, and she wanted to follow Kate to prolong the kiss. She tried her best to keep her rampaging libido under control and locked her muscles into place. If anything was going to happen, she wanted Kate to lead it.

Kate traced her fingers over Parker's forearm, leaving goosebumps in their wake that ran ahead all the way up her arms, over her shoulders, and down her back. She growled quietly, unable to resist Kate's sweet torture. Kate interlinked their fingers and drew Parker's hands toward her own body. She placed them on her own hips.

"I want you to touch me back," Kate whispered.

Hesitantly, Parker skimmed her hands along Kate's waist. A

small tug loosened her shirt, and Kate pushed it up, baring Parker's midriff. The rush of cold air on her overheated skin made her pull back her head and gasp for air. "Are you sure?"

Kate looked up and slowly nodded. "I want us to make love."

She used Parker's shirt to pull her down until their lips met. The soft kiss turned passionate when Kate's warm tongue teased Parker's lower lip, asking for permission to enter.

Her lips parted, and she pulled Kate closer, pressing their bodies together. A sharp wince from Kate made her pull back. "Are you okay? Did I hurt you?"

"No, some parts of me are just really tender." Kate held onto her and prevented her from pulling away any further. "I want you to make love to me, please. There's no point in waiting for me to improve. I won't get any better and as far as things go, today is a good day."

She saw the pleading in Kate's eyes, and it almost tore her apart. She wanted to give Kate everything she asked for and more. "What can I do?" Her voice was husky and thick with emotions.

Kate gave her shirt another small tug and whispered. "Help me undress you."

Parker brushed another soft kiss on Kate's lips before she pulled far enough back to discard her shirt. She gently freed Kate from her shirt, which joined Parker's on the floor.

"This needs to go too." Kate pointed at Parker's sports bra, which promptly followed.

When she stepped closer to free Kate from hers, Kate explored her tattoo again.

"I still can't believe you carry me on your skin."

Parker smiled and trailed soft kisses over Kate's collarbone. She caressed Kate's bare stomach while she reached up with her other hand to free Kate of her bra.

"Of course you can do this one-handed." Kate laughed gently and pulled at Parker's jeans.

Parker slowly maneuvered them closer to the bed, and they

were finally naked.

"Lay down please." Parker pulled the covers back. "Do you like light?"

"No lights, please." Kate settled in bed and pulled a sheet up to cover herself. "My body isn't as flawless as it used to be."

"You're as beautiful as you ever were." Parker joined Kate on the bed and loosened her braid to let Kate's hair fall free so she could run her fingers through it. Kate turned on her side and searched for Parker's lips. They met in a gentle kiss. Kate grunted in irritation when she tried to stroke Parker and got tangled in the sheet she had used to cover herself. She threw them off the bed.

Kate's fingers were still cool when she found the jagged scar on Parker's hip and traced it. "I'm being silly, aren't I? Worrying how I look when you bared your scars to me."

Parker stroked over Kate's jawline with her nose. She nibbled at Kate's ear before soothing the bite with a kiss. "Beauty comes from within. You're the most beautiful woman I've ever seen." Carefully, she settled Kate onto her back and leaned over her. With her free hand, she stroked from Kate's cheek down over her neck and collarbone, following the line of her necklace to the ring and pendant nestled between her breasts. "I love that you still wear this." She traced the tree that she'd given to Kate as a teenage way to lay claim on Kate, much like Kate had when she put her mother's ring on Parker's finger.

"I never took it off."

Parker remembered seeing the pendant in an antique shop out of town. The silver tree intricately woven inside a braided wooden circle was perfect for Kate. Small, colorful gemstones nestled between the branches gave an illusion of the tree holding a color pallet. When she'd entered the store, she knew that she couldn't afford anything, but for some reason, the owner had sold it to her for the meager amount of money she'd offered, which had been everything she had in her wallet.

Parker continued from Kate's breast and onto her stomach,

tracing patterns around Kate's navel. When she started to follow the path her fingers had just taken with her lips, Kate stopped her.

"You need to help me a little here." Even in the faint moonlight, Kate's cheeks were tinged pink. "I've never done this before."

Parker silenced Kate with an index finger gently pressed to her lips. "You can just lie back and enjoy this one."

Kate sucked Parker's finger into her mouth and gently nibbled it before she let it go. "So there will be more than one thing happening tonight?"

Kate's eyes glinted mischievously, making Parker smile. "Only if you're up to it. There's no pressure." She went back to caress Kate's curves and slowly moved downward with her lips. A trail of soft kisses followed, and when she kissed down the valley between Kate's breasts, Parker moaned and Kate buried her fingers in Parker's hair. Kate guided Parker toward her right breast, and she closed her lips around Kate's stiff nipple. Kate sighed softly, and her entire body started to rise under Parker's.

"Don't you dare stop," Kate said when Parker released her breast to give the same attention to her left one.

Parker stroked along the outside of Kate's thigh, and she slowly moved downward, leaving a trail of tiny kisses on Kate's belly.

"I need you to touch me there." Kate's hips bucked beneath her.

She wanted to lower her head again to move on and grant Kate's wish, but she stopped her.

"I want to see your face."

Parker moved up and answered with the kiss Kate demanded. This time, it wasn't sweet. Their kiss was hot and languid, and Kate's tongue teased her own. When she finally buried her fingers in Kate's damp curls at the apex of her thighs, they both moaned. Parker took her time exploring her wet folds, finding Kate swollen and ready for her. Her own body was so ready that for their first time, she feared that she may come without Kate touching her. Parker settled into a rhythm, circling Kate's clit.

Kate wrapped her legs around Parker and sighed. "Go faster."

Parker ignored Kate's plea and slipped down and circled Kate's opening instead. Kate inhaled sharply, and Parker looked up, but the expression of pure bliss on Kate's face eased her worry.

"Need to feel you, closer. Need more. Inside. Please," Kate said breathlessly.

Parker pressed two of her fingers inside Kate's wet center. "You okay?"

Kate nodded. "I won't break. I need to feel all of you."

Their bodies moved together, passionately and tenderly, driving Parker crazy. Kate's breathing quickened, and Parker circled her thumb over Kate's clit in tight firm circles. A guttural moan was the only warning she had before Kate tumbled over the edge and her orgasm clamped down to hold Parker's fingers inside her. One last jerk of Kate's hips made her crest with her and released the pent-up energy.

Kate smiled and sighed. "Can we stay like this for a while?"

All Parker could manage was a nod. She wanted to stay like this forever.

After their lovemaking, Kate became drowsy, and Parker coaxed her into her T-shirt to keep her warm. She really liked the thought of Kate sleeping, surrounded by her scent. She pulled the comforter over Kate, who surfaced enough to plead with Parker not to let her sleep alone. So she wrapped her arms around her and watched her sleep.

Dawn slowly started to lighten the room. She traced Kate's necklace and held the silver Claddagh ring and the hands holding a small sapphire heart. It had been Kate's mother's and meant the world to her. Touching it transported Parker back to the moment Kate had slipped it onto her finger. She had searched Parker's eyes and said, "This means you're taken. This means you're mine."

She hadn't known what to say, so she had cradled Kate's face in her hands and gave her a tender, lingering kiss. They had lost themselves in one another and pulled away only to breathe. Kate had thrown her arms around Parker and pulled her close, not willing to let go. Parker had pressed her forehead to Kate's and whispered,

"Always."

Tears fell from Parker's eyes, moved by the beautiful memory. She released the ring and moved onto the pendant that hung next to it on the chain and ran her fingers over its surface.

Kate stirred next to her and looked at Parker. "I've never taken it off except to get it reinforced a couple of years ago. One of the tiny twigs had almost worn through."

Parker wished she had something of Kate's that she could have carried all those years, but her tattoo was a far more permanent reminder of Kate.

"I want you to have the ring now that we're kind of back together. You're mine for the time I have left." Kate reached for the necklace.

Parker stilled her fingers and tugged the covers around her. Her heart swelled with the possessiveness in Kate's words. "Let us do that when it's light out, there is no rush."

"I really need to pee." Kate looked a bit sheepish when she managed to get out of bed. "And maybe you'd like to sneak off to your own bed now or everyone will know we slept together."

The pink tinge in Kate's cheeks was adorable. Parker wouldn't care one way or the other if everyone in the house knew they'd shared the bed for the night and had sex, but if Kate was more comfortable with keeping it to themselves for now, she was happy to leave. Parker sat up in bed. "Are you okay though?"

Kate leaned down and kissed her. "I'm absolutely fine. It was amazing, but I need some more sleep, and the others will wake up soon." Kate straightened. "Maybe we can do it again tonight."

"You're on." Parker watched Kate swish her way to the bathroom in just Parker's shirt. When Kate closed the door, Parker pulled on her jeans, sports bra, and hoodie. She hung Kate's clothes over the back of the chair and carried the rest of her dirty laundry out with her, leaving no trace of her behind in Kate's room.

Their night and the new level of intimacy made Parker hopeful for their future, hopeful that Kate would warm to the idea of letting her donate part of her liver when she turned out to be a match. There was no way she would give her up again.

Chapter Twenty-Four

THE BABY GRAND BEGGED to be brought out of hibernation. Parker rearranged the multiple photo frames on the surrounding shelves so she could remove the thick protective cover from the lid. She closed her eyes and stroked her fingers over the keys, reacquainting herself with the feeling. She heard the sound of each note in her mind but didn't push the key until the hammer hit the string, not wanting to make any noise.

The silence was deafening in the house after last night's heated exchange. Her early bird father hadn't made an appearance and it was already after nine in the morning. The suspicion that he hadn't spent the night in the house at all grew with every passing hour. There was no trace of his aftershave lingering in the air and the tell-tale scent of brewing coffee in the kitchen had been absent when she'd come down earlier.

"Why don't you play?" Colleen asked.

Parker shook her head. "No, it's probably horribly out of tune after all these years, and I'm not fairing much better."

"I owe you an apology." Colleen squeezed her shoulder.

Parker turned around on the bench to face Colleen. "You don't owe me anything."

"Yes, I do. I don't mean for yesterday, though I probably do for that too. I should have reached out to you, asked if you were okay. Checked in on what happened." Colleen shook her head. "I should have seen the signs for what they were."

"How could you have?" Parker asked.

"You forget I was told to leave and not ever come back by my parents too," Colleen whispered as if the memory was painful for her even after so many decades. "I wanted you to know that you did the right thing not telling them about Mark. You were right that it wasn't your place to tell them."

"That doesn't make Mom any less angry at me." Parker shrugged.

"She'll eventually cool down and see reason." Colleen fiddled with the cuff of her blouse. "Besides, she's a lot angrier at Harry."

Parker wanted to ask how it had gone after she'd left the room, but she stayed silent.

"There's one thing I would really like to understand. Why didn't you defend yourself when we all blamed you? You kept silent then, and you were silent last night. If Kate hadn't spoken up, we still wouldn't know. And please don't tell me that it wasn't your place to tell," Colleen said and sounded frustrated. "That's been going on for far too long in this family."

Colleen looked tired and drawn, even more so than a few days ago. But despite that, she seemed to be the only one so far that understood they needed to start communicating with each other if they wanted to become a family again.

"You needed someone to blame," Parker said and told Colleen the same thing she'd told Kate. "It's not like it made any difference to me after I left. Kate was the one who needed your support. She was heartbroken and struggling with her illness and I still loved her. I wanted her to be able to lean on all of you if she couldn't lean on me."

She fell silent and searched Colleen's face for answers to questions she didn't want to ask but had to know. "How do you think Mom and Dad are doing after all the revelations last night?"

"Your mother was really angry with him. She said she needed time to think and told him to leave." Colleen looked uncomfortable, like she didn't want to be the one telling her.

"Damn, I wouldn't have left them alone if I knew they would take each other's heads off." She closed the keyboard. The euphoria that had lured her there had disappeared and left her defeated.

She'd wanted to repair the relationship with her family not tear it apart some more.

"I think it's understandable, considering he kicked out her only daughter."

"I guess he didn't kick me out. He gave me an ultimatum, and I chose to leave." She wasn't sure where she should stand in all this. She had a long time to think about this and view it from every angle she could think off.

A knock at the door saved Colleen from responding. When she heard Jazmin's voice from the hallway, she felt compelled to join them. Even though Jazmin was truly the last person she wanted to see today. Her persistence for demanding answers that weren't hers to demand was partially to blame for the evening getting out of control.

"I really don't want to cause any more trouble." Jazmin held up both hands when she saw Parker. "I came to apologize for last night."

"That seems to be going around," Parker mumbled. "I can't say I'm particularly happy to see you. Maybe you should leave."

"I know I shouldn't be here, but I need to talk to you." Jazmin scrubbed her face. "But I want to check on Kate to make sure she's all right after yesterday and apologize to her as well. Please?"

"She's in her room." Parker wondered if Kate felt like hiding from the world today, or if she was still sleeping after their busy night.

Jazmin turned toward the house extension where Kate had been staying the past couple of days.

"She is in her room upstairs." Parker pointed to the staircase and led the way.

When Kate didn't respond to the knocking on her door she got worried. Both Jazmin and Colleen crowded into her personal space. She opened the door a crack to see inside. It looked like Kate was sleeping but with all their noise, she should have woken up.

Parker went to the bed and gently stroked her face. "Hey, Kate, it's time for you to wake up."

She didn't respond.

"Don't do this to us, Kate!" Colleen's voice rose with every word. "It's too soon."

Jazmin shouldered Parker out of the way and bent over Kate, her hands moving over the still form in the bed while she yelled over her shoulder, "Someone call an ambulance."

Parker's blood ran cold, and she barely registered her mother and Zoe rushing in.

Jazmin rubbed her fist over Kate's breastbone, and Kate moved slightly before her eyes fluttered open.

"What?" Kate asked.

"How are we doing on the ambulance?" Jazmin shouted.

"Tired." Kate stretched the word in three syllables, and her eyes drooped.

Nobody moved except Jazmin. An ingrained part of Parker's training kicked in and shook her out of her stupor. Her hands badly shook when she pulled out her cell and dialed 911. She stopped shaking and calmed her voice to speak to the operator. Parker related every piece of information Jazmin wanted her to.

Time stretched and contorted strangely. It felt like they waited for forever for the ambulance to arrive though it was no more than ten minutes. She held onto Kate's hand and told her what was going on in the most soothing voice she could muster.

"Stop it. She won't be able to comprehend what you're saying," Jazmin said.

Parker glared at her before she turned back to Kate. Even if Kate couldn't understand what Parker told her, she could hear her voice and know she wasn't alone. It seemed Jazmin had gotten the hint; she didn't tell Parker a second time. Kate's chest rose and fell in a slow steady rhythm, and the sight gave Parker a small amount of comfort. Kate was breathing on her own and reacting, so this wasn't anything serious, right? She was just tired.

"I know what you're thinking," Jazmin said. "But I don't want to risk missing anything. Some people can improve their condition for a short time through sheer willpower, especially if they want something badly enough. And Kate wanted this so badly that it wouldn't surprise me if that's what happened. But if she crashes, going into a coma is a real possibility."

By the time Parker, her mother, and Zoe reached the hospital, Kate had been situated in a room and was hooked up to various monitors and machines. Countless tubes and leads sneaked under her blanket. Harry arrived minutes later. He looked to her mother, but she shook her head.

"It's not the time or place," her mother said quietly. "She would want you here. That's the only reason I called."

Everyone in the room looked so resigned, and Parker thought again about telling them about her getting tested. They'd had longer to get used to Kate's declining health and her possible death. But Parker couldn't accept the situation. She'd just gotten Kate back. She needed to get hold of Dr. Miller and find out what was taking so long with the results. Her hands trembled, and she balled them into fists. She felt helpless and empty. Why did the sweetest person she knew have to suffer so much? Why couldn't she be suffering in her place?

Jazmin entered the room followed by Dr. Miller. Jazmin looked like she wanted to be anywhere but in this room. It made the tiny hairs on the beck of Parker's neck stand on end, and the feeling that something was amiss crept up her spine.

"Kate left detailed instructions behind in case we reached this stage, and she could no longer make informed decisions. It also allows me to speak to you openly about what is going on," Dr. Miller said. "Reaching this point means we have a very short window to find a transplant. Each passing day makes full recovery less likely."

Parker didn't know if she was angry or grateful for the way Dr. Miller delivered the information.

Colleen stroked Kate's hair. "How long?"

"I really couldn't say, Mrs. Cane."

Was it so impossible to give definitive answers? You know why, the professional part of her brain supplied. Life was too fragile, and people fought differently to be sure.

The sudden return trip to the hospital messed with her head. She had unconsciously started to tip her fingers one after the other to her thumb while breathing in. It changed her breathing rhythm and helped her relax. She hadn't needed to do this in forever, but this time, she hadn't even deliberately started it.

"We made the necessary calls to update her score on the transplant list. All we can do now is wait and pray." Dr. Miller continued. "I can respect that Ms. Snow decided she can't take the risk with her career after all."

"Excuse me?" Parker felt like someone had knocked her over the head. What the fuck was she talking about? "I've made no such decision. No one's called me to let me know whether I'm a match or not."

Dr. Miller didn't flinch. "Commander Hazelwood informed me yesterday that she'd talked to you about it, and you'd changed your mind."

"The last time I talked to the commander was in your company during the tests."

Dr. Miller frowned. "But the commander said she called you right before she called me. She said that you were downright rude and hung up after saying you couldn't take the risk with your career. She was angry because she stuck her neck out for you by speeding up the process."

"But I didn't talk to her." Parker leaned against the wall for support. She pulled her phone from her back pocket and checked the call log to see a number she'd never seen before, and the call had lasted for almost three minutes. "No, that's impossible," she muttered and shook her head.

"She called me about half past four," Dr. Miller said like it might help Parker's memory.

Parker checked the timestamp in her call log and tried to make sense of what she saw. The call had connected when she was in the shower with Kate, washing her hair. How was that possible? The whole family were home, and Jazmin had been in the house too. Parker whipped around and saw Jazmin sneaking up to the door, trying to leave unnoticed.

Parker rushed to intercept her and blocked her escape. "What did you do?"

Jazmin looked like a deer caught in the headlight. "I swear I wanted to tell you. That was one of the reasons I came over, but then we found Kate and—"

"You wanted to tell me what?" Parker shoved her forearm against Jazmin's neck and backed her up against the wall. "That you risked Kate's life with this stupid stunt?"

"Jazmin?" Dr. Miller stood by Parker's side and put her hand on Parker's forearm to gently pry her away. "Is that true, Jazmin?"

Jazmin looked at the floor and said nothing.

Dr. Miller shook her head. "Oh, Jazmin, what have you done?"

"I—"

"Don't say anything else. Go into my office and wait for me there. You are not to stop on your way, and you are not to talk to anyone before we speak again. Do you understand me?"

Jazmin nodded. "I'm sorry—"

"It's a little late for that now." Dr. Miller guided Parker out of the way and opened the door for Jazmin. "This should have never happened. I knew they'd become friends over the years, which was why Dr. Callahan wasn't an attending doctor while Kate was hospitalized."

A heated discussion between the doctor and Parker's parents broke loose about possible legal consequences. The words ran together in Parker's head, and she wanted to yell at them to shut up and concentrate on Kate. None of that would help her right now.

"Everyone, this is not helping any of us," Harry said. "We need to concentrate on Kate and Parker. We can decide on any other actions we want or need to take later. Our daughters need to be the most important thing right now."

Unbidden tears blurred Parker's vision. She blinked them away before they spilled over. She needed to keep a cool head if she wanted to help Kate and that was all she'd ever wanted to do.

Dr. Miller turned to her. "Parker—you're a match. You can help Kate."

Parker's legs gave away and she buckled, but Dr. Miller caught her. "No time for that now, Marine. We need to inform the commander." She reached for the door. "Let's go somewhere a little more private for that."

Parker went with Dr. Miller to a break room and waited for her to finish a phone call with the commander. It took an age and with only one side of the conversation, Parker had no idea what was going on with all the medical terms flying around.

Dr. Miller pulled the phone from her ear. "Commander Hazelwood wants to know if you could see her now over at Walter Reed?"

"Yes." Parker nodded. She'd do whatever was necessary.

The call carried on for a few more minutes before Dr. Miller disconnected and turned to her. "Do you have any more questions for me?"

"No." She had no questions. She just wanted to get this done and hoped it would be enough.

"Then we're done. I don't want to keep you. Commander Hazelwood is waiting."

Parker reached for the door handle when she realized that she may not get another private moment with Dr. Miller. She felt her cheeks flush and the tips of her ears burn. She'd turned bright red, and she knew it.

"Are you all right, Ms. Snow? You've thought of something you'd like to ask?"

"I don't know." She bit her lower lip until she tasted blood. "Is it my fault Kate's condition declined so fast? We spent last night together."

"What do you mean?"

"We made love," she whispered.

Dr. Miller smiled and shook her head. "No, Parker, it's not your fault."

Parker felt some of the guilt lift, but she doubted she would ever lose all of it. Saving Kate's life, however, would assuage that guilt still further.

Chapter Twenty-Five

PARKER DRAGGED HERSELF DOWN the cemetery path, her sister's grave like a homing beacon in the distance. She hadn't been here for a long time. Too long. Still, she had no trouble finding Nicole's headstone even though she was so drained, she could hardly keep her eyes open. Twilight cast long shadows and made the place a little eerie.

She sank to the ground and leaned back against the side of the headstone. "Hi, Nic, long time no see. I'm sorry it took me so long. I could apologize and say I was busy with hospital visits and tests. But we both know that isn't true."

The visit to Commander Hazelwood at Walter Reed hospital had robbed her of her remaining energy. She'd sat through a long psych evaluation she was told was only a formality. Her brain was almost too sluggish to think, but it wouldn't quiet down. "I swear, you're never far from my mind, Nic." She let her head fall back against the stone. The resulting sting on her skull woke her up some. "I hope you can see what a wonderful young woman Zoe has become." Parker pulled her legs close and rested her chin on her knees. "She misses you, you know?"

In her mind, she heard Nicole chiding her for disappearing and leaving Zoe and her family behind without a word.

"I know I screwed up, Nic." She welcomed the cold, damp air creeping through her jeans and hoodie, slowly chilling her but keeping her awake too. "Zoe needed me and so did Kate, but I ran as fast and far as I could. But someone should've told me that Kate had gotten so much worse."

An owl hooted in the distance. Her surroundings came to life with nocturnal animals slowly venturing out all around her. Tiny glowing eyes regarded her from underneath a hedge close by, but the darkness was too dense to make out their owner.

"They won't let me help Kate without permission from my superiors. I'm as close to a perfect match for Kate as possible, but they can only go forward with a life-saving surgery if I have consent from the military. Can you believe that?" She fell silent for a moment and stared unseeing into the distance. "What if they say no? I'm so scared." The words fell from her lips before she could censor them. She never admitted her fears. Giving in to them could mean the difference between life and death in her work. But she'd never been so afraid in her life, not even when she'd been wounded and kidnapped in the desert.

Of all the places you could have gone, why did you join the military? She imagined Nicole asking.

"They gave me a home and structure when I needed it most. It's a good life, and I grew to love the service." Parker bounced her head against the stone a couple more times. The slowly radiating pain at the back of her skull helped her to keep her eyes open. Two nights in a row with little sleep had taken its toll. But chancing a nighttime visit from her demons, while Kate slept in her arms was something she hadn't been willing to risk.

You could leave the Corps if they say no. The thought ghosted through her head.

"That would take too long. I'm contracted for another eighteen months, and even if they gave me an early separation, it takes weeks to process out. Kate doesn't have that much time." She slid her fingers into the grass and pulled. The tiny blades cut into the soft skin between her fingers, leaving behind an unpleasant sting. She stared at the tiny drop of blood gathering between her thumb and forefinger. If she didn't start to take better care of herself, she wouldn't be able to care for Kate or anyone else.

The vibration of her phone drew her from her musings. She pulled it from her hoodie and checked the text. "Mom wants to know where I am. She wants to pick me up when I'm done." She stared at her screen, her finger hovering over the answer button. She wasn't in the mood for company. Finally, she locked her screen and as she pocketed her phone, she felt the envelope she'd stuck in there yesterday.

Her fingers were cold and numb and made it difficult to open the envelope. The tingling in her chest increased when the page came loose at last.

My sweet Parker,
After so many years without a word, this letter will probably be a shock. I hope you'll keep on reading, but I couldn't blame you if you chose not to.
While I'm sitting here writing, I feel like you're standing right behind me, your hand resting on my shoulder to give me strength. But when I reach up to squeeze your fingers, all I find is empty air.
My condition has gotten steadily worse over the past couple of years and now my liver is failing. The rising copper levels in my blood are slowly poisoning my body and brain, making me lose my hold on reality a little more each day. Colleen and Helen still hold out hope for a lifesaving transplant surgery, but I know that the chances dwindle every day as I get weaker.
I know I'm selfish to do this, but I want to apologize and say my goodbyes to you while I still can. Sending you away so I wouldn't hold you back in life is my second biggest regret. I can't tell you how sorry I am and how much I wish I had trusted you and your love. I know now that I crushed you that day. You had no one to pick you up and support you. I still don't understand why you took all the blame for the breakup. I didn't only destroy us, I destroyed your connection to your family.
But by far my biggest regret is not going after you and

doing everything to right my wrong. I caused us both so much misery. I sincerely hope that time and distance healed the hurt I inflicted on you.

You were my heart and soul. You will always be. I wish I could've had thirty thousand todays with you instead of worrying about one tomorrow. I wish we could've grown old and gray together.

It's too late for me, sweetheart, but I don't want you to have the same regrets. Don't wait for tomorrow to make something right. That tomorrow you're waiting for may never come.

I'd like to ask one last favor of you. Please make an effort with your family. They miss you terribly and want you back in their life, especially Zoe. She'll give you a hard time at first, but deep down, she'll need you, especially after I'm gone.

It makes it easier to imagine that I'll get to see my parents and Nicole again when I leave this world. And we'll be watching over you and the others.

Goodbye, my love. If I have one last wish, I'll wish for your happiness.

Kate

Parker was no longer alone in her quiet corner of the graveyard. Faint steps echoed on a nearby footpath. She pocketed the letter and wiped her tears away.

"Parker, are you here?"

Her father's deep baritone drifted over before she had a chance to get up and duck out of sight. His steps quieted when he walked onto the grass.

"There you are. Didn't you hear me calling?"

"I heard you just fine." Parker grumbled. She remembered Kate's words to make an effort with her family. She should start now but letting go of the past was hard. "I came here to have some quiet time to think, but you can stay if you like."

"Anything I can help you with?" Harry sat next to her.

"Not really." She shook her head. "Well, maybe... How did you cope with knowing there was nothing more you could do for Nicole? Looking at Kate, I'm going insane. Why was I sent home? How can help be so close and yet unreachable?"

Her father turned, an unreadable expression on his face. "I can't pretend to know how you feel. Losing a child is devastating. But this would be like me losing your mother, and I just can't imagine that. She hasn't spoken to me for twenty-four hours, and it's wrecked me. I'm a broken man, and no matter what I've done or will do to make up for my mistakes, it'll never be enough."

For the first time, her father's drawn features and the dark circles under his eyes registered. He looked like shit.

"What do you mean by making up for your mistakes?"

He looked away and scratched at a dirt spot on his pants. "They didn't want you to know. Mom, Colleen, and Kate all had different reasons, but I didn't agree. You had a right to know, you had a right to make your own decision..."

What was her father trying to say? "Why didn't you call and let me know? Why did I have to find out by accident?"

He sighed deeply. "And what we did to you and Kate was so unfair. We tore you apart. Kate merely caved first to the pressure we put on you both." Harry continued like she hadn't spoken. "We couldn't understand how the two of you could have fallen in love with each other. You were practically sisters, and it just seemed wrong. But I've seen what it's done to Kate. And your choice to stay away spoke volumes."

Parker didn't say anything when he stopped speaking. She wanted to retreat into her hoodie to create a physical barrier between them. The darkness had cocooned them in and disconnected them from the outside world. It seemed Harry had gone somewhere else in his mind and needed to get rid of what was weighing on his soul. All she could do was wait for him to continue.

"After Kate's last episode, I realized we were running out of time if I waited much longer. I knew that she wanted to see you again. She hardly talked about anything else when she was delusional." Harry looked at her, his eyes clear and focused. "A few years ago, I ran into a man I knew from another lifetime, back when I was a sniper on a mission so deep behind enemy lines, I was certain if I saw another living soul other than through my scope, it would be the end of me. I'd just climbed a tree to check if I had a clear shot to my target when I saw a lone friendly soldier through my scope. He was staggering through the jungle looking as if he was about to fall over. I couldn't be sure if it was a trap or if he was the unluckiest soul alive since there wasn't much chance he would stay undiscovered for much longer. I had a decision to make. Stay and complete my mission even if it meant that soldier died before my eyes or help him and risk exposing us both."

"Since you said you met him again, I take it you helped him," Parker said.

"I did. I gave him water and took him with me into my sniper's nest until my mission was complete. I didn't see him again after we were collected from my rendezvous point. When I met him again, I was surprised to learn that he was a high-ranking officer. I called him and asked him if he could help me get you home."

"Who did you call?" She ran through a mental list of names and dismissed everyone she came up with.

"I'm sorry. I promised never to tell."

"Did you consider what implications that may have on me?"

"Does that really worry you, now that you're here?" he asked.

"No." Of course she didn't care. Kate was everything to her. "I'm worried I won't get the permission I need for the surgery."

Harry squeezed her thigh. "Have I told you how proud I am of you?"

She couldn't stop a small smile. "Oh?"

"I know we don't deserve any credit for the woman you've become, or for the career you've built. But your selflessness to help Kate is astounding. I wish I could've done it so you didn't have to put yourself at risk, but I'll support you both in every way I can. Even if your mother doesn't want me around, know that I'm only a phone call away. We should never have stopped you being together. I'm sorry it took me so long to see that."

"Thank you." She was too perplexed to say anything else.

"If you ever want or need a civilian job, you'll always be welcome to join the family firm."

This was all too much information, too much of an about turn from what she expected from him. "What's changed your mind?"

"I realized that pride, especially false pride, can be very dangerous, and it may have cost me my family. I want to make amends if it's not too late. "I was wrong and I'm sorry, so very, very sorry."

All this time wasted. Her anger. His pride. She wrapped her fingers around Kate's letter and sighed. It was time to start afresh. "Let's go home, Dad."

Chapter Twenty-Six

A MIXED SENSE OF déjà vu and foreboding settled over Parker when she walked down the hospital hallway. It got worse when she found her father sitting next to Kate's bed. He'd driven her home last night but hadn't come in.

"Did you sleep okay?" Her father stood up.

"I guess so." Compared to the other nights she had. She'd managed five hours before she woke, and her body refused to go back to sleep, but it was much better than most other nights. "What about you?"

Harry stretched. "These old bones aren't made for sleeping on the office couch. I probably should look for a hotel, but it feels like that would be admitting defeat."

"You think it will take Mom that long to come around? Why the office couch? I thought you had a downtown apartment."

"She wrote me an email last night asking for a temporary separation." His shoulders slumped. "Next thing, she'll be asking for a divorce. I've seen it hundreds of times. The apartment is occupied until the end of the month."

Parker didn't want to be the reason that her parents' marriage ended after all they'd been through together. "You shouldn't give up. I can talk to Mom if you think that'll help."

"Does she know you call her Mom behind her back?"

She smiled and shook her head. It had slipped out once before, by accident.

"Don't talk to her, no. It's something your mother and I have to work out." He squeezed her shoulder. "But for now, it's probably best if I'm not here when the cavalry arrives. Let me know when you get any news regarding the surgery. I'd like to be there for you and Kate." He left and closed the door quietly behind him.

Parker settled next to Kate's bed and held onto her hand. Her fingers felt cool in her slightly sweaty palms. So much had happened since she'd come home. In all that chaos, she wondered if she and Kate could really have a chance when all this was over. Parker knew that she was doing this for the right reasons, and that she'd be doing it even if she and Kate couldn't be together. But she also wondered how it might affect her career and the course of the rest of her life.

Dr. Miller came in to check on Kate. She was barely able to follow verbal commands.

"Has she been any more alert while you were here?" She checked the readout on a monitor.

Parker shook her head. Kate had looked like she was asleep and that was easier to bear than the thought of Kate's mind slowly slipping away and leaving behind an empty shell.

"I didn't think so, but you shouldn't stop hoping."

Dr. Miller's face was a steady mask of neutrality, and it frustrated Parker that she couldn't read that woman any better than the first day they had met.

"Did you get any news regarding the surgery clearance? I know it's still early and Saturday to boot but time is ticking." Dr. Miller adjusted Kate's IV.

"No, I haven't." She pulled her cell from her pocket and checked, just to be sure she hadn't missed anything.

"As Kate's primary case worker, they'll let me know, but you'll get the notification sooner. I'll only get it after the consent has been finalized." She buried her hands in her coat pockets.

It looked like she wanted to say more but stayed silent. As the silence between them became unbearable, Parker asked, "Is there anything else?"

Dr. Miller's cheeks colored slightly. "After what transpired yesterday, we think it would be a good idea to have Kate transferred to Walter Reed for the surgery, if it goes ahead."

"Why? Isn't that more complicated?" Parker frowned.

"We can't say how extensive the consequences of Dr. Callahan's actions are. We think it's better that way, especially given the legal ramifications of her behavior."

Parker wanted to ask how it would be better, but she bit her tongue. She just wanted to get into surgery.

"I promise nothing much will change for you," Dr. Miller said. "And I have some privileges left over there, so we can guarantee Kate's care will continue to the best of my ability. We're taking Dr. Callahan's actions very seriously. She's been suspended, pending a thorough investigation."

Zoe entered the room without knocking, closely followed by Parker's mother and Colleen.

"I'll leave you to it," Dr. Miller said and left.

It didn't take long before she felt claustrophobic in the little room. Her mother and Colleen were deep in discussion and hardly acknowledged her, too preoccupied with Kate's state, but Zoe eyed her like she expected her to have an answer to it all. When she couldn't stand it any longer, she excused herself under the pretense of making a call and left the room.

Her feet carried her down the hallway on autopilot into a small waiting area with two ancient-looking vending machines. Nothing in them called to her, but she fed enough coins into one and pulled a soda can out of it. The can was cold, and she emptied the too-sweet liquid in a few long pulls. It settled like a lead balloon in her stomach. All this inactivity made her feel out of control, and tears of frustration burned in the corner of her eyes. The delicate walls of the soda can gave way under her closing fist, making a high-pitched crinkling sound.

She pitched the crushed can into the empty trash bin in the corner with a little too much force and was instantly rebuked by a low clearing of a throat. She hadn't noticed the woman sitting next to the door when she'd entered. If she'd learned one thing during her own time in the hospital, it was that people needed to talk. The acute state of being in limbo, of not knowing or not being able to change what was happening to people and their loved ones seemed to heighten the need to connect to strangers.

However, she had no desire for that today. She needed answers herself, and everything was moving far too slowly. She pulled her phone out and made the call. It was time to stop waiting and take action.

***

Parker came to a halt at Kate's room, hardly able to draw enough air into her lungs. She held onto the door frame with one hand and pressed her head against the wall, as if it was all that kept her upright. The words of her superior's aid replayed in her head over and over, threatening to pull her under. *Admiral Pike is on leave until the end of next week. He can't be reached until then.*

Everything was slipping out of her reach again. Kate didn't look strong enough to hang on for another week. The pain and despair took her breath away. She couldn't breathe, she couldn't think. She clawed at the door frame instead of her own skin, which she wanted to flay off. She pulled back and struck the wall with all the strength she could muster. Her fist landed with a resounding thud next to the door, and the plaster gave way. The pain settling in her hand slowly crawled up her arm and gave some sweet release to the turmoil inside her.

She drew her hand back. Another punch and she'd be able to fill her lungs with air again.

"Hold it, captain!"

A familiar voice filtered through the haze and instantly tapped into her training. She froze in position, not sure she'd really heard the words, or if it was just her mind playing tricks on her.

"Captain?"

A hand as strong as her own closed around her wrist and

slowly started to lower it.

"Turn around and look at me."

Parker turned to see Linda standing in front of her, concern etched on her face.

"What are you doing here?" Parker took in Linda's unusually disheveled appearance.

"Suzan's blood pressure got worse two nights ago, and she was admitted to the hospital. The doctors couldn't control it, so they had to do a C-section." Linda inspected Parker's hand. "It doesn't appear to be broken, but you should get it checked."

Linda began to lead Parker along the corridor.

"Wait." Parker stopped and turned to look at Linda. "The baby's been born?"

"Yes." Linda's expression transformed into the goofy happiness only a newly minted parent had. "A healthy baby girl born at 2355."

Parker momentarily dismissed her own predicament and hugged Linda. "I'm so happy for you, my friend." She pulled away. "But didn't you say you were expecting a boy?"

Linda shrugged and grinned. "Seems like nature had other ideas."

"Do you have a name?"

Linda shook her head. "Not yet but tell me what's going on. Is everything okay with Kate?"

Parker gave a quick recap of the last couple of days and finished with the information that the Judge Advocate General, the man who would ultimately decide Kate's fate, was unreachable at the moment.

"Oh, I see." Linda slowly nodded. She tugged Parker's arm. "Come on. Don't you remember that I told you to call me if you run into any trouble on that front?"

Parker had a vague recollection of Linda's offer, but Parker had only just found out and was still processing the news. Linda stopped at a door, reached for the handle, and hesitated. "I really want to help you, Parker, so I'm going to let you in on a secret. But it's really important that it doesn't leave this room."

Parker nodded, and Linda opened the door. She followed Linda into the room and saw her commanding officer dressed in jeans, running shoes and a washed-out sweater at the bed beside Suzan. He looked younger without the uniform. What was he doing here?

He was fussing over her and the tiny bundle in her arms and didn't look up to acknowledge their arrival.

"Would you like to explain that?" She grasped Linda's wrist as she moved to go past Parker.

"No, not really," Linda said.

"Linda." Parker clenched her jaw. Linda looked toward their CO with more familiarity than Parker felt comfortable with. A muscle spasmed in her back, and she realized she'd unconsciously come to attention. Her body now protested with all the pent-up tension she'd been holding in.

"You asked if I wanted to explain, and I don't." Linda snatched her wrist away and rubbed it. "But I will, because you're my friend, and knowing will help you. I kept the secret of why you left, and I'm going to need you to do the same." Linda looked at Suzan for a moment before she turned back to Parker. "Jacob—Admiral Pike—is family."

"But he's your commanding officer." The words were out before Parker's brain caught up, and she wished she could reel them back in.

"Would you let me finish?" Linda's gaze drifted back to her wife. "Jacob is Suzan's uncle." Linda sighed. "I know I shouldn't be working under him. But when he was appointed Judge Advocate General, he became my boss by default."

"The appointment usually only lasts one term, three years," Admiral Pike said as he approached. "We didn't want to risk Linda being loaned out to another branch of the military. That would most likely have entailed her being stationed somewhere else—away from Suzan."

They looked like they expected some sort of response from

her, but she didn't have one to give. She felt like the walls were moving in on her again, her capacity to process new information diminishing fast. But now that she knew, she spotted the faint resemblance between Suzan and the admiral. They had the same nose and similarly shaped eyes.

"I couldn't bear the thought of her being stationed somewhere else again." Suzan straightened the baby's tiny cap. "Or have her work for a different branch, like you. I couldn't bear being responsible for Linda losing what she loves so much."

Parker clenched her fists. That the Marines had abandoned her and loaned her out to the Navy without an explanation or an end date was an incredibly sore subject for her. The room fell silent.

The little girl in Suzan's arms woke up and let everyone in the room know that she demanded attention with her high-pitched cry.

"I think we may need to find the nursery." Suzan's nose wrinkled like she'd smelled something unpleasant, and she looked at Linda. "Can you help me up, darling?"

Linda held the newborn in one arm while she supported Suzan with her other. They slowly moved toward the door, with Suzan having great difficulty walking even with Linda's support.

When they passed Parker, Linda leaned in and whispered, "This is your chance to talk to him. We'll be a while."

The quiet click of the closing door indicated this was her chance. It was now or never.

"How have you been, captain?" Admiral Pike regarded her with interest. "Settling back in okay after deployment? I know you still need to get debriefed. But I'd hoped that an uninterrupted Thanksgiving holiday with you family would have been nice."

Parker didn't have time for niceties and small talk. "Why did you bring me back, sir?"

"Why don't we sit down?" He gestured at the two visitor chairs around a small table next to the window. "I think it's time for us to talk." He ran his hand over his short-cropped hair that started to recede at the top. "Do us both a favor and drop the sir for now. This won't be an official conversation."

She almost protested. As much as she wanted answers, she didn't want to talk to him in a purely private capacity. She appreciated that he was there as Suzan's uncle, but Parker needed her commanding officer. He was the only one who could help Kate.

She followed him but waited until he was seated before she pulled back a chair and followed suit. She took the time to gather herself and pull on the armor she used in court. Her mind cleared, and she knew exactly what she wanted to know.

He was clearly struggling to decide where he wanted to start, and she had a feeling he was already regretting the offer for them to talk.

"Sir, I would like to say something."

"Jacob, please."

"Okay, Jacob." Parker took a deep breath, closed her eyes, and let the air drift out slowly before she opened them again. "When I came back, I learned that my adopted sister was very sick. Her liver is failing, and she needs a transplant to survive. She's on the waiting list, but the doctors think she may only have days left, maybe not even that." She took a deep breath to control her shaking voice.

"I'm so sorry. You can take as much time as you need," he said and straightened like he was back into his professional persona.

"Thanks. But I actually need something else."

"Oh?" He looked at her with interest.

Parker called up her courage. "I need your permission to be a living donor for Kate. I'm a match, and it would save her life." She tried to read his reaction, but he was a more skilled litigator than she was, and she found no reflection of his thoughts on his face or in his body language. "Kate is much more than just my adopted sister. She was my lover before I joined the Marine Corps."

"I know." He nodded and looked away. "I know a lot more than you think and not because it's in your file, but because I know your father."

"What do you mean?" she whispered. Her father had said he'd

pulled in a favor, but he'd been reluctant to tell her from who. Parker didn't know if that would make things better or worse for her.

"I met your father a long time ago in a god forsaken place."

He went on to recount the story Parker had heard from her dad the previous night. He regarded her in silence for a moment before continuing. "I sat through endless debriefings hoping to find out what went wrong. By the time I'd finished, your father had been processed out. We only met again years later in a civilian courtroom at opposite ends of a case."

"How did you know who he was?" Parker's curiosity was peaked. She didn't know much about her father's military past. She'd never cared enough to find out.

He laughed a deep belly laugh. "Believe me, I needed to find out who'd saved my scrawny nineteen-year-old ass. There was no way I'd forget his name unless someone put a bullet between my eyes."

Parker bit her lower lip to not laugh at the graphic description.

"We met for a match of golf after the case was over, and we still do occasionally."

"Golf?" Parker had never heard her father mention golf before.

"I don't think it's his favorite pastime. He attends more for the business side of things but I'm not entirely sure. Anyhow, he told me about his family, and I told him about Suzan and Linda. Back then, I didn't know they knew Linda."

"Small world."

He sighed and relaxed back into his seat. "I knew about Kate being ill and on the verge of losing her fight. Harry had told me. He also told me that the two of you used to be much more than sisters."

Parker swallowed. She knew no one cared these days, but she didn't advertise her sexual orientation.

"I have no judgment, Parker. Life happens. And Harry didn't tell me until very recently when he asked me if I could help him to bring you home for a few days."

"Sir?" Her mind stumbled over what he said. Her father had asked for a few days, but she'd been pulled from her current assignment and stationed back in DC. "A few days isn't the same as a reassignment. Why?"

"Jacob, remember?" He shook his head. "Because I'm a meddling old man. When your father called me, I looked at your record. You spent a lot of time on assignment, far more than what is required of you. Between Harry's plea to get you back and what I'd learned from Linda about you and Kate, I thought you could use some time to be close to them."

Parker grimaced. Why had Linda talked about her with the admiral?

"Don't be mad at Linda. She probably has no idea that I put her vague accounts about a friend who joined the service after she got her heart broken together with your name. Besides, with everything going on here, I imagine you haven't slept too well lately–the dark circles under your eyes are testament to that. I wouldn't be a very good superior if I sent you back out there before you were ready for the challenge, would I? If I'd been your CO back when you were injured, I wouldn't have sent you back so soon."

Parker's jaw clenched. She didn't want to get back into the reason why she'd fled the country after only a couple days at home.

He looked at her inquisitively, and she wished she could hide her welling emotions better. But she was afraid it was all out there now, her armor pierced, leaving her soul exposed.

"The desert is more comfortable for you, isn't it? You know how to function there, and it gives you comfort." His words were a quiet statement, and there was little for Parker to add, so she stayed silent. "Some soldiers have trouble coming back here where their life intersects with the civilian world, so they keep going back out there."

Parker knew he was trying to ask her if she was struggling with PTSD without actually saying it. And she probably was, but up to now, she'd found it hard to admit it. Unless she posed a threat to herself or others, the military wouldn't interfere unless she asked for help.

"No one could fault you if you were struggling, considering what you've been through." Jacob said.

She knew he was right. She'd known for a long time. But she'd been too afraid to ask for help. The stigma was one thing, but the reason she'd tried to hide it was deeper. She'd been afraid that someone in a white coat would find her too broken to repair and declare her medically unfit and process her out. And where would that have left her? The Corps was the only thing that had kept her sane and together. Losing that had been an unbearable thought a week ago.

But things had changed. *Everything* had changed.

She'd made a promise to herself and Kate to change her destructive ways. "Yes, you're probably right. I do struggle when I'm back here. It's easier for me over there." Parker closed her eyes and inhaled slowly. "I think I may have PTSD."

"I didn't think you would admit to it." He cocked his head.

Parker nodded. "Where do we go from here?" This wasn't the conversation she'd thought they were going to have, but it couldn't be stopped now.

The silence in the room stretched her nerves to the limit. "Sir, I need to know if you'll let me go ahead with the surgery. Kate doesn't have time for us to go back and forth, or for me to have psych evaluation after psych evaluation. I'd honestly appreciate it if you could just come out and say whether or not we can move forward."

He tilted his head. "I don't think I can."

Parker's heart plummeted through the floor, and her blood ran cold. That couldn't be it. It couldn't be over. The edges of her vision started to blur and darken. "No. No, no."

"I'm sorry, Parker, I think you misunderstood."

"What?" she whispered.

"I mean I can't deny you the surgery. I'll sign off on it. Not doing so would be cruel."

The black around her vision started to recede, and she was able to focus on the admiral and his words again.

"But."

Ah, the price. Whatever it was, she was willing to do it.

"I have a couple of conditions. First, you'll stay in DC so I can keep an eye on you for as long as you serve under me. I owe your father that much at least. I also want you to see someone for your PTSD. We have great people who can help you, and it's no longer stigmatized like you think it is."

"I don't like taking prescription drugs." Parker looked away. It had been a problem on multiple occasions, her over sensitive system didn't cope well with them at all.

"There are other ways and techniques to deal with it. I want you to give it an honest shot before you say it won't work for you."

Parker nodded. "I'm not against trying, but Kate can't wait for me to quiet my demons."

"I'm well aware of that. I'll settle for your word, Parker. No running away when it gets tough."

"That I can do."

"And one other thing," he said. "I can't promise you that it won't have an impact when your next evaluation comes up. That depends on how you heal and how they judge the situation. Worst case, they may discharge you on medical grounds or put you on a permanent desk job until your contract is up."

A laugh bubbled up in Parker's chest, and she didn't manage to hold it in. "I basically already have a desk job. The court room is hardly a battlefield."

"We both know it can be when you're embedded with a unit. But that's not the point right now. I just wanted you to have all the information."

Parker nodded. "Thanks, I already know. Doctor Hazelwood explained all the ins and outs to me and the potential consequences it can have. I'm willing to take the risk. I couldn't live with myself if I didn't do this, you know?"

"I understand where you're coming from, and I think what you want to do is admirable. I'll see to it that the appropriate papers get moving today. The hospital should have it all sorted within a few hours as soon as I sign off on it."

Parker could hardly believe her ears. She wanted to fall around the admiral's neck but thought better of it. *This is it. We're gonna do this, Kate!*

Chapter Twenty-Seven

PARKER WAS EXHAUSTED BY the time she made it home. Admiral Pike got the ball rolling straight away, just as he'd promised. Due to Kate's critical state, the doctors at Walter Reed scheduled the transplant surgery for the following day. The less Kate waited, the better chance she had to fully recover. The speed with which things had unfolded over the past couple of hours made Parker's head spin.

Kate would be moved to Walter Reed, and all that was left for Parker to do was pack her stuff and show up at the hospital at 0700 hours with an empty stomach. She was equal parts relieved, elated, and terrified. It left her in a strange state where she had too much energy to rest but was too mentally exhausted at the same time.

Since Parker was about to lose a piece of a perfectly functioning organ, her body would need to readjust and make up for the missing part, therefore she'd need all her energy reserves for the recovery process. Regardless, Parker couldn't settle.

Besides, she wanted to have a word with her parents. She wasn't naïve. She'd made arrangements long ago in case anything happened overseas, and she didn't come home or came back in a state in which she couldn't make any decisions. It was time she told her parents about the arrangements and let them know where the papers were kept. Just in case, Parker told herself.

It took her less than ten minutes to pack a go-bag. She was ready to go.

The house felt empty when she made her way back downstairs. She thought everyone else was at the hospital, but she called out anyway. As she'd expected, no one answered.

"Some alone time is good," she murmured to the empty living room. A few quiet moments to let her emotions catch up with the unfolding events of the day might be helpful.

She walked toward the sunroom and halted when she passed the baby grand. Zoe's school portraits through the years caught her eye. She picked one up and studied it closely. Zoe looked more like her mother with every passing year. Parker picked up an old family portrait. They'd rented a beach house for the summer. They were all barefoot in the warm sand and bright sun. Nicole was already pregnant with Zoe when the image was taken, making it the only photo that captured the whole family.

She fell onto the piano bench with a thump. The memories of her sister and her during that last summer added to her emotional rollercoaster. They'd been just far enough apart in age to have a stupid teenage rivalry, and they'd never really clicked. Nicole was gone before they had the chance to become friends.

The call to play was strong. It had always soothed her soul. She pulled the cover up just far enough so she could open the keyboard cover. Her fingers stroked over the black and white keys begging her to play. With no one in the house, it didn't matter that she was out of practice and her play rusty at best.

The first chord was tentative. She didn't expect the instrument to be tuned. To her surprise, the first notes weren't horribly out of tune. Someone had obviously cared for the instrument during her absence. The music was muted through the heavy layers of protective covering, but something was slightly off, and it wasn't her playing.

She got up and uncovered the piano. She folded the cover and placed it on a nearby armchair. Opening the piano lid was easier than she'd expected. As soon as she looked inside, she saw what was causing the mild disharmony. A clear plastic tube filled with rolled up paper lay across the strings. *How long has that been there?* Parker pulled off the lid and carefully extracted the contents.

Her hands trembled when she unrolled the pages. All paintings of Parker. She didn't need to see the signature in the lower corner to know it was Kate's work. Her style unique and familiar enough that she would've known who it belonged to without identification.

The first drawing showed her wearing dress blues, holding Kate in her arms wearing a light summer dress. It had never happened, but it was deeply touching that Kate had pictured them together after Parker had left.

It was one of many shared moments between them that had never happened, milestones each of them had spent alone. Another picture showed them in their mid-twenties, maybe. Her and Kate standing under a lady justice statue, probably marking the moment she graduated from law school. The third image of her in uniform with captain's bars, and Kate looking adoringly at her. Another showed them both sitting on the piano bench, playing together in the here and now.

All of the drawings had two things in common: Parker still had longish hair, and there was no visible evidence of Kate's progressing illness.

Parker gathered the drawings, wondering why they were hidden in the piano. Had Kate wanted them to be close to the other family photographs? She propped the first drawing onto the music rack, fiddling for a moment to make sure it stayed upright and didn't tip over. She put the rest of the artwork back into the tube and placed it in a part of the piano where it wouldn't interfere with any strings or her play.

Parker sat back down, the excess energy vibrating beneath her skin had intensified and needed escape. Her hands still shook when they settled back onto the keys, the opening bars of "Ain't No Sunshine" filled the room, the earlier hesitation gone from her play. She paced it slower, the overall pitch lower bordering on the side of jazz.

She focused on the drawing of her and Kate embracing and let her eyes drift closed. The smile on Kate's face was the last thing she concentrated on before she gave herself over to the music. She played for Kate, the memory of them together and the secret teenage love they had shared in a time when society had shunned them.

She sang softly. Her eyes pricked with unshed tears. She carefully pulled back on her self-control and let everything inside her flow out and into the song.

The melody and lyrics reverberated through the room and washed back over her. Goosebumps formed on her arms, and an icy shower ran down her spine. She felt phantom heat permeate the side of her body where Kate used to lean against her as she played for her as a teenager. But the feeling disappeared too soon.

The fear and uncertainty of the past few days bled into her voice and built the intensity of her despair before the music carried it away and the tension ebbed to a level she could endure.

When the last notes faded away, the presence of another person in the room registered. She no longer felt wired, but it had left her raw and exposed. She pulled her self-control back around her like a security blanket, afraid she might need it when she turned around.

Zoe stood in the doorway, open mouthed.

"I'm sorry. I didn't hear you come home." Parker's voice was thick with unshed tears.

"Mom brought me straight home after we had to leave the hospital. I'm not allowed to see my friends. I'm grounded after the school incident, remember?" Zoe shrugged.

"Why didn't you say anything when I called out?"

Zoe slumped against the door frame and buried her hands in her pockets. "I didn't hear you."

"Really?" Parker wondered if Zoe had really not heard her or just plain ignored her.

"I was wearing my headphones." Zoe pointed at the pair hanging around her neck and connected to the phone in her hand.

Zoe seemed irritable tonight, and Parker wasn't sure what had brought that on, though Kate on the verge of life-saving surgery or death was probably a good enough reason.

"I'm just so tired of hearing Grandma and Grandad argue all the time. It seems like it gets worse every year, or maybe I'm just getting more aware of it." Zoe hung her head.

"What do you mean?" Parker turned to face her properly.

"Why do you even care? You disappeared and left me behind!"

"It was never about leaving you behind." Parker exhaled. "It—"

"Have you any idea what it was like here while you were gone? Do you? It was never the same. My birth mother is dead, and her sperm donor never cared enough to learn my name. Do you really think it didn't leave marks on them when Nicole died? Or when they lost you to the military? Or when they've been watching Kate, who they love like a daughter, begin to die?" Zoe sniffed. "Will they get divorced now?"

So that was what had Zoe all twisted up. The Thanksgiving blow-up didn't only affect her and Kate. Even if she was glad everything was finally out in the open, she hadn't thought about the consequences. Zoe was stuck in the middle and couldn't get away. "I'm so sorry, Zoe. I don't have an answer to that."

"I always wished they had to work late so I didn't have to hear them argue all the time." Tears spilled down Zoe's face. "Now Grandad's not home to argue, but I miss him."

Parker's chest tightened, watching Zoe in so much pain. She got up and pulled her into an awkward hug. Zoe wrapped her scrawny arms around Parker in a vice-like grip as if she was afraid she could disappear.

Zoe blinked up at her. "Can I come live with you and Kate if they split up?"

"Um." Parker moved them to the piano bench to give herself some time to come up with an answer that wouldn't hurt Zoe's feelings.

"I'm sure Kate wouldn't mind. She's always been there for me."

Parker shook her head. "Zoe, we—"

"I guess you'll both need time to recover first, huh." Zoe let go of her. "Although, I could help both of you while you get better after the surgery."

"What?"

"Grandma explained to me what's going to happen." Zoe used a sleeve to wipe at her nose. "You're going to have surgery to help Kate get better."

"Yes."

"You'll really do it?" Zoe's voice was suddenly small, like she was afraid to hope. "You won't lose your job and stuff?"

"It'll be up to the Marine Corps if I'm allowed to stay. How do you know that?"

"I heard Grandma and Granddad argue about it in the hospital. I hear a lot of things that they think I don't."

"Be careful with what you hear, not everything is what it seems if you hear it out of context." Parker motioned with her hand. "And of course I'll have the surgery to give Kate a chance to live, even if it means my future has to change."

"You're different from what I imagined you to be." Zoe stared at her for a long time. "I don't remember you much from before. I only know what everyone else told me, and they all see you different. Now I'm not sure any of them really ever saw you at all."

The wisdom from a fourteen-year-old stunned her speechless, but she'd always thought Kate knew her. Her parents knew her as well as any parents could know their child.

"Can you play some more for me, please?" Zoe asked. "Kate always wanted me to hear you play."

They uncoupled from the hug completely, and Parker turned to face the piano. She settled her hands back on the keys and let them find their own melody. She was almost surprised when she heard the opening notes to a song she'd composed herself many years ago. The hesitant notes of friendship drifting on the air slowly grew into a solid base before the first notion of deeper feelings awoke within. The first longing fluttering around the edges and then the kiss, gentle and slow, weaved into the melody. The song enveloped her, absorbed the rest of her tension, and provided an outlet for old and new feelings that coursed through her.

She had no idea how long she was playing when she heard the front door close loudly. She let the melody fade to an end and stilled.

Zoe frantically wiped at some leftover tears that clung to her eye lashes, as though she didn't want anyone else to know that she'd been crying.

"Please don't stop. I've missed that so much." Her mother stood in the doorway.

Without a word, Parker resumed playing. She closed her eyes again and let the melody carry her away once more.

After her mother sent Zoe to bed, Parker beckoned her to the living room. She'd brought down her paperwork to go through it with her mother and tell her what kind of arrangements she'd made in case something didn't go according to plan.

"I know it's a lot to take in, I'm sorry. I changed a few things when I was at the hospital yesterday, so they should no longer cut you off from all the information," Parker said.

"I know it's selfish of me, but I knew that you would go through with this if there was half a chance." Her mother worried the tissue to bits in her hands. "That's why I couldn't tell you. I was so afraid that if something went wrong, I'd lose you too. Hiding behind Kate's wishes was just an easy out."

Her mother didn't meet her gaze and almost flinched away when she reached out and pulled her into a hug. "Oh, Mom."

"You have to understand; it's like being asked to choose between my girls. I just couldn't do it." Her mother sniffled on her shoulder. "Are you mad at me now?"

"No, Mom." She hugged her mother closer before letting go so she could look into her mother's eyes. "I get it. It was an impossible decision to make."

"I should have told you anyway. You had a right to know,

regardless of my need to protect you."

"Yes, you should have. Can you do me a favor and not spend the entire day in the hospital tomorrow? Do something nice with Zoe. There's absolutely nothing you can do for us while we're in surgery. I don't want you to sit there waiting and worrying, Mom."

"I don't think I can promise that. I'm your mom—even you've said that tonight," her mother wiped at the tear that ran down her cheek. "It's a mom's privilege to worry about her children."

She held Parker in a tight embrace and pressed a kiss on the top of her head before she left to go to bed. The tentative support that had come out in the family since their holiday blow-up let her hope for a brighter future.

Chapter Twenty-Eight

PARKER HAD PULLED ON her workout sweats and an old hoodie. There was no sense in wearing anything else since all she would do was take it off again when she arrived at the hospital. She pulled her shoes on as quietly as she could, not wanting to disturb anyone in the house.

Her father said he'd pick her up. She didn't want anyone to come with her since all they could do was sit around and wait. The surgery would take hours, and there was no need for any of them to waste the day.

She turned the key as quietly as she could in the front door, but the bolt snapped back and echoed through the hallway. Before she could manage to pull the door open, light footsteps hurried over the upstairs hallway and rushed down the stairs. Zoe jumped off the bottom step.

"Please be careful. I couldn't bear it if anything happens to you." Zoe buried her face in her shoulder. "I love you, and I don't want to lose you again."

Parker's heart flip-flopped. She hadn't heard Zoe say that since she was four, and she hadn't expected to ever hear it again. "Love you too, pumpkin." The old nickname had come out of nowhere.

"Hey, I think I'm a bit too old to be called *pumpkin*."

They both laughed. "Just a bit." Parker ruffled Zoe's sleep-mussed hair.

"Can I come visit you later?"

Parker picked up her bag. "I'm not sure if that's a good idea."

Zoe made a face. "Please, I need to know you and Kate are okay."

"Why don't you ask your grandma? If she thinks it's a good idea, you can come visit." Parker reached for the door again. "I'm sorry, Zoe, but I really need to go, and you probably should get back to bed."

Her father's car was parked at the curb. They drove to the hospital in virtual silence, and she was grateful for the lack of small talk. It gave her a chance to think. Her nerves were tingling with anticipation and uncertainty. She was sure of her decision but was uncertain of what the future held.

A soft touch at the shoulder startled Parker. "What?"

"You didn't hear a word I said, did you?" Her father looked at her.

She shook her head.

"I didn't think so." He gripped the steering wheel with so much force that his knuckles turned white. "I asked if you wanted me to come inside with you?"

Parker looked up and saw that they were at the front entrance of the hospital. "No, I can make it on my own." She knew he'd hated hospitals ever since Nicole had died in one. She'd been surprised to find him visiting Kate as many times as he did.

"Are you sure? I don't mind coming in with you."

She forced a smile. "Maybe you could use the time to talk to Mom. There's nothing in there you can do. Visit tomorrow if you've got time."

Harry gave her a one-armed hug over the middle console of the car before she got out and walked into the building.

Doctor Hazelwood had given her directions the day before, and she had no trouble finding where she needed to go. A nurse was already waiting for her when she made it to the department and pointed her toward the room she would be staying in.

Kate lay in one bed surrounded by machines and multiple IVs. She looked peaceful. Parker smiled, glad that she had a chance to see Kate before they went into surgery.

"You need to get changed into those." The nurse pointed at

the flimsy hospital gown on the empty bed. "And take these." She gave Parker a cup of pills. "Water is on the table, if you need any, Captain Snow, but only use enough to swallow the pills. You'll be transported to the operating room in an hour. Your left wrist, please."

Parker held out her hand and the nurse fitted a temporary bracelet.

"Here you go. I'll see you when you get out of surgery. You should use the time to get settled the best you can. You'll be with us for a few days."

"Yes, ma'am," Parker said to the nurse's commanding tone, which was familiar and reassuring.

"Don't get smart with me." The nurse gave her a stern look. "One hour." Then she left.

Parker stowed her go-bag in the cupboard beside her bed and locked her phone in the tiny safe inside the closet.

Parker settled on the edge of Kate's bed and took her hand, careful not to disturb any of the attached lines.

"I hope they were gentle when they moved you." Parker stroked the back of Kate's wrist, the only place not covered by tape or stuck with needles.

"We were. We couldn't risk stressing her any more than was absolutely necessary." Commander Hazelwood stood in the door in a white coat with Dr. Miller, who was dressed in civvies.

"Good morning, ma'am." Parker got up and saluted.

"You should get ready." Commander Hazelwood came over to her. "Do you have any last questions for me?"

Parker pointed toward the pills. "Have they taken into account my sensitivity to any kind of medication?"

"They go by your height and weight. No one wants you waking up during the surgery. There's nothing in your medical record that states any allergies. I'm sure everything will be fine."

Parker grimaced.

"She's doing better than we hoped." Dr. Miller inspected an IV bag. "But I'm glad the waiting is over. Her body couldn't take this much longer."

"But she's strong enough for the surgery, right?" Parker asked.

She nodded. "Yes."

Commander Hazelwood gave her the pills and handed her a cup of water. "Take them. We'll monitor you closely."

Parker swallowed the pills with a mouth full of water. "Done."

"I'll wait for you outside," Dr. Miller said.

"See you in a few." Commander Hazelwood took the empty cup from Parker. "You should get changed and lay down. The meds will make you drowsy."

Parker took the gown from the bed and eyed it warily. It didn't leave much to the imagination.

Commander Hazelwood made a couple of notes in a chart. "You'll have laparoscopic surgery today. It'll make recovery easier and should keep your career safe too. You'll feel a bit strange the first couple of days, and you'll be very tired until your body gets used to the changes."

Parker nodded. She'd heard this speech twice already. "Is there anything else I need to know?"

"You need to sign these." She held out some papers. "They're consent forms for the surgery. They also give us permission to continue with old-fashioned open surgery if there are any complications with the laparoscopic method."

Parker knew that too. She skimmed the text before she put her signature underneath and handed it back. "Anything else?"

"No. I'll see you when you get out of surgery." She gathered her things and made her way to the door. She opened it to reveal Parker's mother, Colleen, and Zoe on the other side.

"You should all still be in bed." Parker gathered the things she was supposed to change into, and light-headedness kicked in, telling her that the pills had started working.

Her mother squeezed past Colleen into the room. "You didn't for one moment think I would let you go through this alone. You're my daughter."

"We talked about this, Mom."

"No, you told me what you wanted, and I didn't agree." Her mother stopped in front of her and put her hands on her hips. "Listen to me, Parker Lorraine Snow, you're not shutting us out again."

"Fine." The fuzziness in her head grew, and she wasn't up for the argument. "If it makes you feel better, you can stay. But I need to get changed, so excuse me." She made her way to the tiny bathroom and was glad to close the door between them.

She made quick work of what she had to do in the bathroom. The gown left her too exposed for her liking, and she wished she'd thought to bring a bathrobe. She folded her clothes in a neat pile she could stuff in the closet before she got in bed.

Her hope that she would be alone with Kate when she left the bathroom was short-lived. They were all still there. Zoe had sat down on a chair close to the window, while Colleen was sitting on Kate's bed. Parker's mother was walking up and down the room, radiating nervous energy.

Her mother looked her up and down. "You don't look so well."

"I'm fine." Parker grinned at her. "They have awesome drugs here." Rainbows had started to creep onto the edge of her vision.

"Oh my god, are you high?"

"Not sure. They gave me a bunch of pills." Parker tried to get hold of one of the rainbows to pull it out from her field of vision.

"Oh yes, you're drugged up. Come on. We need to get you into bed." Her mother wrapped her arm around Parker's waist and tried to pull her toward the hospital bed.

"But I don't want to lay down, I want..." She couldn't remember what she wanted to say, and the bed suddenly looked very inviting. "Bed."

Her mother maneuvered Parker into bed and drew the covers up. "See, that's much better, isn't it?"

Parker nodded, no longer able to gather coherent thoughts to speak and let her eyelids drift close.

Loud noises and persistent jarring rose Parker from her drowsy state. Her surroundings had changed, and white lights flashed overhead as she was moved. Where was she going again? Oh, right. The OR for surgery.

"What? Did you say something?" Her mother's face appeared over her.

"Kate."

"Right behind you." Her mother's voice was now disembodied.

Parker turned her head and was able to make out another moving shadow a little behind her. She wanted to reach out, but her body wouldn't obey her command, and her arm fell uselessly back to her side.

Her mother was there in an instant and picked up her hand. She squeezed it gently. "Everything will be fine. Stop fighting the medication and sleep."

Parker swam through the muddy dregs of her brain. Nothing much made sense. Where was she? Hospital. Why? She got shot. Nope, that was a while back. *Think, Parker, think.* Kate. She was here to help Kate. The tension eased, and an invisible pull started to drag her down again when the movement suddenly stopped.

"I'm sorry, Mrs. Snow. This is as far as you're allowed to go," someone said above her head.

"Can you give us a moment?" her mother asked.

"One minute. The surgeons are getting ready."

"Don't disappear on me," her mother whispered and tried to hug her.

"Okay," the man said, "we need to go."

"Come back to me."

"Semper fi," Parker whispered.

Chapter Twenty-Nine

VOICES DRIFTED IN AND out, and nothing made sense. Parker tried to hold on to single words, but they ran through her mind like water through open hands and faded away too quickly to understand.

She had no idea how much time had passed when more words seeped into her mind. The voice was familiar, but the words didn't make much more sense. But something was distantly familiar about them, like she hadn't heard the voice in a while. She clung to the familiarity, and let it pull her in. The moment she stopped trying, the voice got clearer, and the words fell together into a sentence she started to understand.

"Is it normal that she's sleeping so much? She hasn't been awake since she came out of surgery."

"She was awake briefly after the surgery. I was there and talked to her," someone else said.

Parker had no recollection of being awake and talking to whoever that voice belonged to. She squeezed her eyes tighter and tried to remember her last clear thought. It took a while for her mind to come up with anything but eventually, it started to come back to her.

"This isn't normal, Dr. Hazelwood."

So, the second voice belonged to Dr. Hazelwood, the commander. She'd spoken to Parker after the surgery. How long ago had that been, and why did her body not want to obey her? She wanted to open her eyes and tell them that she could hear every word, but nothing happened.

"Mrs. Snow, I know you're worried. It's not uncommon for people to sleep so long after this type of surgery."

Why hadn't Parker recognized her own mother's voice? Was she that out of it?

"I haven't seen her awake or even move since you brought her back from surgery yesterday," her mother said. "That's too long, surely?"

Something distorted the sound in Parker's left ear. Maybe that's why she hadn't recognized her mother's voice. Something also irritated her cheek, but it wasn't enough to make her body move. Why couldn't she just open her eyes? It was like her brain was awake, but her body was still in deep sleep.

"I suspect that your daughter hasn't rested much at all recently," Dr. Hazelwood said. "Every person reacts slightly different. I'm certain she'll be fine as soon as her body has had a chance to rest up and get used to the changes. She's young and healthy, and she'll bounce back quickly once she's fully awake."

"You really think waiting is the best thing we can do?"

Parker drifted off again before she could hear an answer.

***

The next thing that caught Parker's attention was a sharp knock.

"It's nice to see you again, Mrs. Snow."

Parker immediately recognized Kid's voice. When she got out of here, she needed to encourage him to apply for the bar. He had the skills no doubt, but they both knew he was procrastinating.

"Lieutenant Callahan, I wish I could say the same. Are you here on behalf of your sister?" Her mother's voice was icy.

"No, Mrs. Snow. I'm here to see how my partner is. She saved my life, didn't she tell you that? I had nothing to do with what my sister did, and she'll have to answer for her actions. But I'm not here to talk about her. How's Parker doing?"

Parker heard shoes squeak and imagined Kid shifting from one foot to the other like he did when she called him out on something. It was something she'd never seen him do around anyone else.

"I'm not sure," her mother said. "She's not been awake since the surgery."

"Parker is stubborn, she'll be okay. She dragged me and my co-pilot out of a crashed chopper even though she was told not to go back because it was on fire and was about to blow up. I owe her."

"Would you like to sit with her for a while?"

"I would very much like that," Kid said. "She waited for me when I came out of surgery after they shipped us back to Germany. She made sure I didn't wake up alone."

A calloused hand closed around hers.

"You aren't alone, you hear me, Raven?"

She fought against the maelstrom that wanted to keep her under, but her body wouldn't budge. Her eyes stayed closed. She couldn't even make her hand squeeze back. The harder she tried, the harder it seemed to become. She drew a long and even breath and was relieved that at least that part of her body complied with some form of voluntary command.

"You were there with her, weren't you?" her mother asked, her voice trembling.

"Excuse me?"

"When my daughter was kidnapped."

Parker felt him tense through his hands around hers.

"Yes." His one-word reply was clipped.

"What happened?"

"That's need to know," he said.

"*I* need to know," her mother said, a hint of steel in her voice. "I sometimes think I don't recognize my own daughter anymore."

That wasn't a surprise to hear. After ten years apart, how could they know each other? They hadn't much talked about how they felt toward each other; everything had revolved around Kate since she came back. In her mind the incident had little to do with her parents. Their relationship had suffered long before that. She didn't think what had happened had impacted that at all.

Kid had struggled a lot in the beginning. They weren't supposed to tell anyone what had happened, and it had weighed on him.

"Please," her mother said.

Parker knew Kid's hesitation on a subconscious level and wished once more that she could break out and say something herself.

"Mrs. Snow, I hope my mother will never learn the details of what happened to us. Not because I don't trust her with the information, but because I love her and wouldn't want her to have my nightmares. None of us can change the past. We can only make different decisions in the future. Be there for Parker when she needs support and give her space when she needs to process. That's the best my family could do for me, and I'm sure Parker would appreciate the same thing."

Parker was glad he hadn't given into her mother's pleas. The relief that washed through her body threatened to pull her under again. Her subconscious startled when music started to play out of nowhere. It took her no time at all to recognize her own song, the one she'd played on the piano for Zoe the night before she went into the hospital. She must've recorded it.

"Zoe, turn your phone off. Now," her mother said.

"I'm sorry, Mom, it's just a message about homework."

It was Kate's love song. The melody stopped, and she missed it. She wanted to know how it would continue now that Kate had the surgery. *Oh right, it'll only continue if I compose a new movement.* For that, she needed to wake up, now. And before she did any of that, she needed to find Kate and bring her home.

Chapter Thirty

SOMETHING WAS DIFFERENT WHEN Parker's senses engaged this time. The sludge in her head was mostly gone, and the distinctively musky scent in the room was new. She had a visitor that hadn't been in her room before, at least not while she'd been trapped somewhere between wakefulness and sleep.

There was another essence in the room, faint and almost hidden by the smell of disinfectant. But she was sure it was there, the fragrance she would always associate with Kate. Other sensations registered in Parker's mind. Her back hurt all over, and her lower abdomen was throbbing. Even breathing was slightly uncomfortable.

"Will she be okay? I can't believe they didn't tell me that she wasn't awake."

Kate sounded strong. *It worked*. Relief washed over her.

A low chuckle came from her other side. "Take it easy, Kate, you're not technically supposed to be out of bed yet," a man said.

"Is Parker going to come through this unscathed?" Kate caressed Parker's cheek. "I couldn't forgive myself if there are consequences because of what she's done for me."

"She'll be fine. She's almost ready to wake up, I'm sure," someone said. "You should have some time with her, but you have to be honest about your own limitations. We can't risk you overdoing it."

Parker felt the hesitation in Kate even though she couldn't see her. Kate was probably trying to weigh the consequences if she didn't leave when she got tired. Parker hoped that Kate wouldn't take any stupid chances.

"Okay," Kate said.

The sheets on her left moved and Parker felt soft, warm fingers on her hip, leaving a fiery trail. Parker's muscles fluttered and twitched under Kate's delicate touch. A dull ache radiated from her lower abdomen, but it ebbed away when her muscles relaxed again.

"What are you doing? Looking to see if we didn't forget to put the bandages in place?" the guy asked.

Kate pulled her fingers back. "Um, no."

Cool air hit Parker's overheated skin. A shiver ran down her spine. Kate's fingers traced the old scar where her skin was hypersensitive and gave her a jolt. Her eyes were still closed, but the fog in her brain was gone, and for the first time since she'd gone into surgery, she felt like she could really open her eyes if she tried.

"I need to know that her art is still okay." Kate's finger traced the outline of her tattoo. "I know it's silly, but I feel like she has someone to watch over her, even if she wakes up alone. It makes me feel connected to her somehow, knowing that she has a piece of me on her skin." Kate's hand settled over the ink raised skin like she wanted to protect the tattoo from prying eyes.

"It's not as silly as you think," he said. "I haven't walked in your shoes, but you obviously care a great deal for her. I can see it in your eyes."

Kate gave a light laugh. "It's that obvious, huh?"

Parker felt the sheet being tugged back into place, and the slight chill receded. The male voice sounded familiar, but she had trouble placing it. It was like she knew him, but his appearance would be so unlikely that her mind simply refused to make the connection.

Parker made a deliberate effort to open her eyes, but they wouldn't budge. Like someone had glued them shut. She balled her hands into fists in frustration.

"She moved. I'm sure she moved." Kate's fingers closed around her hand and lifted it. "I'm not going back now. I want a little more time." She brushed her lips over Parker's knuckles and placed a trail of tiny kisses down the back of her hand to her wrist. "Can you hear me, Parker?"

Yes, I can hear you. She couldn't say it out loud, but she managed to pry her eyes open and blinked against the bright fluorescent light overhead. Everything around her was blurred, and she couldn't make out much more than broad shapes. She turned her head toward Kate's voice. She spotted her seated next to the bed but could only make out her red hair shining like a beacon against her pale face.

"Hey, sleepy head, welcome back." Kate squeezed her hand. "You gave me quite the scare."

Someone moved on her other side, and she heard quiet tapping against a surface, as if someone was checking the readout on a machine. Parker swallowed, and it felt like she had broken glass stuck in her throat. "Sorry." Her voice was hoarse. Her vision started to clear. She could make out the worry lines around Kate's eyes and mouth.

"How are you?" Kate let go of her hand and touched her cheek.

Parker breathed in deeply and tried to move to assess her body. Everything seemed to be in working order, though she still felt sluggish, and movement was slow. She also allowed herself to acknowledge the pain and followed it back to its origin. It wasn't as bad as she'd thought it might be. It was more like a dull ache after a strenuous work out. "I'm fine, I think. I'm a little uncomfortable, but I'm not in any real pain. I guess whatever they're giving me is really great in taking care of that."

A laugh came from her other side. "They've taken you off most of that, so you probably won't feel so great soon enough. I told them about our hypersensitivity to drugs and pain killers. In this case, they seemed to make you sleep a lot."

Now it made sense. "Mark?" She smiled when her brother came into focus. "It's more like they stuck me in a fucked-up suspended space between sleep and alertness." Parker immediately regretted speaking when her throat hurt more than the rest of her.

Mark came closer and used the bed controls to move her to a seated position. He held a cup with a straw. "Here you go. Small sips, so you don't throw up."

She grunted. The first tentative sip of the ice-cold liquid running down her throat felt like heaven. She wanted to drink down the entire cup, but she heeded Mark's warning and stopped when the cold liquid had numbed her throat. "Thanks."

"I'll leave that here." He put the cup on the small bedside table. "Just take it slow. How are you feeling?"

"A little fuzzy still. Like my mind and motor function don't inhabit the same body."

"You didn't cope too well with the morphine, I'm afraid." He scratched his five o'clock shadow. "Didn't that come up during the pre-op?"

"I told them." She looked back at Kate, searching for her hand on the bed, and entwined their fingers.

"I guess it wasn't in your medical file, so they didn't take it too seriously," Mark said. "It should have been noted down in your permanent file after the surgery in Germany."

Kate yawned, and she blinked a couple of times.

"Hey, are you okay, honey? You look really tired." Parker brought Kate's hand to her lips and kissed it. Kate gave her a sleepy smile so beautiful that it made Parker's heart race.

"I'm doing so much better." Kate took her hand again and kissed the back of it. "I just tire easily, but that's nothing new."

"You're really doing okay?"

"Yes, I'm doing fine. I'm sore. They had me walk a few steps today, but I hardly made it to the bathroom. The doctors said it looks really positive, and they have me on about a dozen different medications so your liver can feel at home with me."

Parker smiled. There was little indication left that she was barely able to follow simple commands a few days earlier.

"I should go, but I don't want to leave you."

"I'm not going anywhere, not again. I'll be right here tomorrow."

Mark came around the bed and disengaged the brakes on the wheelchair Kate sat in.

Kate held onto Parker's hand like she didn't want to let go. "Sweet dreams. Don't you dare not wake up tomorrow. We've got so much to talk about."

"I'll be here, I promise." Parker sighed as she watched Mark wheel Kate away. Warmth spread through her heart at the sight of some of her family together. She would be here tomorrow, and the next day, and the day after that. She was going to be there for Kate forever.

Chapter Thirty-One

PARKER WOKE RESTED AND with a clear head early the next morning. The pain had reduced to a dull throbbing she could manage, as long as she didn't try to move too much. She hadn't said anything last night, but she'd been a bit worried when Mark told her that she'd been taken off most of the pain medication.

A myriad of nurses and doctors came and went throughout the morning, each one needing something else from her or making sure she was doing okay. Dr. Hazelwood apologized that she hadn't taken Parker's claim to be oversensitive to most medications more seriously. Part of Parker wanted to be angry, but she understood that they had to be cautious with information that wasn't on her medical records. She'd made sure her affliction would be noted formally.

"Can I check your wounds before I leave?" Dr. Hazelwood made a note in the chart she was holding.

"Sure." Parker pushed down the sheet and revealed the god-awful hospital gown. She needed to find something else to put on. This thing made her feel half naked. She supposed there was little they hadn't seen, but she wanted to go to the bathroom without baring her entire backside to the world.

"This may sting a bit." Dr. Hazelwood lifted the corner of one of the smaller bandages right under her sternum.

Parker watched what she was doing. The bandage came off and left a light orange frame around the incision that was held closed with a neat duo of two black knots. They seemed to have bathed her abdomen in that strange orange stuff they used to prep the surgery area. She couldn't wait to take a shower and wash it off.

"It all looks good." Dr. Hazelwood placed a new bandage on the first of the small incisions. "These will barely leave a scar if you care for them properly as they heal." She moved onto the big bandage now and repeated the process.

It hurt more than the others but was nothing she couldn't handle. At four and a half inches, this one was held closed by an ant-like row of black stitches. A bit of blue thread poked out at either end and something that looked like sticky tape was plastered all over the bright red incision line.

Dr. Hazelwood cleaned the wound before she placed a new bandage on it. "It's important that those stay dry and clean, captain."

Parker nodded. "Can you tell me how Kate is doing?"

"No." Dr. Hazelwood made a few more notes in her chart. "I know she probably wouldn't mind me telling you, but I don't have her permission and I haven't managed to check in on her today. I know she came through surgery with flying colors and is recovering remarkably quickly. But I don't know anything more specific."

Damn. Parker needed specifics. She couldn't bear not knowing how Kate was, but it wasn't like she could get up and go find out. "Could you ask someone to let me know, please?"

Dr. Hazelwood nodded. "I'm sure another member of your family will be there. I'll tell them. Now get some rest so *you* can make a quick recovery too."

"Sure thing, Doc." Parker released a breath and settled back into bed. All she could do was wait.

***

A knock and a loud bang startled Parker out of her drowsy state. When the doctors told her she would feel tired and exhausted after surgery, she hadn't taken them too seriously, but they were right. Her sleep had been restful, thankfully. The last time she'd been unconscious under pain meds, her demons had free rein of her subconsciousness, and it had driven her to the edge of despair.

An orderly rolled Kate in, on a hospital bed, and a nurse followed, rolling some fancy looking machines in behind them. He positioned the bed beside Parker, and the nurse hooked Kate up to them. The nurse completed some checks and adjusted the IV drip before they both left the room.

"Hey, darling, how are you doing today?" Kate turned to look over toward Parker.

Parker's heart fluttered in her chest. Kate had called her that the night before, but Parker hadn't registered it with her addled state of mind. "I'm much better. Thanks for asking." She smiled at Kate and reached out, but Kate was too far away for them to touch. "How are you doing?"

"This is keeping me happy." Kate pointed to the IV bag. "The doc says I'm doing remarkably well. None of them had expected me to bounce back so quickly."

Parker wondered how often Kate had worried about her condition and the long-term effects it could have on her. A part of her wanted to ask, while another didn't think she had the right to intrude that way into Kate's personal life. Until now, their relationship had been in that weird, suspended state based on the assumption that Kate's time was running out. But now things had changed, and Parker had no idea where she stood.

"Penny for your thoughts."

Kate gave her one of her half smiles that had melted Parker's heart as a teenager. It still did.

The door opened, and her mother looked in. "Oh, Parker, you're finally awake! And Kate is back too. This is wonderful."

She walked in and dropped her handbag on the small table beneath the window. Parker looked back to the door to see her father enter. He closed the door behind him and took a seat quietly. She hadn't expected to see both parents in the same room anytime soon. Had they patched things up already?

"Where's Colleen?" Kate asked. "I didn't see her yesterday or today."

"I'm so sorry, honey," Parker's mother said. "Colleen isn't feeling well. She saw her doctor yesterday, and he thinks it's just general exhaustion, but with you fresh out of surgery, no one wants to take the risk that she may be sick and give you something."

"I understand." Kate's smile faltered.

Parker looked around. "Where's Zoe?" She'd expected Zoe to insist on visiting them.

"We were told to be careful because of Kate's immune system being suppressed after the transplant. Harry and I thought it best if she didn't come here in case she'd picked something up at school or from her friends."

"Bet that didn't go over so well." Kate pulled up her blanket like she wanted an extra layer of protection.

Her mother huffed. "I swear she's turning out to be the hardest of all of you with her teenage rebellions. She got angry and told us she won't talk to us until you're both home."

Parker laughed. "Are you sure about that, Mom? Maybe you don't remember the things Nicole and I got up to?" She looked at Kate, who blushed pink. They'd gotten up to quite some mischief, but if they were caught, Parker always covered for Kate.

"Mm, possibly." Her mother made a dismissive gesture with her hand and went back to her bag. She pulled Parker's iPad out and placed it on the nightstand next to her. "I brought this yesterday, but I didn't want to leave it while you were still sleeping. I was afraid someone might take it."

Parker nodded. "It's all good. I just want it to look for apartments. I still need a place to stay when I get out of here."

"Our door is always open for you, Parker," her father said. "I know it's not been easy in the past, but it's your home."

"Thanks, Dad. I appreciate it, really. But I need my own place. It'd be great if I could stay until I'm fit enough to move." There was no way she could stay at home. This was the first assignment in a long time where she wouldn't have to share her living space, and she was looking forward to setting up her own place. "I'll be staying for a while, so I'm looking for an affordable place nearby." She had no intentions of moving so far away that she wouldn't see them regularly and easily. After Kate, Zoe was a huge reason why she wanted to stay close. She'd already missed too much of her life.

"You could move in next door," her father said and smiled. "The old Madame Fourie place is empty, and the ground floor is freshly renovated following Kate's design plans. It's plenty big enough for you and Kate—if you wanted to recover together." He glanced at Parker's mother. "And then your piano's close by if it started calling to you again. Helen told me she heard you playing the other night."

"Please say yes, Parker," Kate whispered. "I want you close."

She shrugged. "I guess that's a yes, Dad."

"To be fair, the upstairs is a bit of a work in progress. But the downstairs bedroom is done." Her father sat down in one of the visitor chairs. "And I hope you'll really come over to play. I've missed your beautiful music around the house."

"I'm just sorry I missed the whole performance. Zoe hasn't been able to shut up about it since," her mother said. "We've both really missed your music."

She joined her dad and put her arm around his waist. It looked like they'd had some time to sort things out, after all. Parker could tell that her mother meant they'd been missing more than just the music. It was clearly her way to encourage Parker to take her dad's offer without pressuring her.

"You didn't tell me you still played piano." Kate looked at her almost accusingly.

Parker shook her head. "We've had more important things to worry and talk about than me playing again."

"Crap. We could've talked about it anytime. I wanted to ask you to play for me, but I didn't want you to feel obligated." Kate bit her lower lip.

"I played the night before the surgery. It was the first and only time I've played since I came back." Parker felt heat creep up her neck. "And it shows." Finding Kate's artwork hidden inside the instrument had inspired most of her play that night.

"It was beautiful," her mother said.

Parker smiled at Kate. "If you don't mind a few off-key tones, I'll be happy to play for you when we get out of here."

Kate beamed at her. "I'm looking forward to that. As long as I can sit right next to you on the piano bench...like I used to." Kate winked.

Parker's heart fluttered in her chest. *Was Kate flirting?* Parker nodded, unable to respond with words.

"I'm sure those few off-key notes will go away with a little practice. I'd love to keep you company."

Parker swallowed hard. She wanted to change the subject—with her parents in the room, flirting wasn't really on the agenda. Her heart beat into her throat, and she was afraid she would blush when she looked at her mother. "You two look like you've made up."

They looked at each other, but neither said anything. Parker watched with interest. She'd learned to read people over the years, and she could see them conferring without exchanging an actual word. It made her long to have the same kind of deep understanding with another person, with Kate.

Her mother cleared her throat. "I was here when they brought you out of surgery, and I knew something wasn't right. They told me you were just sleeping off the remains of the anesthesia, but you were too still, too deeply asleep. A mother can tell, you know."

"She called me," her father said. "I came immediately. When you'd hadn't woken up by the time Kate was alert, we called Mark and asked him to come."

"I don't think I would have known what to do if Mark hadn't been able to explain to us what was happening with you," her mother said.

"Good thing our son became a doctor and that he found us when he did." He embraced her mother.

"After the doctors listened to what Mark had to say and reduced your meds, your father and I sat next to your bed for hours. If that damn monitor over your bed hadn't been bleeping away, showing you were still alive, I would have lost it." Her mother dropped into the chair beside her father.

"That's the funny thing about clarity," her father suddenly said. "We're so often blinded by expectations and perception that we lose sight of what's really important in life."

Her mother nodded. "I was so angry at him that I didn't let myself see what happened through his eyes. I'd been equally frustrated with your moping after the breakup. What if I'd been the one who'd told you to clear your head? What if my words had made you leave? Would I have told him what was said in the heat of the moment? Would I have gone after you to apologize? I'd like to think that I would. Hindsight is always twenty-twenty. We were all so hung up on the fact that you two practically grew up as sisters. We should have protected you and focused on the fact that you aren't related." She took his hand. "Your father is my rock. I've loved him since I was sixteen years old. He's been with me during the good times, and he's carried me through the bad times. Without him, I would never have made it through the depression I had after I had to give up Mark and then again when Nicole died. Seeing you in that hospital bed, still and unresponsive, scared the shit out of me, Parker."

Kate yelped, and her hand flew to her mouth. They'd never heard Parker's mother swear before.

"All of this has given me clarity on a few things." Her mother let out a long breath. "A mother can only hope that her children find someone to share their lives with, a partner that gives them the same love and support I received." Her mother looked between Parker and Kate. "If that's what you are to each other, who are we to judge you?" Her mother let go of her father's hand, reached into her handbag, and pulled something out. She walked over to Kate and held out what she had taken out of her bag. "Colleen said you'd want this back as soon as you got out of the ICU."

Kate took the necklace and held it against her chest. "Thank you. This always made me feel whole when Parker wasn't around."

Parker turned her mother's words over in her head, her thoughts going in too many directions. She couldn't settle on one train of thought long enough to follow it through to its conclusion. But the one thing that shone out to her was that she and Kate finally had her parents' blessing. If they wanted it, they could be together, with no judgment and no shame. Her heart skipped. If her giving up a piece of her liver was all it was going to take to get here, she wished she'd done it years ago.

Chapter Thirty-Two

THE EARLY MORNING SUN danced on Parker's face and warmed her skin. She slowly moved from early morning drowsiness to wakefulness. It'd been a quiet night, and she felt rested.

Parker stretched her body carefully. She knew how she could move or turn without creating too much discomfort. The nurses thought she was exceptionally stubborn when she'd refused any additional pain medication before sleep. She heard steps and opened her eyes, turning her head to see Kate coming from their bathroom.

The bright sunshine made her blink a couple of times to adjust to the sudden light intensity. But what she saw was well worth the momentary discomfort. Kate had turned her back to her and was looking out the window into the waking day. The golden-orange morning light formed a halo of light around her. Kate's sleep-mussed hair looked like it was on fire and was the most beautiful thing Parker had ever woken up to.

Kate had replaced her hospital gown with Parker's gray T-shirt and her cut off sweats. Parker had tried wearing both items yesterday, but the elastic was too close to her bandages. She turned onto her side and savored the magnificent view for as long as she could before her position became too uncomfortable. It looked like Kate was in a world of her own, and Parker didn't want to startle her out of it, but she was curious about what captured Kate's attention so completely.

She came up behind Kate and gently placed her hands on Kate's hips.

Kate tilted her head to one side and looked back over her

shoulder. "Good morning, sleepy head. I was wondering how much of the day you were going to sleep away."

Kate's smile warmed Parker from the inside out and made her forget that their room was a little cold, particularly since she was only wearing a tank top and nothing on her feet.

"Good morning to you." Parker rested her chin on Kate's shoulder and looked outside. "What's fascinating you this morning?"

Kate moved back until her back just barely touched Parker's front. "I'm looking at today."

"Today?"

"I've spent so much of my life worrying about tomorrow and the what ifs that I've been neglecting the todays, the here and now. And I sacrificed the best thing in my life by telling you to leave." Kate's whisper didn't hide the tremor in her voice.

Her entire body trembled against Parker's. She took a deep breath and dared to hope that what had happened over the past few days had given them the power to change their future. Parker was sure of her feelings and her hopes to share that future with Kate, but that didn't mean Kate felt the same way in the light of a new day.

"What I want to say is—"

Parker held her hand up. "Let me go first, please."

Kate half-turned. "Okay."

"I need you to know that this," Parker touched her own and Kate's bandages softly, "doesn't mean you owe me anything, Kate. I need you to understand that I don't expect anything from you— you're not beholden to me."

The expression on Kate's face went blank before it changed into something that Parker had a hard time interpreting. It made her feel even more uneasy. Kate turned and looked at her.

She looked sad. "What if I want you to expect something from me?" Kate's lower lip trembled, and she bit down on it. Kate took her mother's Claddagh wedding band from her necklace. "I want you to have my mother's ring back." She held it out to Parker. "I never wanted it back in the first place. It belongs to you."

Parker wanted to take it, badly. She'd missed it. But she didn't want it as payment or out of pity. She shook her head, but Kate took hold of Parker's hands. She wanted to ask if having it meant the same thing as it had before Parker left. Did it come with the same commitment Kate had once given her? But the words stuck in her throat.

The heat radiating from Kate's fingers on her right wrist were in stark contrast to the cool metal Kate slipped onto Parker's finger. Kate looked deep into Parker's eyes and held it up for Parker to see.

"See, still fits you perfectly," Kate said.

Parker swallowed against the sudden dryness in her mouth. "You should turn it around."

Kate glanced away and her shoulders sagged slightly. "Have you already forgotten what it means if I turn it so the heart will face you?"

"No, I haven't." She shook her head. "My heart *is* taken." Heat crept up her neck.

"Oh." Kate sighed deeply and smiled, but it didn't reach her eyes. "Do I know her?" The sadness in Kate's face seemed to be replaced by curiosity.

Parker closed her eyes. "I'm not quite sure if she wants me. But you still hold my heart, Kate. You always have. It's okay if you don't feel the same way, but I want you to know." Parker didn't dare open her eyes.

"Look at me," Kate whispered. "Open your eyes, I want to see your gorgeous baby blues."

She squinted through one eye.

"Open the other one too, please." Kate tugged on the hem of her tank.

Parker opened her other eye to see Kate's smile radiate brighter than the early morning sun.

"My darling Parker, you stole my heart when I was fourteen years old, and I never took it back. What's happened over the past decade and the past few days hasn't changed a thing for me, and I want you to hold my heart forever. I love you." Kate took Parker's hand and turned the ring around.

Parker cupped Kate's cheek gently and brushed her thumb over her soft skin. She looked into Kate's eyes and marveled at all the emotions and feelings, the love and tenderness, that were laid bare for her to see. She wanted to shake herself for not seeing it before. She leaned down and inhaled the scent that was so distinctively Kate. A fiery trail ran down her chest and settled in the depth of her belly. It was pleasantly humming when she leaned in even closer and pressed her forehead against Kate's. This moment, this simple connection made Parker feel like she had finally come home, her home.

Kate brushed her lips over Parker's to deepen their connection. Her hands settled on Parker's hips, and Parker wrapped her arms around Kate in a tentative embrace. She didn't want to ruin the moment by causing Kate any pain.

"Are you okay?" Kate drew away.

"Yes, why?"

"Because you're crying."

Parker reached up and found the traitorous wetness on her cheeks. "I'm just so very happy." She wiped the moisture away. "It won't all be easy, I know that. We're very different people to who we were a decade ago."

"I'm not naïve." Kate kissed Parker's cheek. "But we've got time to find out who we both are now. You might not want me in a few weeks when you realize that I'm not that great a catch—unemployed and on sick leave for the foreseeable future."

Parker laughed and regretted it immediately, when pain shot through her body. "I disagree. You're amazing. And it's not like I don't come with baggage. Who knows what lies ahead for my career."

"I still can't believe that you risked everything for me."

"Believe it. And believe that I won't ever walk away from you again." Parker took Kate's face between her hands and tenderly brushed her lips over Kate's. Their kiss deepened and chased the pain, uncertainty, and misunderstanding of the past days, the past decade, away. Kate held her tighter as if she knew that would ease the heartache they'd both been through.

Parker pulled up for air. "You're my everything, Kate. I love you, and I'm going to spend the next sixty years showing you how much you mean to me."

Epilogue

Six months later – Memorial Day Weekend

PARKER SAT AT THE baby grand piano in her and Kate's living room playing the recent addition she'd composed to continue their story. It had been almost too hard to capture the pain and despair their separation and Kate's illness had cost them both. She'd almost refused to include it in the music, but Kate had insisted it was part of their story and without it becoming part of the composition, their story would be incomplete. Kate sat next to her countless hours until they'd both worked their emotions into the piece, the heavy melody climaxing and breaking into something soft and hopeful through their recovery. The sounds slowly grew stronger as their strength and connection did the same. The last notes reverberated through the room and faded away through the open patio door.

"It becomes more beautiful each time you play it." Kate leaned into Parker's side and captured her lips in a soft kiss.

"You become more beautiful with each day," Parker said and stole another kiss before she tugged a loose lock of Kate's shiny red hair behind her ear. "It was a wonderful surprise from Mom and Dad to have the baby grand moved over here."

When they'd been released from the hospital after the transplant surgery, they'd moved into the neighboring house to recover and be close to their family. When Parker had seen what Kate had done to the place, she'd fallen in love with it all over again. Three months into their recovery, Kate had drawn up plans for the second-floor renovations, letting her know, a little sheepishly, that there would be an art studio where the upstairs sitting room had been.

"That was beautiful, but Granddad wants me to let you know that the guests are arriving," Zoe said as she wiped at the corners of her eyes.

"Thank you." Parker turned to Kate. "Are you ready?"

"For a BBQ cookout with all our family and friends?" Kate laughed, and the sound made Parker's heart flutter in her chest. "As long as I have you by my side, I'm ready for anything." She tugged Parker from the piano bench and handed her a wrapped package.

"What's that?" She took the object and gently shook it.

"Open it and you'll see," Kate said and walked off toward their kitchen. "I'll get the pasta salad from the fridge and you, darling, need shoes."

Parker unwrapped the package to find it was the painting of her and Kate sitting at the piano, the one she'd propped up on the sheet music stand when she played the night before the surgery. Now it sat in a silver frame.

"Do you like it?" Kate asked when she came back with a bowl in her hands.

Parker placed the frame carefully on the piano. "It's very thoughtful. I love your art, you know that. I just wish you would let me support you so you could paint full-time."

"I know, and I love you for that. And maybe I'll let you one day, but I enjoy my job as an interior designer too. I always have."

Kate had started working full-time again six weeks ago. Her medical checkups went well, and she'd recovered quicker than the doctors had thought possible.

When they made it outside, guests where already milling though the yard. Her dad had taken down the fence between their backyards when the weather had improved. It made going from one place to the other even easier, and the opened space was perfect for the cookout.

Kate radiated with happiness next to her as they walked hand-in-hand to greet people.

"You can relax," Kate whispered into her ear. "I'll let you know when I get tired so you can rescue me. That may be sooner than you think." Kate grinned mischievously and bit her bottom lip.

When she looked at Kate now, it was hard to believe she'd been on Death's doorstep just six months ago. Her skin color was almost completely back to normal and her too-skinny body had filled out a little in all the right places. Heat raced through Parker's body, and she swallowed hard. In that cream-colored sun dress, Kate looked downright divine.

"Don't look at me like that." Kate elbowed her softly. "Or I'll be the one dragging *you* inside."

"Bossy." Parker melted. When they'd reached the state in their recovery where there were no longer restrictions, Kate showed her how she intended to make up for lost time, and they'd barely emerged from the bedroom for sustenance.

Mark walked up to them with Ben by his side. "How are my two favorite sisters?"

"Great, how are you?" Kate asked.

Mark and her parents had fallen into an easy relationship throughout her and Kate's recovery, and it had transformed into a real family bond. He and Ben were fully accepted as part of the family and now split holidays between them and Ben's family.

Mark leaned in. "You passed your last checkup with flying colors. You're fully recovered, and there will be no restrictions on your service. You'll get the official notification in a few days."

Parker felt Kate stiffen. She put her arm around Kate's waist and pulled her against her side. Kate seemed to relax a little. She didn't want Parker to leave the service, but she struggled with the dangers inherent in Parker's role. A clean bill of health meant she could be sent on deployment again, and she hadn't yet figured out how to soothe Kate's worries about that. One thing for sure, she wouldn't be volunteering for that anytime soon. But if they sent her orders, she could hardly refuse.

"Thank you, Mark." Parker gave him a one-armed hug. "I'm

grateful to be deemed fully recovered."

They talked a little while longer before they went for something to eat. The amount of food her parents had prepared was unbelievable. But then she looked at the plates piled high by their guests and worried that it might not be enough.

She saw Admiral Pike talking to her father while her dad kept the grill going. Kate had invited her co-workers, who were all very happy to have her back. Parker left her to catch up with them and ran inside their house to get some sodas. She'd thought that days like this, with all the alcohol around, would be a challenge, but they really weren't. The bigger challenge was to find something non-alcoholic to drink. The few sodas her mother had put out had flown off the drinks' table.

The embargo on alcohol after the surgery was temporary for her but permanent for Kate. She'd never been much of a drinker, and she'd happily given it up entirely.

Kate met her halfway back, took one of the cans from her, and drank from it greedily. "I really needed this. All the talking is making me thirsty."

"Me too." Parker had downed a glass of water in the kitchen before coming back out.

"Hey, where did you find those?" Zoe ran up to them and pointed at the Coke can in Parker's hand. "I wanted to get one for Melody and me, but there aren't any in Grandma's kitchen.

Zoe's friend Melody joined them, but she didn't make eye contact.

"Hi," Melody said, barely loud enough to be heard over the chatter filling the backyard.

She seemed painfully shy. Parker had realized that Zoe and Melody were as good as inseparable when she'd recovered enough to focus on something more than Kate and herself. She looked over the crowd and saw Melody's two moms talking to her mother at the other end of the yard.

"Check our kitchen. The patio door is pulled closed so no one wanders in there, but it's not locked." Parker thumbed over her shoulder toward the house.

The two were off in an instant.

Kate laughed. "Teenagers. Zoe only seems to have two speeds: fast and faster. I wish I had that much energy."

Parker laughed too. She just hoped they wouldn't forget to close the door again. With Kate on immune suppressants, they'd decided it would be better if they controlled who went into their house.

"Who is that?" Parker motioned toward the tall, middle-aged woman who stepped out of her parents' house and looked around like she was a little lost.

They watched as Colleen appeared at the woman's side, took her hand, and tugged her away toward a secluded part of the yard.

Kate grinned at her. "I think that's the woman who has Colleen smiling every time her phone pings with a new message lately."

"Oh?"

"They met at a conference, but I don't know her name or what she does." Kate shrugged. "It doesn't matter, as long as Colleen is happy. I want her to find the same happiness we have. She put her life on hold long enough."

Something hit Parker at the back of her leg, and she turned around. A wooden cube with numbers painted on it lay at her feet.

"What's that?" Kate asked and picked it up.

She raised an eyebrow at her and tilted her head to the blanket not far away where baby Katelyn and Linda sat. While little Katelyn stretched her arm out toward Kate, Linda tried very hard to look everywhere but at them.

"Did you lose something, sailor?" Parker asked. She took the cube from Kate and tossed it at Linda.

Linda raised her hands in surrender. "Hey, I couldn't risk you two corrupting my kid. You're looking at each other like you want to tear each other's clothes off."

Heat crept up Parker's cheeks. She'd done her very best to

keep her hands off Kate.

"Oh, and you aren't looking at your wife like you'd like some alone time with her?" Kate stepped in front of Parker to face Linda as if she wanted to protect her from Linda's teasing.

Suzan laughed as she walked past them and joined Linda and Katelyn on the blanket with a full baby bottle in hand.

"I hope that never stops," Suzan said and passed the bottle to Linda.

Parker stepped closer to Kate and embraced her from behind. Kate leaned back into her, and Parker settled her chin on Kate's shoulder. They gently swayed as they watched Linda hold Katelyn on her arm and give her the bottle, while Suzan fussed over them both.

"They look so happy," Kate whispered and pushed back gently against Parker.

"Yes, they do." She kissed Kate's ear.

"A perfect little family unit." Kate pulled Parker's arms tighter around her.

"Hm." She kissed Kate's neck, not missing the wistful tone in her voice. Children were something they hadn't talked about yet. She knew teenage Kate had wanted a family of her own one day. But Kate hadn't said a word about it since they'd been back together. But Parker saw how Kate looked at Suzan and Linda with their child every time they were around.

Kate sighed deeply. "I thank the Universe every day that I have you back in my life, darling." She leaned her head back and captured Parker's lips for a sweet, too short kiss.

"So do I." Parker savored Kate's scent.

Kate stilled in her arms. "What would you say if I told you I wanted a child?" Kate whispered.

Parker turned Kate around and held her face between her hands so she could look into Kate's eyes. They glistened with unshed tears, and Kate's lower lip began to tremble.

"I love you, Kate. I will always love you." Parker leaned in and kissed the tears that escaped before she brushed her lips over Kate's. "And I will love our children just as much."